OTHER WORKS BY THE AUTHOR

Plays Published

Fresh Horses

The Hitch-Hikers (commissioned adaptation of Eudora Welty's short story)

Asian Shade

Ghosts of the Loyal Oaks

The Trading Post

Character Lines

Rib Cage

Quail Southwest

Patrick Henry Lake Liquors

Screenplays Produced

Ghost Cat (Discovery Communications, Animal Planet)

The Retrievers (Discovery Communications, Animal Planet)

The Only Thrill (Moonstone Entertainment)

Vital Signs (Twentieth Century Fox)

Permanent Record (Paramount Pictures)

Fresh Horses (Weintraub Entertainment Group)

BLUFFING

A Novel

Larry Ketron

Bluffing is a work of fiction. All of the characters, names and incidents are the products of the author's imagination or are used fictitiously. Any resemblance to actual events or to persons, living or dead, is purely coincidental.

Published in the United States by
CLASS
Publishing Division
P.O. Box 2884
Pawleys Island, SC 29585
www.ClassAtPawleys.com

ISBN 978-0-9911124-1-8

First Edition

Cover art by Michael Francis Gay. Cover design by OBD.

*Thanks to my readers and editors,
most notably Dale Davis, Gayle Edwards,
D'Ann O'Donovan, Annie Pott, Trish Taylor
and, of course, Linda.*

PART I

Chapter 1

I tried to call Marty Sequatchee the other day from my home on Cherokee Lake in East Tennessee. There was no answer, but that was no surprise. Marty had been hard to reach for years, and I rarely made the effort anymore. But while rummaging through a closet, I ran across his name in an old *New York* magazine, and the past came crashing down on me like drums and cymbals. So I picked up the phone.

I'd tried to call about six months ago after I overheard a woman in a movie line talking about a picture she'd seen way, way back. She didn't think the movie was awful, she said to her companion, but she didn't exactly compare it to *Casablanca*. I almost said, "Excuse me, Marty Sequatchee wrote that script. He's a friend of mine."

No, I didn't say it, even though it evoked a Proustian moment. So did seeing Marty's name in that 1980's magazine as I turned the musty pages. I started thinking about my old friend, and, of course, about the murder that shocked us soon after we met.

If the killer hadn't been caught, Marty might have been next. I didn't blame myself for the death, but if something had happened to Marty, well, I might never have gotten over it. After all, Marty was involved only because of me, Jay Bluffing, Esquire ... and loafer.

We hashed it and rehashed it, over and over. Who wouldn't? We broke it down again and again, usually in an Upper West Side bar, talked about what he was doing the night I was doing so and so and about what I was doing when this or that happened. We pieced it all together in detail, right down to the fluke that trapped the killer.

I first met Marty in Central Park one Sunday morning. A bunch of mostly average athletes were getting up their weekly touch football game, six on six, and they were a man short. I hadn't intended to play, wasn't dressed for it, but being an accommodating sort, I stepped in to even up the sides. At least I was wearing sneakers.

I had joined in like this a time or two before. You could meet anybody. One Sunday I played on a team with an ex-Yankee pitcher, a charming, compact lefty who had won a few World Series games in his time. Imagine, a former star like that playing football in Central Park with pretenders. Yes, some players were above average.

But a year of Sundays had come and gone since then. The 1980's were past their midpoint. Over the course of this latest game, I got to know Marty Sequatchee some. I was easy to get along with, a better-than-most athlete myself, and Marty liked that.

Marty was a superb football player, maybe the best in the park. Tommy Kloover rivaled him, but you had to give the edge to Marty. Fast, quick. Lanky with great hands. He could throw, catch, defend. He must have intercepted four or five passes that day, leaping to bring them in, then running like liquid. He played and moved with exceptional skill. Plus, he took it all in stride with no showboating, no dancing in the end zone. But you couldn't call him a talented kid, exactly, because he was nearly forty. I never would have guessed it, but somebody kidded Marty about it at the end of the game.

I wasn't even close to forty; I was thirty-eight. A lawyer, not practicing at the moment, I was up from Kentucky and living, as was Marty, on the Upper West Side. Marty was from Tennessee, so there was a casual familiarity between us, especially since I had gone to college in Marty's home state before law school.

Leaving the park at 79th Street that morning in early October, I learned Marty was a writer. Plays were what he loved to write. They were produced in small but professional theatres all around town. In those days there were two hundred theatres like that. They were considered Off- and Off-Off-Broadway.

"Can you make a living doing that?" I asked as we tossed back and forth an old Wilson NFL ball with Pete Rozelle's signature on it.

"No," Marty said, "you have to do something else to make money." He didn't take the opportunity to say what the something else was, in his case. I would find out later about Hollywood.

Some of those little New York theatres were reputable houses and did first class work. Frank Rich would come down from *The Times* and write a review. That was an important event; it could make a writer's reputation, a theatre's, too. Of course, many of the showcases were rat holes, and Frank never showed up.

Marty was starting to cast a new play the next morning, Monday, so I mentioned my kid sister Kate, Kate Bluffing, who was in town on an extended stay. She wanted to be an actress. When I asked Marty if it would be possible for her to get an audition, he couldn't have been nicer.

Standing there on Central Park West, he found a golf pencil between two cobblestones and wrote down my sister's name on the inside of a discarded ice cream wrapper. He told me to tell her to come down to the theatre anytime the next day. He'd see she was worked in. On the bottom half of the paper, he wrote his own name and the name of the theatre. He ripped that part off and gave it to me.

"What's the address?" I asked him.

"She'll know where it is," Marty said. "I'll look forward to seeing her."

Farther along on the walk home, alone now, I rounded the corner of 79th Street onto Columbus, and there were Kate and a girlfriend of hers having brunch outside at a café. I joined them, gulped a glass of ice water, and sipped Kate's Bloody Mary. It was so spicy my eyes watered.

"Who won?" Kate wanted to know. She was twenty-eight, almost a full ten years younger than I. Whatever our parents were doing for all those years in between, they weren't having babies because we were the only two kids. Our mom and dad were high school sweethearts and had been married fifty years. James Bluffing owned a service station and garage, and Esther kept the middle class house and raised us kids. She had once been a telephone operator back in the days when you heard, "Number, please," but that ended when she married.

Kate pulled her long, blonde hair away from her face and forehead and off the back of her neck. She tilted back in her chair like a circus performer and absorbed the warm autumn sun.

"We did."

"Were you the hero?" She glanced at her friend Patsy, a luscious brunette with eyes like syrup and matching lips and hips. The two had known each other only about six months but had become good friends. I remembered the moment Kate introduced me to her new pal. Hubba hubba.

Although ... I didn't fully trust Patsy. I felt that if I loaned her twenty bucks after running into her at the dry cleaners, let's say she left her purse at home, I'd never see the twenty again. Just a hunch. Maybe the wickedness I suspected was part of her appeal. God knows she was appealing, and if she needed twenty bucks, all she had to do was ask.

"Jay grew up playing football and was always the hero in games," my sister said. I loved it when she bragged about me, especially to someone like Patsy.

"Not this time," I told them, "not by a long shot. Another guy. Someone who will interest you, Kate."

"Oh?"

"A writer of plays."

"Does he have a part for me?" she said, not taking it too seriously. "Maybe. I got you an audition."

Her eyes, or at least one of them, narrowed at me. "Is this a put-on?"

"No, you have an audition tomorrow at a theatre called the TASSQ." I was digging through my pockets, trying to find that little piece of paper.

Kate kept studying me. What I hadn't realized was that this was a big deal.

"Are you telling me you got me an audition at the TASSQ, swear to God?"

"Tomorrow. Anytime. He said just to show up."

"Who? Who said?"

"The writer. His name is Marty Sequatchee. Sequatchee. Could I make that up?" I found the sticky piece of paper that proved it.

Kate stared at me a moment more, then looked at Patsy who was staring at me, too. Then the girls stared at each other. Then Kate reached across the table and took both of my hands.

Suddenly very sincere she said, "Jay. You played football with Marty Sequatchee and got me an audition for his new play?"

"What have I been saying?"

She squealed a little, rose to lean over and kiss me.

"I did good, huh?"

Patsy was making pinging sounds with her glass by tapping the rim of it with a manicured fingernail. She was excited, too, apparently, and it was her way of squealing.

"Marty Sequatchee is a real playwright," Patsy said.

"He writes movies, too," Kate added.

"I don't know," I said.

"What does he look like?"

"Marty? He's a good-looking guy, I guess. Dark complexion, dark hair, dark eyes."

"Uh-oh," she said. "A brooder."

"Not at all. He's upbeat, funny, a lot of positive energy. He's from the sticks, like us. He's about my age, but he seems younger."

"You seem younger, too, old man," said Patsy. Then she chomped down on a piece of celery and chewed. I wanted to cut the stalk into pieces and feed them to her, slowly.

"Tomorrow, anytime. This is good," Kate said.

"Marty was happy to do it."

Patsy folded her arms across her mid-section, lifting her breasts with her forearms as she did so and pointing those delectable babies in my direction. "What about me?" she wanted to know. It was a simple question that would lead to murder.

Chapter 2

Patsy was an aspiring actress, too, I had forgotten. She worked part-time for some area TV commentator as a secretary or assistant. I thought of her in that capacity, if I thought about her occupation at all. Wrong. Actress.

So Monday morning all three of us showed up downtown at the TASSQ. The letters stood for Theatre At Sheridan Square. Why wasn't it just called the TASS? Maybe because the Q gave it a certain distinction, that extra something. Without that extra something, what are you? The Q was for cachet. There was another more famous theatre at Sheridan Square at the same time, but the TASSQ was the other one.

I had to tag along to ask Marty if it would be okay if my sister's friend auditioned too. Kate and Patsy thought it was unbelievably gracious of me to do it, but I didn't mind at all. You meet somebody the way I had met Marty, playing a sport or at a party, say, it cuts through barriers and protocol.

I once met a heart surgeon, Norman Coles, while playing softball in Riverside Park. When I was Norman's patient years later, I was very relaxed, not the least bit reluctant to say anything, ask anything, since Norman remembered those softball Saturdays, too. I enjoyed special care and attention. I even got a full explanation of the ventricles and valves, the pulmonary artery, the aorta, the whole arterial system.

Norman and I had been two-thirds of that renowned combination, Sequatchee to Bluffing to Coles (Marty played softball, too). That's the reason Norman would someday take the time to explain the most fundamental aspects of the living, beating heart to me. He couldn't do it for every patient; he'd never get anything done.

Anyhow, I walked into the theatre lobby, Kate and Patsy trailing me, and asked to see Marty.

"He's in the theatre," a chubby girl said. She was in a ticket booth with bars on the window, but I could tell she was chubby and her hair was dirty. She was reading Faulkner's *As I Lay Dying*, and by the frown on her face, it seemed to be giving her fits. I pointed toward what I guessed was the theatre itself and headed that way.

"Wait. You can't go in there. What do you want?"

I told her, and we bounced some words off each other for a moment or so. Then Kate, Patsy, and I walked up a carpeted staircase where we had been told to go. One or two stairs creaked with our footsteps, and the oak banister was worn as smooth as an Irish bar.

At the top of the stairs was another lobby. Six or eight young people and a couple of older ones were sitting or standing around. They were all reading from typed pages, studying lines or scenes, and most of them were smoking. Almost everybody smoked in those days. It was even legal. I smiled at the skinny kid behind a table and told him why we were there and that the girl downstairs was getting a message to Marty.

"Yeah, okay," he said, blinking eyes that were hooded and too close together. "Marty mentioned her." He went back to some sort of schedule in front of him for a moment, then organized some papers on the table.

I referred to a couple of wooden fold-up chairs that had just become vacant and said to the girls, "Y'all might as well sit down."

I had spoken too loudly, disturbing people who looked at me oddly. One female in particular scrunched her cute little nose. Maybe it was my southern accent. I doubted she'd scrunch her nose at Marty, but then his accent was not as noticeable as mine. Kate and Patsy took the chairs. I went over and sat on the top step just in time to see Marty Sequatchee climbing the stairs.

"How you doing, Jay?"

He arrived, I stood up again, we shook hands. Marty's eyes were sharp and acute, and he liked to use them on people. "Not like me to take more than I'm offered," I said, "but Kate brought a friend of hers. Would it be possible ...?"

"Sure. Might be a little wait is all."

Marty was holding coffee in a cardboard cup. The coffee was vibrating some, like calm dishwater when a truck suddenly drives by outside the kitchen window. I realized the hand was trembling a little, barely noticeable, and wondered for a moment if Marty were a drunk. No, couldn't be. He looked too good and was too much of an athlete.

Marty caught me noticing the minor tremor and said, "Auditions make me nervous. I'm hearing the words spoken aloud for the first time, and they're awful. Besides, people have to be rejected. Who am I to say, 'Sorry, you're not good enough to speak my precious lines.'"

"I'm sure actors and actresses understand, don't they? It must happen all the time." I didn't know what I was talking about, but it sounded logical.

"Yes, it happens all the time, and no, they never understand. They can't afford to understand. They can't allow it because then they'd have to tell themselves they weren't right or they weren't good enough, and you need too much confidence and daring to do what they do. They can't admit to anything that undermines those qualities." He searched my face to make sure I understood.

"Whatever happens with these two," I said, referring to Kate and Patsy, "please don't angst over it. They just appreciate the opportunity."

Marty slapped my shoulder. "You really want to know why my hands were shaking? I quit smoking eight years ago, and I'll want a cigarette till the day I die."

I never smoked, but I pretended I understood.

"That pass you caught yesterday, long over the middle, that was a great catch."

"Thanks, you called it," I reminded him.

"Yeah, the old banana play. It can't be stopped if there's no free safety. You playing next week?"

"Hadn't thought about it."

"Nine o'clock, every Sunday. How about I meet your sister and her friend?"

We crossed over to Kate and Patsy. I made the intros. The girls thanked Marty for the opportunity and so forth and, nodding kindly, he fixed them up with "sides," the script pages with which they would audition. Sides, okay. I was not fluent in the vernacular.

There are people who shake their heads, seemingly for no reason. It's as though they're having thoughts they don't approve of or they don't like the situation they're in or the people around them, and barely perceptible head-shaking is a way of expressing disapproval. Not Marty, he nodded a lot, as though he liked everybody and everything.

His profile reminded me of Cochise or somebody, except he smiled more than Cochise, probably. But he did have a strong, straight nose. Both Kate and Patsy were impressed with him, charmed by him, but they didn't make fools of themselves. I was grateful for that. I also felt the playwright could have either one of the girls for the asking. Marty had the young man at the table write down their names. They would be squeezed in as soon as possible.

Both said later they liked the parts they read and felt they had done well. Neither was cast.

Chapter 3

The next Saturday night, I stood on a corner with Kate beside me and a phone to my face talking to Marty. I could tell from his raspy whisper he and Patsy were in his bed with the action over for the time being.

Kate and I had decided to hop a cab down to the village and get a late bite at an all-night restaurant on Barrow. It had the most extensive menu of any place on the planet. Anything, anytime. It was all good and we both loved it. It was a comfortable, bohemian place, especially about two or three in the morning, especially if you were really hungry.

Yes, I was with my sister on a Saturday night. Kate had recently broken up with her boyfriend, a loser, and she and I spent quite a few nights together. Me? There was a girl I'd call every once in a while but not too often. I always had my eyes open, though.

Of course, I wasn't as good-looking as Marty. Or as tall. Or a writer of plays and movies. If I were, I'd have been in bed with Patsy. But I wasn't. Kate, with her blonde hair, blue eyes, and bone structure, stole the show when it came to us Bluffing kids.

They said sure, they'd love to go eat. Marty said to come on up, they'd be ready in ten minutes. He lived in a brownstone on West 85th.

The door on the second floor was ajar. "We're here," I said, coming in behind Kate and closing the door.

It was a one-bedroom apartment, medium size, with a brick wall or two and a fireplace with a huge mirror hanging over it in a simple frame. Reflecting the opposite wall, it made the apartment look twice its size, a common trick in Manhattan. The room was sparsely furnished. There was a wheat-colored sofa and a couple of comfortable club chairs the color of the insides of a chocolate-covered cherry. An art deco lamp looked like something they advertise in *The New Yorker*, a full page all to itself. There was a clunky oak desk, the kind where you sit to pay bills, not write scripts. Marty must work in the bedroom. I peeked around the corner, into the kitchen. It was larger than you'd expect and had full-sized appliances.

Marty came out first, dressed and smiling. Why shouldn't he be smiling? "Hey, guys." He went to Kate first and pecked her on the cheek. He turned to me and we shook hands.

"Nice place, good stuff."

"Macy's," he said. "Say, did you call before?"

"Huh? Yeah, I'm the one who said let's go eat."

"No, before, before that."

I looked at Kate to be sure. "No, we called the one time."

"Somebody called and hung up, is all."

Then Patsy came out from the bedroom, all sultry and satisfied. We greeted her, and she said she was glad we called. Turned out she and Marty were supposed to have gone out to dinner earlier but, what with one thing and another, hadn't made it. They had snacked on cream cheese, Triskets, and grapes, but it was after midnight now and they were really hungry. Sandolino's, that was the name of the place, sounded perfect.

During the ride downtown Marty told us a little more about the hang-up call and amused Kate and me by telling us what had happened just before my invitation.

I was right: they'd been lying in bed. When he replaced

the receiver after the annoying call, Patsy asked him if he was nervous. No, he wasn't nervous, it was just a wrong number ... and no cigarettes.

Then suddenly they heard a noise in the bathroom which was off the bedroom. Toiletries clinked together and something like a can of shaving cream fell into the sink. Patsy jumped as if she'd just stuck her finger in a light socket. She asked Marty who in the world was in there and grabbed an extra pillow for her chest. He told her it was Bob, and Patsy was appalled Marty had a roommate who had sneaked by them at who knows what point.

"Bob's my cat," Marty had told her. "He knocks things over. He's not a klutz, he's just not careful." Marty called Bob in from the bathroom. He entered with a swagger. He was a gold job, handsome and not one to miss a meal. Marty introduced Patsy. Bob stared, blinked, then shot out of the room, his body at some weird angle to his head.

But now our taxi passed 14th Street, nearing the Village. Everybody was quiet for a moment.

"I like cats," Patsy said. "If I were an animal, I'd be a cat. A jungle cat."

No argument.

I was sitting up front with the driver, and when we stopped at the restaurant, I paid him. Marty climbed out with the girls and didn't offer to take care of the fare or even split it. It didn't really bother me; maybe he planned to pay for the return trip. Then I found myself hoping the guy wasn't cheap, a moocher. That kind does not make a good friend.

Inside, Marty pointed to a particular table, halfway back and against a wall. The place was loud with voices. Dishes clanked everywhere. The four of us were seated and ordered a ton of food. Steaks and eggs, pancakes, toast and muffins, on and on. Everybody ate part of everybody else's, and it was an awfully good time. We were serious some but mostly silly.

There was room-temperature wine and icy beer, orange juice and rich coffee.

Patsy and Marty were about as handsome a couple as you're likely to find. Handsome with panache. Beside me sat beautiful Kate. I wanted to put a bag over my head.

At one point Kate reached across the table, took Patsy's hand and admired an amethyst ring.

"Is this new? It's lovely."

Patsy took her thumb to the stone, turned it to the underside of her finger. "It was a gift."

To rib Marty, I said, "Hmmm, the competition."

"I don't buy much jewelry," Marty said to all of us but especially to Patsy. It was probably meant as a warning, even though it was said in jest.

"It was given to me by a friend who was leaving town. I didn't even want it."

"Yeah, who would want an old thing like that," Kate said.

Patsy took Marty's hands in her own, looked at him with Aphrodite eyes. "He's gone, baby. He's gone."

I was thinking, Honey, I believe you. Tell me the earth's hollow with a giant hamster spinning it from inside, I wouldn't question it.

Our waitress dropped by to refill the coffee cups. She was tiny with ears of an unfortunate size. Patsy twisted the purple ring off her finger.

"Here," she said to the waitress, "I want you to have this." The waitress took it, looked at it, wondered what the gag was. "It's yours. If you don't want it, throw it away."

"You're giving this to me?"

"Yep. Please take it."

The tiny girl examined the ring. Was it hot or something? She hesitated, then said, "Okay. I will." And she walked away with it.

"That was unnecessary," Marty said.

"I didn't want it." And that was that.

Marty said he loved Sandolino's, and I felt there was a story behind why, and why this particular table, but I didn't ask. We laughed and talked about a lot of things, mainly entertainment. We all thought a song from several years before, "Every Breath You Take" by the Police, was maybe the best popular song we'd ever heard. We touched on politics, but didn't get into it far enough to rile anybody who might have disagreed with somebody else. It came up I was an attorney. Marty wanted to know why I had come to New York and wasn't practicing law. Just taking some time off, was my answer because I didn't want to go into it. Why punch the party in the mouth?

It was rollicking fun. I suspected Marty had many good times like this, with women, food, drink, and laughter, even though he was careful not to get out of hand, too loud or rowdy. He didn't seem to have a writer's eccentricities, especially a southern writer's. The guy actually seemed normal.

About a quarter of two, we were finishing up. Kate asked Marty about a movie called Learning the Body. I'd never heard of it. Apparently it was about medical students in the 1930's and Marty wrote it.

"I liked it," Kate told him.

"It's awful," Marty said. "I've written three movies and worked on several others, and they're all awful. You know what I say about the movies I've written so far? They were supposed to be good."

The check came then, interrupting the conversation, and we wouldn't get back to Marty's Hollywood career that night. Marty pinched the check from the table, reached into his pocket.

"Let me split that with you," I said.

"You got the cab." Marty pulled his hand out of his pocket, his fingers wrapped around a folded bundle of bills, mostly tens and twenties. He must have been carrying six or seven hundred dollars. He didn't mean for us to notice the wad, but we did.

Marty wasn't the flamboyant type, so the accidental flash of so much cash embarrassed him.

I didn't know it at the time, of course, but Marty was nearly broke and worried sick about it. Maybe it was the real reason his hands shook sometimes. He had made hundreds of thousands of dollars, but some bad investments and a crooked financial advisor had cost him everything. The cash he carried in his pocket did not reflect the true state of his affairs. There was not a lot more where that came from.

In the cab as we sped uptown, Marty said it would not be easy to get up in the morning to play ball in the park.

"You think you'll make it?" I asked.

"I'll be there," Marty said with defiance. "I have to be there. I have to play. You're coming, aren't you?"

"I didn't think I would."

"Sure, come on. One of these days it'll be too cold, too much snow and ice, it'll be over. Then not long after that, we'll be too old." He tossed his head back and laughed, even though it wasn't really a joke. "Up until then, you play."

We dropped Patsy off first. She lived in a pre-war building a few blocks from my place. She was on the fence about whether or not to go back home with Marty. I figured the looming early morning game made her decide to go home and sleep in her own bed, not be disturbed as Marty got up and dressed for combat. Marty didn't protest.

Then we swung over to my building. The cab drove off as Kate and I trudged up our front steps.

"She gave away that beautiful ring," Kate said.

"Yeah, wasn't that strange?"

Chapter 4

That Sunday morning was crisp and clear. Perfect football weather. We warmed up, chose up, played for nearly two hours. It wasn't the best game of my career; I needed more sleep than that. Yeah, yeah, Marty sparkled, even after he fell on his knee and twisted it. Years later he would tell me he tore some cartilage that day. Of course, over the years scar tissue developed, arthritis set in, the usual.

We found ourselves leaving the park together again. I noticed a minor limp.

"Hurt?"

"Knee. I should wear braces, pads at least."

"Why don't you?"

"I'm so excited, so anxious to get out and play, I don't want to take the time to put them on."

"You don't want to take the time," I said back to him.

"I just want to play."

Okay, maybe the guy was a little peculiar. We stopped at a water fountain long enough for Marty to soak his turquoise bandana, fold it, and apply it to his eye.

"Feels like there's something in it, won't come out."

That would turn out to be a cornea scratch from the point of the ball that had hit him during warm-ups. We walked on.

"My phone was ringing when I came home last night.

Another mystery call. Probably nothing but I couldn't help feeling it was a bad sign."

"It's easy to imagine the ominous when you're alone and awake at nearly three in the morning," I said, wise and worldly.

"Yeah, it didn't keep me up. I tortured my teeth and gums for a minute and went to bed. Fun last night, glad you called."

"It was Kate's idea, not mine. If I had been you, I would rather have been left alone."

"No, we were hungry."

"Gorgeous, isn't she?"

Marty, still holding the bandana to his eye, stopped us and turned to me.

"Did I overstep?"

"What do you mean?"

"Asking her out. Were you going to ask her out?" Marty was appalled to think he might have blind-sided me.

"Not my type," I lied. Patsy was every guy's type, are you kidding?

"I'd feel terrible if you were eyeing her and I jumped in ahead."

"Stop it. She's yours."

"You know how we play the game, Jay," he said, gesturing back toward the football field. "You call your own fouls. If it was pass interference, tell me."

"I've known her six months, Marty. If I were ever going to ask her out, I would have done it by now."

"Okay. Good."

"It probably broke her heart I never asked her. I'm just glad she's recovered enough to start seeing you."

"Okay, I understand," he said. "She was living in mortal fear you might make a play for her, and she'd have to squash you like a bug. Now she feels more secure you won't bother her since she and I are seeing each other."

I refused to respond. Marty laughed from the gut up and pretended to hit me in the ribs with an elbow.

We crossed Central Park West and started to part ways. We shook hands, and Marty said, "Women, right?"

"Women," I concurred. The word that seemed to say it all. Except I had a question. "Ever been married?"

"A live-in girlfriend for six years, close enough. When we broke up I told her I'd always think of her as my first wife."

"What happened?"

"That's a long and woeful tale. What about you, where's the mother of your children?"

"Still looking."

A few days later I heard through Kate, who heard through Patsy, Marty was hobbling around with a patch over his eye. I meant to give him a call to check on him but didn't. I picked up the phone a time or two but figured Marty was probably busy with his new play, and Patsy, and dropped it.

I didn't show up in the park the next Sunday morning. I assumed Marty wouldn't be there and, anyhow, I ached all over, had jammed my thumb, and needed a "bye" week.

Nothing much happened in my life over the next couple of weeks that fall. But that was about to change.

Chapter 5

I was standing on the southeast corner of 57th and Sixth waiting for Don Toswell. Don was a short, stocky fellow, shorter even than I. He was from Teaneck, New Jersey and was once a high school wrestler. We had met "on the hill" at the University of Tennessee as freshmen, were good friends for those undergraduate years. The Yankee and the hillbilly, they called us, with plenty of immature snickers. Then Don went to business school, I went to law school, and we more or less lost touch.

But now, every year or two, one would phone the other. We didn't need to get together; we'd just let our voices reach back and touch a by-gone time.

I had called him when I first moved to the city a couple of years before, but we hadn't seen each other yet. Then Don phoned and wondered if we could have a quick lunch. So I stood there on the corner, looking around and waiting. I flexed my thumb a few times. It was still sore. It had looked for a few days like the Hindenburg, but I kept icing it. It was finally getting back to normal size. Still hurt though.

I didn't know exactly what Don's job was. He worked for a company called Boseman, Goddard and Hall. I asked him one time what he did for them and the answer was, "Analyze accounts." Who knew what that meant?

"I show up and tinker, then pick up a hefty check. The next week I do the same thing," Don had said.

A woman, toothpick thin, stopped and lit a long, menthol cigarette with a silver Dunhill lighter. She was elegant and there was something Audrey Hepburn about her, right up to the black and red hat she wore. Unless that was a flying saucer on her head.

As I was observing her, a man bumped into the back of my shoulder and hurried on down the street. He was a squat somebody in an oversized cardigan sweater, sort of a cocoa brown, with vertical yellow stripes. He didn't stop, didn't glance back to say "excuse me," nothing. He just kept on going, either oblivious, rude, or both.

Then I saw Don sauntering up Sixth. Same Don. Expensive, stylish attire, but all of it looking somehow misplaced on him. His tie, with an oversized full Windsor knot, was loose at the neck, the sleeves of his suit jacket a quarter of an inch too long. His top-of-the-line Cole Haans were scuffed.

He had a friendly though somewhat cocky smile. We shook hands and were glad to see each other, didn't even have to say it. We just looked each other over for a moment.

"Okay if we just have a hamburger here?" He was referring to the Bun n' Burger there on the corner. It was a chain, gone now. Great burgers, the meat sort of in a delicious ball.

We went in. It was almost one-thirty and the place was jammed, but a couple of stools opened up at the counter and we grabbed them. We ordered hamburgers, fries, and Cokes and sat without a word for a moment or two. Then I said, "What's on your mind, Don?"

"You mean why I called you? Can't I just call you?"

"You can, but you didn't just call me. Something's on your mind."

"My wife is screwing her boss. I guess I need some legal advice. Before I go to a real lawyer, I thought I'd talk to you."

"I don't know what to say, Don."

"Just what I want to hear from my lawyer. Is that what you do in court? They say, 'Your witness.' You stand up, 'I don't know what to say.'"

"First of all, are you sure?"

"Yes. I'm sure. I want to fix it so she gets absolutely nothing. I want the house, the cars, the kids, everything. Can I get everything and leave her with nothing?"

"Not a chance."

"Then the legal system is not working."

"Have you confronted her? Has she admitted it?"

"No. No to both."

"But you know."

"I followed her. Hotel on the Upper East Side, The McNoel." He knew the exact address off Second Avenue and spat it out.

"That's where they meet. Afternoons, of course."

"How can I help you?"

"I don't suppose you can. I just needed to tell somebody. Can't very well tell any of my real friends."

By that he meant friends, neighbors, coworkers he sees every day. Couldn't very well tell them. Maybe the divorce could be for irreconcilable differences, period, and no one would ever know.

"Well, you could tell me this — do I go to a lawyer first or do I confront Susan first and tell her I'm going to a lawyer?"

"I'd tell her what I know and what I intended to do."

"Get her reaction, huh?"

"Well, yeah, I suppose she'll react."

The food came. We didn't really say too much more about it. At one point, chewing and staring off into nowhere, Don said, "Thirteen years."

There's a Suzie, Sue, Susan, in every man's life, usually his past. How many times had I heard some guy say, "Suzie left me for some fool with a Corvette." Or, "I was going to marry Sue till I realized she had slept with everybody I knew." Or, simply, "I wonder whatever happened to Susan?" Every guy has a Suzette somewhere, a Suzie Q. Don's was still around, living under his roof, but maybe not for long.

Back out on the street I said, "How old are your children now?"

"The boy's ten, the girl's eight."

Rather impersonal, wasn't it? "The boy" and "the girl." He could have said their names, especially since I had forgotten both of them. But he didn't. Maybe he was mad at the kids for having a mother who was fooling around.

"Thanks for listening," he said and we shook hands again. He grinned, then took off down the street. I stood there in the full sun, watching him melt into the endless pedestrian flow.

"Whatcha looking at?"

I turned to Marty, who was standing right beside me.

"Hey, Marty. Just said good-bye to a friend of mine. Where are you going?"

"Have to pick something up," he said, vaguely pointing to the building on the corner, "then I have to get downtown."

"How's the eye?"

"Healed up. Just a scratch. Worried me for a day or two, though."

"I heard you were wearing a patch."

"An eye patch. Everyone looks at you like you're some pretentious phony. Nobody thinks for a minute there's really anything wrong with your eye."

I didn't ask about the knee; I wasn't his mother. "Too bad your season ended early."

"Ended? No, I'm still playing, I wasn't hurt that bad. Where have you been, last couple of Sundays?"

Just like the pros, the real players showed up and played the game. Eyes, shoulders, knees, ankles, forget about it. Just play.

"One thing and another," I said.

Marty didn't press me about it. I wasn't the missing nail in the horse's shoe that caused the battle to be lost. The games went on without me.

"Say, what are you doing this afternoon?"

"No plans."

"How would you like to see the first run-through of the play?"

"Run-through" was a word I'd heard here and there. You couldn't live in New York City without hearing it, especially if your live-in sister was trying to act.

"You mean you're up and running already?"

"No, no, still two more weeks of rehearsal. We're just going to take a look at the piece, top to bottom. A handful of people will watch, maybe five or six."

I told him I'd be delighted. Marty said to come with him up to his agency; the building was the one on the corner above Bun n' Burger. He'd pick up his package; then we'd take a cab downtown together.

So we went in, to the elevators, caught one, started up. "I've never seen a play in rehearsal. It sounds like fun."

"It'll be awful," Marty said, "because it's so early in the process. But you can get the gist of it."

Marty used the word "awful" a lot when talking about his work. I wondered if every word he wrote really was awful or if he was just naturally self-effacing.

The elevator stopped several floors before we were to get off and a young woman stepped in. She was tanned, from a tube or a spray, I suspected. Her heavy eye shadow shouted "Queens!" She had mussed-up hair and seemed harried, then flustered. She had a Ticonderoga pencil in her mouth like a bit, manila folders in both hands. She hesitated, did a little stutter step, stared right at Marty. She didn't bother to turn and face front. Nor did she bother to give me so much as a glance.

The doors closed, the car rose, and, still staring at Marty, she said, "One of the zaniest days of my life: I look like this, and I have to run into you." She said it with the pencil still between her teeth. She was excited, as though she'd just bumped into a major celebrity.

Marty didn't say a word, just smiled at her. The elevator stopped again. Doors opened and we walked out.

"What was that about?" I said.

"She thought I was somebody else."

"Who?"

"I don't know," Marty said. "It happens every once in a while, people mistake me for God knows who."

"I think she thought you were a movie star."

"Ah, things like that happen to everybody."

"Not to me. I'm just plain old Jay Bluffing. Period."

At the front desk a bored receptionist handed Marty a big, purple envelope. "You just missed the producer," she said. "He dropped this off himself and had a brief word with Stassie." I didn't know it at the time, of course, but Stassie was Marty's agent.

"Sorry I missed him," Marty said, but I didn't believe for a second he meant it.

"You could have passed him in the lobby," the receptionist said. "Did you see a short guy in a big, brown, button-up sweater with yellow stripes?"

"No," Marty said.

"I did," I said, smarting a little from the "short guy" comment, since I had never exactly cracked a tooth on the crossbar of a goal post. "He crashed into me on the corner. I thought he was just some jerk."

"I'm sure he is," Marty said.

A couple of minutes later we were in a cab headed for Sheridan Square.

"What kind of a name is Sequatchee?" I said. "Indian?"

“Cherokee.”

“I guess you’ve heard all the Bigfoot jokes?”

“Not necessarily. What’s yours?” Marty said.

I started to apologize but let it go. I was sure Marty had been called everything from Sasquatch to Sequins.

“There’s a county in middle Tennessee, you know, called Sequatchie, but it’s spelled with an ‘ie.’ Mine’s ‘ee,’ probably the original spelling. It might mean ‘hog trough,’ ain’t that attractive?”

“So you’re part Cherokee?”

“Maybe, but it would be way back. Or maybe some old patriarch in the family just took the name. You Irish?”

“Irish, German, Scottish, you name it.”

“American.”

“That’s me,” I said. “American.”

Another American we both knew had only a few hours to live. If we had only known ...

Chapter 6

There were four or five girls in that play, most of them honeys. And they were all talented, from what I could tell. They wowed me as the performance, well, the rehearsal, proceeded. There were a few men in the play, too, different ages, good actors, I guess.

I sat in an aisle seat about halfway between the stage and the last row. Marty had said to sit anywhere. Sitting beside me were Kate and Patsy. On the ride down Marty mentioned the girls might be there. Kate had a job at a funky, hip clothing store on Broadway called Pauline's Dream, but the owner liked her and let her come and go as she pleased.

Specifically, I was on the aisle, then Patsy, then sister Kate. A dozen other people were sprinkled around, slumped in seats. Maybe they were friends or tech workers. Ordinarily, rehearsals would take place in a room somewhere else in the theatre because another show would be performing on stage at night and that show would own the theatre till it finished its run. But Marty's play was the first of a late-starting season, so no other furniture or sets were in the way.

I didn't think what I saw was awful; I thought it was darn good. Very down-homey. Once in Louisville when I was a kid, I saw an amateur production of a play by William Inge. Marty's play had that kind of flavor to it. At this run-through, there were no frills, no stage lighting or costumes or make-up. Just the bare bones.

There were plenty of mistakes, or it seemed like that to me. Lines were missed, "dropped" in theatre parlance, and once somebody turned and started talking to somebody who wasn't even there.

The director was a smooth, low-key, intellectual fellow with a high forehead and rapidly thinning hair. Thinning, even though he was only about thirty. He watched from the second row. A time or two he stood, placed the palm of his hand on his forehead, and quietly said, "Okay." Everybody on stage stopped what they were doing. Then the director, his name was Wayne Galafant, would hop up onto the stage and whisper something into somebody's ear. Then he'd jump down again, take his seat, and the acting would start again.

Marty was sitting in the back, in the last row. I never heard a peep out of him the whole first act, not that I expected to. The dramatic tension up there on the stage kept mounting, even with the flubs and interruptions. Then the act reached a climax, and that skinny kid from a couple of weeks ago, the one with the hooded eyes, said, "End of Act One." Turns out he was the ASM, assistant stage manager.

I began to applaud. Others joined in, reluctantly, it seemed. Had I broken some sacred rule? Then Patsy put her hand on my forearm, smiled without showing teeth, and said, "I have to make a phone call." These were the days before cell phones, of course, so she either had to find a phone in the theatre she could use or go outside to the corner.

I let her squeeze by me but didn't flatten as much as I could have. I wanted to make sure she brushed me, brushed her nipples against me, touched me, and she did. I quietly took a deep breath and inhaled her sweet scent. I managed not to faint, but it took will power. Good gracious, I thought. I watched her slink up the aisle.

Would she be alive today if she hadn't gone out to make that call? No one would ever know.

Marty had disappeared, and I wondered if he'd crawled under a seat. He would say later he had gone upstairs to drown himself in the men's room sink, but had chickened out.

Patsy didn't return for the second act. Kate and I sat through the fifty minutes with the empty seat between us. At the end, someone else started the applause, and I joined in. Maybe I hadn't been such a rube, after all.

Marty came down the aisle, not smiling, and stopped at my sister and me. "I warned you," he said quietly.

"I thought it was very good," I said, actually meaning it.

"It was, Marty," Kate said. "It's a very good play."

"You guys," he said, then he laughed a little. He kissed Kate's cheek and shook my hand. "Patsy couldn't stay, huh?" He was obviously a little hurt. Who wouldn't be?

I looked at Kate.

"I don't know what happened to her," she said. "She was just going to make a call. I guess something came up."

"I'll see her later," Marty said.

"I'm curious, Marty, is the play autobiographical? Is that a piece of you up on the stage?" I wondered.

I should have known better. The question was too personal in the first place and certainly too complicated. I realized that as soon as I heard the words coming out of my big mouth.

Marty laughed but it wasn't his usual free and open laugh. It was a quiet, forced little sound. "Don't think I'm those characters or that I've lived those situations. Don't watch any play or movie of mine and think, 'Ah, that's Marty! That's Marty saying it, doing it, thinking it.' If you do that, you'll be wrong most of the time. Maybe Flaubert was Madame Bovary, I don't know. But I say if you're the writer, stay yourself out of it, as best you can. You'll be in it enough without trying.

"But if you can't avoid associating me with the piece because you know me, because we're friends, then at least take the other road. Instead of looking for me up there on the stage, look at me down here — maybe the work has made me who I am." Then he flipped his hand back and forth in front of my face, pretending to slap me.

"Point taken," I said. When anybody started talking about Flaubert and Madame Bovary, I dove for cover.

"We're going to give the cast some notes, probably take about an hour. Don't know if you want to stick around, but if you do, there's a bar across the street on the corner. I could join you there for a drink in a little while," Marty said.

Kate and I looked at each other and said we'd see him there. Marty continued down the aisle, jumped up onto the stage where everybody had gathered for their note session. I escorted my sister outside into a breezy afternoon.

On the sidewalk I said, "I wonder what happened to Patsy?" The question was loaded, and I didn't even know it.

Chapter 7

Barney's, an amazing clothing store, ultra expensive, was on 17th Street in the old days, not too far from where we were. Kate wanted to go there and browse while we waited for Marty. I would have been fine sitting in the bar behind a pitcher of beer, but if we did that for an hour, we would just about have our fill by the time Marty arrived.

So Barney's it was. We went in and split up, agreeing to meet at the same entrance in half an hour. I had no intention of doing any shopping but ended up buying a beautiful wool Yves St. Laurent sports jacket, charcoal and classy, thirty-eight regular. I loved that jacket. It hangs to this day in the back of my bedroom closet in Tennessee, and I'd still be wearing it if it fit.

I met up again with Kate. There I was with my snazzy box inside a fancy shopping bag, but Kate hadn't bought anything. "What'd you get?" she said.

"Just a jacket. Show it to you later. See anything you wanted?" I felt guilty.

"There were these shoes," she said, but then she just shook her head.

"You want them?" "No, no."

"Let's go see them."

"You don't want to see women's shoes."

Of course, I didn't. But I let her lead me back, and I bought the shoes for her. They cost more than a Cadillac, but so what? Kate put the shoes in the bag with the jacket.

Okay, I had money. I had made much of it several years before on one particular situation. There was a five-hundred acre horse farm outside of Louisville, and I was negotiating its sale to a wealthy Kentucky gentleman who loved horses and loved the land. Everything was in place, we were ready to close. I was going to make plenty. It was a good, honest, fair deal, and everybody was happy.

But a few days before the papers were signed, my girlfriend took me to see her father. My girlfriend. She was a southern belle all the way. That means pretty to look at as long as you don't look too closely and see the sharp edges softened by makeup, the hard eyes expertly enhanced, and the selfish streak flowing through her blood like a third kind of corpuscle. Educated at Ole Miss with a four-year degree in nothing, she had come home again to be daddy's little girl, and was.

Her daddy was a real estate developer. He had built scores of houses, not one at a time but by the neighborhood, and money piled up around him like dunes at a beach. It seemed he and several of his friends were wanting to get into the "horse trade" as he called it, and was there any way I could maybe shift the deal I'd been working on toward them, instead of toward the fella who was about to purchase that prized property? They would make it worth my while, if it could be arranged. His daughter was in the room, sitting quietly. I looked at her, her name was Susan, and she shrugged and batted her eyes. All this was way above her head, she was saying.

I worked it out. It wasn't easy. Legal but not easy. I would never forget the look on the old Kentucky gentleman's face after the land was ripped out from under him. Such severe disappointment. Disappointment in losing the land and disappointment in me, too.

The man said, "People who try to save what we have are called sentimental, and sentimentality is ridiculed. I got rich never having to destroy anything or anybody. Not many wealthy men can say that. It's why I have such wonderful memories." He walked away. He looked back once, and his eyes stabbed me in the heart.

I tried to pretend I didn't know what the man was talking about. Okay, I sold the land for more money to somebody else, give me a break. Aren't other people allowed to raise horses? Less than a year later the bulldozers and land movers rolled in, and that horse farm is a sprawling mall now, the Jewel of Kentucky, they call it.

Back during its construction, a flatbed truck hauling a John Deere Caterpillar to the site lost control on Interstate 65 and rammed into a Ford pickup. The driver of the pickup was killed and burned beyond recognition. It was the gentleman who was supposed to have bought the land in the first place, until Jay Bluffing put the pea under one of three walnut shells and moved the shells around with sleight of hand.

Reneging on the original deal was something I would never get over. The older man's death in such a horrifically ironic way, well, how many nightmares would I have about that?

But, yes, now I had money. I wasn't set up for the rest of my life, necessarily, by that deal and others, but I could buy a sports jacket and a pair of shoes at Barney's.

Kate and I took the quick ride back down to the Village and were sitting with frosted glasses of draft Budweiser when Marty came through the door with two girls from the play. Happy hour was over, but the presence of these two young women made me happy indeed. We all shared what was left of the beer, and Marty ordered another pitcher right away.

One of the girls, the youngest of the pack who had been on stage, was Louise MacArthur. She looked about twenty-one or -two. She turned out to be distant and aloof, a little sulky.

Maybe the notes had been rough on her, for all I knew, even though she had the smallest of the parts in the play. Or maybe she was insecure because she was so much younger than the rest of them.

She had one of those short haircuts, short as a man's. It curved just right and fit her round head very well but too short for me. But she had a perfect theatrical face and was easy to look at. It was Kate who told me, later, about the theatrical face. It meant she had large features, eyes, mouth, and nose. Who wouldn't appear to, having so little hair?

It was the other one, Rebecca Norse, who attracted me. She wasn't quite as lovely as Louise, certainly not as young, but she sparkled with good energy and a sort of goofy sense of humor I just loved. I pegged her for about thirty-two. She was real, an honest-to-goodness good girl, I could tell. She had slid in next to me, just the luck of the draw, at our table opposite the bar, and for the whole time we were there, more than an hour, our thighs were constantly touching and rubbing against each other. I was aware of it, and I think she was. Maybe not. Her hair was a very dark brown. It fell as far as her neck, then curled under itself. Every once in a while she wrapped a strand of it around an index finger, then unwound it after making herself a moustache with it for a second or two.

We talked about the play. Kate was kind, but I lavished praise on the writing, the performances, the direction, everything. Most of the time I was telling the truth. Said I couldn't wait to come back and see it during a real performance.

What was the play about? Set in late 1965 in a newsstand in a town in eastern Tennessee, it was about a rootless, unfocused young man who dallied around getting into minor trouble. He worked at a gas station but hung out at the newsstand. He was basically a good kid but naturally rebellious. He charmed the girls and read the magazines, played the pinball machines and talked about going either to California or Florida or New York

City. When a friend of his dies tragically in a farming accident, the young man goes off and joins the Marines. He didn't know a war was looming but the audience, they knew. They knew what was ahead for him.

I thought the play was aiming to be a microcosm of American life during those mid-years of the sixties. The young were a little rough around the edges but basically innocent. Elvis, then the Beatles, had caused tremors but the biggest eruptions were still to come. The times they were a-changing.

I refilled my glass and recalled a movie from decades ago called *Bus Riley's Back in Town*. The stories of Marty's play and that movie weren't the same, although the movie featured a kid, Bus Riley, who had just returned to his Midwestern town from the Navy. There were a few vague similarities, but mainly it was the tone. The movie was written by William Inge. I didn't think for a second Marty saw Inge's movie and then went off and wrote the play. But Inge did write that picture, not long before he killed himself. Today, of course, his movie and Marty's play have both fallen into obscurity.

Jay Bluffing, film historian, mentioned the Inge movie to Marty, asked him if he'd seen it. All Marty said was, "There are only so many stories out there. Polti says there are basically only thirty-six dramatic situations."

Who? What? I let it go; I was out of my field. Ask me about the ever-expanding legal doctrine of strict liability, I could talk to you about it for an hour.

Louise, the young one, left first. Nobody seemed upset about it. A few minutes later, Kate said she had to go, too. She had been quiet through several glasses of beer. I knew why. It made her sad to talk about the play with the writer and cast members when she wasn't a part of it. On her way out the door, she bumped into Wayne, the director, who was coming in. He smiled at her, engaged her for a moment. I thought she was going to come back over to the table, but she didn't. She left.

Wayne joined the table, briefly. He seemed to have a lot on his mind. After a glass of beer which he didn't finish and a few superficial words, he rubbed his forehead with his hand, tossed a couple of bucks on the table, and left. I realized the director had come in to say one thing and one thing only to Marty. He said, "Think about that speech on page twelve."

When Wayne was gone, Marty said, "He wants me to cut everything but the title."

Rebecca, Becky, thought that was hilarious and slapped my thigh as she laughed. "I thought the play was the thing," I said, not knowing anything about the line's origin or even exactly what it meant.

"The play's the thing, but the director's the boss," Marty said. We were having an exuberant, easy time. The bar was filling up and we were filling up with it. Marty ordered some French fries with brown gravy for the table and some fried calamari and that sounded good.

Becky reached for the Barney's bag. Kate would have taken it with her, but she had forgotten about it. I had forgotten about it, too, I was so wrapped up in Becky.

"What's that?" Becky said.

"Oh, a jacket."

"Can I see it?"

I wasn't going to stop her. She pulled out the box, opened it and was impressed. "Gosh ... beautiful."

"Thanks."

Marty glanced at it. "Well done, Bluffing."

I appreciated that because Marty's own style was tasteful, subtle, and comfortable. Of course, it didn't matter, since he was one of those bastards that looked good in anything.

Becky had moved on to the shoes. She had the lid off the box. She dug past the tissue paper, pulled out a black pump. At least, that was my word for it.

I knew what Marty was going to say. "Those'll go great with your new jacket. Never knew a man with a size five foot."

Okay, I didn't know he was going to say the second part but was glad he did because it made Becky laugh and laugh, and the more she did, the more she pawed me. Not that she was doing it consciously, but who cared? If Marty had an infectious laugh, Becky's could start a pandemic.

Then she broke poor Bluffing's heart. She quit laughing and said, "Gosh, I was supposed to meet Harry uptown."

"Harry?"

"My boyfriend." She gathered her pocketbook and things, bumped the table with her knees scooting out, started fishing for some money to contribute.

"Forget it. It's paid. Get out." That was Marty. Deep in a financial hole, he was still picking up checks.

"Thanks, Marty." Then to me, "Good to meet you ..."

The hesitation was enough to finish me off. "Jay," I said.

"I'm sorry," she said, apologizing for forgetting my name. "I just know Harry will be mad. Bye."

We each made a lame attempt to stand as she left. Then we settled and drank some more.

"Boyfriend," I said.

"Don't you hate that word when it's not referring to you?"

"Yes," I said, "and it usually isn't."

We didn't stay much longer. We took a cab uptown to 72nd and Broadway and split up. Marty headed west to visit someone on Riverside Drive. I watched him cross Broadway carrying the black soft-leather briefcase from Coach, which he usually lugged around. It was stuffed with scripts, books, pens, and papers. I watched the sun sink like the Monitor did in 1862.

This October had been a warm one, but when the sun turned in this early evening, the air got chilly fast. I strolled up 72nd Street toward Columbus on the way home, "people watching" while pretending not to.

Inside the apartment, I called for Kate. She wasn't home. I hauled out my new jacket and slipped it on. There was a full-length mirror on the back of the bathroom door. I went in and checked myself out. Not too bad.

I heard the front door opening and came out to model the jacket for Kate. She came in, wan and weeping, leaving her keys in the door and leaving the door half open.

"Jay, Jay ... Jay ..."

"What is it? What's happened?"

"Patsy's dead, Jay. She was murdered in her apartment." She grabbed me, clutching the sleeves of the coat. She cried harder, her face buried in the wool, and I could feel the material getting smudged with mascara and wet from her runny eyes and nose.

Chapter 8

Marty never thought he'd become a great or famous writer, a remembered one, or one even too highly praised. He was mostly right. But for the years he worked and wrote, he did well. His contemporaries knew him, he got plenty of press, and the public, all in all, never seemed disappointed with his plays. You didn't see many cartwheels from people leaving the theatres, but nobody asked for their money back, either. His movies? Mostly painful disappointments.

His main problem, he told me, was that everything he wrote was soft. It was a term in his line of work that meant nothing he wrote was hard hitting enough, bold enough, risky enough. The highs his characters reached weren't in the heavens, and the lows they fell to didn't put them at the gates of hell. Too many people of power in "the business" considered him tepid, mild, soft. And there was nothing he could do about it. He wrote true to himself, and that's the way it came out. Marty probably longed to be outrageous and insane, but he wasn't. Maybe his eccentricity was in doing it his way while knowing it would take him only so far. If he were outrageous and insane, he could reflect that in what he wrote and solve his problem. He wasn't and he couldn't, period.

Oh, he was tough enough. He had backbone, fortitude, determination, resiliency. You had to have those to survive.

And he was a sweet guy most of the time, seldom impolite or rude. And his writing was too soft. It's why you've probably never heard of him.

There were lots of things about Marty that took me years to learn. You had to drag personal info out of him most of the time. Ten or twelve years before I met him, he drove up to New York City in a beat-to-hell '65 Chevy with about six hundred dollars in his pocket. He had graduated in June from UT with a liberal arts degree, worked the summer at a hotdog joint, saved his money, and cruised into New York in September. He stayed at the old YMCA on Eighth Avenue and 52nd Street. Down to his last dime, lonely, jobless, and ready to head back to Tennessee, he met a girl, an actress. She invited him to stay at her place and he did. She happened to know somebody who knew somebody who knew somebody else and within a week, Marty was working at a boutique ad agency, now long gone. The job was a lucky break.

"You only got it because you were charming," I suggested.

"Well, and smart," he said.

"And likeable and handsome, don't shortchange yourself."

Kidding aside, Marty was highly creative ... and would have had a good attitude. Then, of course, after he was hired, he probably worked harder than anybody else in the company. Yes, some people have all the luck.

His days were spent in the office, but he started writing scripts nights and weekends. They were awful, according to Marty, and every place he sent them sent them back. Until finally some artistic director, an aging, rather sad fellow running some dump on disgraceful 42nd Street stumbled across Marty's latest effort. He read it late one night and, drunk, phoned Marty at home. He demanded to meet the writer and talk about the play that very night. Marty wasn't about to say no.

So just after one in the morning, they met at a friendly, noisy restaurant in the Village to set in motion what would be

Marty's first production. The place was called Sandolino's. Gulping coffee but not yet sober, the artistic director, gay as a gingerbread house, confessed he had been struck more by Marty's unusual name printed on the cover than by the merit of the script itself. Marty accepted that. Whatever got you noticed.

But about six weeks later the play opened and ran six performances. It was a disaster, of course, but it was the beginning for Marty Sequatchee.

Marty was thinking about all this, he told me later, as he rode a slow, lumbering elevator to a sixth floor apartment on Riverside Drive that early evening after the run-through. He was greeted at the apartment door by the artistic director who had given him his first chance once upon a time. The man was toothpick thin, bald, milk-white, and dying. His tattered bathrobe hung on him like a terrycloth tent, and his tons of pills jiggled like jellybeans in their plastic containers in his pockets. But I'd bet his tired blue eyes twinkled for a moment at the sight of Marty.

Marty embraced the old guy, then stepped back and took a long look at him. "Most people won't hug me," the sick man said. "Afraid they can catch it that way."

While Marty visited with the sad chap who had given him his start, Kate and I were trying to come to grips with the news about Patsy. I called Marty's apartment, knowing he wasn't there but intending to leave the distressing message. I decided against that when Marty's voice came on. After the beep I just said, "Marty, it's Jay. Call me or come over. I need to talk to you right away." Then I tried to get more of the story from Kate and console her. The best way to console her was to let her talk.

After she had come home from downtown, she took a short nap. Then she went out again, intending to go grocery shopping. She decided to take the slight detour and stop by Patsy's place, maybe find out why she hadn't returned for the second act of the play and also to see if she needed anything from the Pioneer market. When she turned onto Patsy's block, 74th between Columbus and Amsterdam, she saw several police cars, marked and unmarked, down toward Patsy's end of the street. Her heart started pumping faster and her step quickened. It was like seeing a fire truck screaming toward your neighborhood and knowing in your gut it's your house that's burning.

Kate knew something had happened to Patsy. By the time she got to Patsy's building, she was out of breath from running. She started up the stoop but was stopped by a young, overweight cop.

"Whoa, whoa ...," he said, gripping fat fingers around her upper arm.

"What's happened?"

"Who are you?"

"I'm a friend of Patsy Holton. She lives in this building."

He kept holding onto her arm. He looked up to the top of the steps and said, "Sir? Friend."

A detective in a cheap brown sports coat was writing seriously in a pocket notebook as if he were taking an essay test. He closed the notebook and put it inside his jacket as he clomped down the steps. He had what used to be called a crew cut. His cheeks were splotchy red with rosacea. He was big and tired, and his neck seemed to hurt.

"You were a friend of the victim?" He tried to ask it with some understanding and tenderness.

"A friend of the victim?" Kate said, looking to the uniformed cop, looking at his fingers squeezing her arm, then looking at the detective again. "A friend of the victim? I'm Patsy Holton's friend."

"Miss, I have some bad news."

So, of course, he told her. It was a good thing the other cop still had Kate by the arm, she said, because her knees buckled, and she would have crumpled to the concrete. The detective walked her over to a gray sedan. They stood outside it. He asked her a few questions, wrote down some of her answers. He told her Patsy had been killed in her apartment, didn't offer much else.

"How?" Kate wanted to know. "A break-in or what? And how?"

"She was hit pretty hard a time or two, then strangled, apparently. All I can say at the moment."

"Was she attacked? I mean, assaulted? Sexually assaulted?"

"She was not completely dressed. Please don't ask me anything else."

He took Kate's name, address, phone number. He told her he was sorry and sent her on her way. Dazed, she started home. She was sobbing by the time she came in the door.

She and I talked about Patsy's parents. They were divorced. Her mother lived in Latrobe, Pennsylvania, where Patsy was from. Her father, who knew? Had they been told? How do you go about informing parents of something like this? An officer goes to see them. Or they get a phone call.

I made a drink of Jim Beam over lots of ice and we shared it. Patsy was dead. Murdered in her own apartment in daylight. Hard to believe.

After the drink went down, I had to get out. I thought maybe if I walked over toward Riverside, I might run into Marty. I knew approximately where he had headed, and besides, you run into everybody on Columbus or 72nd Street or Broadway or thereabouts. I ambled back down Columbus, turned and headed down the north side of 72nd. I saw and said hello to the guy who cut my hair, the guy who did my laundry, and a female bartender from the All State Café who remembered me, I suppose, because I was a pretty fair tipper. Saw them all in the course of half the block. New York City, U.S.A., small town America.

But I didn't see Marty. I canvassed a four- or five-block area, then ended up in front of his building up on 85th. I sat on the front steps for a few minutes, my head in my hands. It was getting dark. What had happened? Did her intermission phone call have anything to do with her murder? Who was it she called? Had there been a break-in at her apartment, a struggle? The cops hadn't been forthcoming.

All this and a thousand other thoughts were spinning around in my head like plates on the ends of pointed sticks. Then I spotted Marty coming home. He was legging it my way with his head down, so he only saw a few feet in front of him. He loped like a lone wolf, following a scent. I stood up and waited.

Marty looked up, saw me, tossed out a salute. He knew how to salute. His four years of college had been interrupted by a three-year stint in the Army, a year of it in Nam, though I didn't know that at the time.

Getting closer he said, "You again?" He was smiling but stopped at the look on my face. "What's wrong?"

"Marty, it's Patsy Holton. She's been killed."

Marty just stood there. His mouth opened, but nothing came out. Then he closed his eyes, shook his head, and winced as though someone had just rung a bell at his ears. But the street was quiet and still. I looked up the block, then down it. Didn't see another soul, nobody even walking a dog.

"How did it happen? Was she hit by a car?"

I had said "killed" not "murdered," so it was a logical question. "Marty, she was murdered, strangled in her apartment sometime this afternoon."

"Let's go inside," he said.

Upstairs, Marty's hand shook as he unlocked his door. I was trembling a little, too. Marty managed to open the door, and we went in. His cat pranced in from somewhere, jumped up on the oak desk, slipped on some loose pieces of paper, popped down again. The papers floated to the floor. "Easy, Bob," Marty said quietly and with no authority.

The phone started ringing. Marty wasn't in any hurry to cross over and answer it. Did he even hear it at first? He tossed his keys, dropped his briefcase onto his desk. When he did, the package he had picked up earlier fell out, onto the floor. He didn't even notice. He took off his windbreaker jacket, flung it over one of the cherry-cream colored chairs.

Then he answered the phone. "Hello," he said. There was no response. "Hello, goddamn it!" he yelled. He looked over, shook the receiver at me as if to say, "I could kill this guy," but he didn't say it. He just replaced the receiver and exhaled like a horse. "Somebody's playing a game. This calling and staying on the line and not saying a word."

Caller ID was years down the road. In those days you talked about "tracing a call." You saw it on TV cop shows all the time. "Keep him on the line as long as you can so we can trace the call," said a cop very quietly as he put on cumbersome headphones and clicked-on a boxy reel-to-reel tape recorder. Maybe the cops still do it if the caller has blocked his number from flashing across the caller ID, but you never hear about it. Ancient technology.

"What do you want to drink?" Marty asked, heading for the kitchen.

"Any bourbon?"

"Plenty."

It was even my brand. Marty poured each of us a stiff one and, drinks in hand, we sank into the two living room chairs. We were quiet for a few moments. Ice clinked in our glasses, a lonely sound.

"How'd you hear about it?"

"Kate went by her place. Cops all over."

"Details?"

"No. You'll be hearing from the police. We all will."

Marty sat there slumped for a moment more. Then he set down his glass, stood up and went into the bedroom. He came back in a few seconds with a bed pillow in a blue linen case. He brought it over to me, and I didn't know if he was going to suffocate me or what. He held it up, indicating I should take it. I did. I pressed it against my own face, inhaled, then gave it back to Marty.

"Yep," I said, "that was her."

Chapter 9

After another drink or two and some miscellaneous chatter about Patsy, I got up and moved around. I picked up off the floor the envelope that had fallen out of Marty's bag.

"Let me see that," Marty said, still slumped in his chair.

I handed it to him. He opened it, removed a script bound with two brass fasteners. He scanned a cover letter, snickered sarcastically.

"What is it?"

"A film script. Somebody thinks I might be able to rewrite it, turn it into something they could actually shoot."

"Who thinks so?"

He handed me the cover letter. It was from the producer, from Hollywood. Well, Beverly Hills. He seemed to be a big Marty Sequatchee fan. At least, he loved a movie called *Mostly Sunny and Warm*, which Marty had written. It had been released a few years before. I hadn't seen it, hadn't heard of it, and according to this guy, I was really missing something. Marty's "sensitive touch," his "delicate hand," the "dazzling, quirky dialogue of *Mostly Sunny and Warm*," was exactly what the enclosed script needed.

I put down the letter. "Sounds like he wants to nominate you for the Nobel Prize for literature."

"He's probably lying. Maybe not, but probably."

"Lying?"

"Chances are he never even saw that movie of mine. Did you?"

"I'm sorry, no."

"Nobody saw it."

"Then ...?" I was trying to figure why the Hollywood guy would offer all the praise.

"My agent," Marty said, with mild contempt. "My agent told him."

"Told him what?"

"About the movie, *Mostly Sunny and Warm*."

"So your agent, having seen the movie, tells him all those things about it, then the producer repeats it back to you?"

"Not exactly. My agent probably never saw the movie either. I told her those things, which she turned around and told the producer."

"Then the producer turns around and writes to you your very words?" I didn't know if Marty was putting me on or what.

Marty slapped at the letter with the back of his hand. "Sensitive, delicate, dazzling, quirky. Jay, I swear to you, those were all words I used when my agent asked me how she should talk about that movie with this cad."

"What a business," I said. "But he does want you to write for him."

"Not yet, he doesn't. I'll have to go to L.A., meet with him, meet with the studio, give them my take on the project, tell them how I'd make it wonderful."

"When will you decide if you'll go? After you've read the original script a few times?"

"What? I decided I'd go when I first got the call that vaguely mentioned the project. Of course I'll go. I'll jump through their flaming hoops like a Ringling Brothers' tiger. It's how I make a living, Jay. Besides, these jobs don't come along as often as they used to. It's the first nibble I've had in six months."

He could have said then and there he was drowning in debt and back taxes and desperately needed this rewrite deal. But he didn't and I had no idea.

I reached for the script, Marty gave it over. I read the title, turned the page, sipped from my glass, flipped through several more pages. The format of a screenplay is common knowledge now days. Any maid at a Motel Six could read a movie script. Most maids are probably writing one. But back then, it was an odd-looking layout to anyone who wasn't in the biz. And I wasn't.

"You want to read it?" Marty said.

"Sure, I'll read it."

"I can't dive into it until after the play opens, I might confuse my wee little brain. So take it home and read it. Tell me what you think."

"Don't know if I'll be able to make heads or tails of it."

"Naw," he said, "don't get bogged down in all the terms and crap. Just read the dialogue."

"I'll read it," I said again.

"I'll tell you a secret, though. That script there? Never be a movie. They're going to pay me a load of money to rewrite it, maybe, but it will never be a movie."

"I don't get it, how do you know?"

"Because I know the producer involved. Or I know of him. He'll never be able to get this movie made. He's made movies before but not in a long time. He walks out of a room in Hollywood, they whisper, 'He's over.'"

"But what if you take what's here and make it great?"

"Doesn't matter. Scripts don't get movies made, people get movies made. The main guy behind this one isn't going to be able to make it happen. Often true in the theatre, too. As often as not, it's the writer, for example, not the play. Or the director, not the writer or the play."

It was confusing. What business isn't when you look at it from the outside?

Marty, down and sad, said, "It's all so meaningless. I mean, Patsy was murdered today and what are we talking about?" Was he suddenly "sensitive" or cynical?

"I'm cynical sometimes, sorry," Marty said. "Don't know about your business, but in mine, cynicism is a shield. A little cynicism is probably healthy, don't you think? What I never want to be is bitter. I run into these old theatre people who never quite made it, you know, never achieved what they had once hoped they would. God, the bitterness, the hate. I don't want that ever to overtake me."

"Old and bitter. May neither of us ever experience it," I said.

"Whatever happens, accept it, live with it. No matter what, there have to have been good times, right? So someday, ancient, may we sit rocking back and forth thinking about the good times, the good friends. I'll think about people like you, Jay, and the beautiful young women ... like Patsy."

We were getting as soppy as red-eye gravy. The third fellow with us had wrapped his arms around both Marty and me. He had started out in the kitchen, but was sitting on the table in the living room now, encouraging us to talk, to say anything, to let it out. He had started to strongly influence the conversation. His name was Jim Beam.

"I visited an old friend of mine on Amsterdam. He's almost dead." He continued and told me about the visit to the director who gave him his start, about that first production, about the pharmacy now carried in the sick man's bathrobe pockets.

"Him, Patsy," he said. "Do friends die in threes?" He asked, looking warningly at me.

"How'd you feel about Patsy, Marty? Okay to ask you that?"

"You mean, did I love her?"

I shook my glass, and Jim shivered.

"These girls, all these girls," Marty said. "I have a theory.

I think it will be many years from now before we can assess it. This one, that one. Did I love her? Or her? Ask me in twenty, thirty years. Patsy? I doubt it, simply because I didn't know her long enough. Can you fall in love in two weeks? Okay, maybe. But probably not, not really."

"All these girls." He used the expression with me as if I, too, had my pick of the female populace. Didn't Marty realize we were a little different in that regard? Okay, I wasn't exactly clawing the walls, but Marty could walk into a party, alone, and walk out with just about any young lady of his choosing. I was more likely to walk out, early, with a handful of cold-boiled shrimp, plucked from the top of the ice. But at the occasional New York City party I attended, the shrimp were huge and excellent.

"Did you think there was something ...," I couldn't finish the sentence. I didn't know exactly what I was trying to say.

"Something a little nasty about her? Maybe even something untrustworthy?"

"Yes," I said.

"Yes." We stared at each other through a whiskey haze, neither of us wanting to say more. Maybe we were both thinking the same thing: the girl is dead, let's not start picking at her.

"Jay, I don't think I would have married her. I don't think we would have grown old together, her watching me become angry and bitter. But I liked her. We had fun. She had become a friend. And sexy? I don't think I have to tell you."

No, he didn't.

"Hard to believe she's dead," he said, sipping drink number five or six.

I agreed. Hard to believe and terribly sad.

"There's a stain on your new jacket." He gestured to my lapel.

"Kate cried on me. It'll come out."

"Sure," he said. "But even if it doesn't, Jay, so what?"

Chapter 10

On the way home that night I stopped at a phone booth and called Daisy Leiber. It only took a few short minutes for me to convince her I should come over to her place across town. She had just stepped out of the tub, was painting her toes, hadn't planned on going out or seeing anyone this night, but she caved in soon enough.

I didn't tell her someone I knew had just been murdered. I didn't want to play that trump card. I figured if she didn't want to see me for myself, I'd let it go. I didn't want her to have me over because she pitied me or, for that matter, because she wanted some details on an Upper West Side murder.

I caught the cross-town bus on 86th Street, took a transfer slip. I could have caught a cab, but a bus felt right. I wanted the warmth of the bus and some people around me, strangers, vulnerable folks like me, living the city life, getting by, surviving, always meeting people, many times losing them forever, one way or another.

Besides, the slower ride would give me a chance to sober some and Daisy's toes a chance to dry. She lived on 48th near Second, consequently the transfer, but this time of evening traffic was slack, and you could make yourself comfortable on an uncrowded bus.

We churned through the park, crossed Fifth, continued

east. But after another stop or two, I was impatient. I bailed and took a cab down to Daisy's. I'd sobered faster than I thought I would, and I could blow on Daisy's toes till they dried.

The doorman on duty was the one I didn't like. The fellow wasn't pleasant. Every time he called up and announced me, one corner of his lip raised a little like he was pretending to be Elvis. I couldn't figure it. Did Daisy have men in and out of here all the time and this doorman was sick of it? Or maybe he wished he was the one going up to her apartment instead of me. Or maybe Daisy didn't tip him enough at Christmas, pick one. But doormen were usually pleasant, and that's how they were supposed to be, dammit.

When Daisy opened the door, I was going to say, "Never told you this, but that doorman down there bugs me."

I didn't have the chance. She took my hand, pulled me in. "A girl's been murdered on the Upper West Side, near you. It's all over the news."

We stood in front of the TV, watching the hubbub and the reporting for a couple of minutes. Every fifteen or twenty seconds Daisy said, "God," and shook her head. A shocked Preston Hondonada made a brief statement. He was the pseudo-suave, partly Hispanic television commentator Patsy assisted. He worked for one of the local network affiliates, did exposés on slum landlords, corrupt city councilmen, that kind of thing. He was overcome with emotion. It seemed real. He stumbled over his words and garbled them, but of course, he always did that, even when he was reading, always spoke with a mouthful of gravel. How do these people get these jobs? When the news moved on to something else, Daisy clicked off the set.

"I knew her."

"You did?"

"She was a good friend of my sister Kate."

"No!"

"We were together this afternoon. Kate, Patsy, and I."

"God."

I went on, sketched the picture for her: Marty's play, Patsy's leaving at the half, and so on.

"You didn't kill her, did you?" Daisy said, just to be on the safe side.

"No."

"The cops must be looking for you right now." She seemed to take a step away from me, could have been my imagination.

"Huh? I said I didn't do it."

"No, I mean to question you."

I knew a little something about cops, detectives, investigators. Honest, hard-working men and women for the most part, professionals who really wanted to make a positive difference in the world. They wanted life to be safe out there (it wasn't), and they wanted criminals to pay.

But still, it was a job. They did the job, cashed their checks, ate home-cooking, repaired the kitchen sink, played Yahtzee with their kids. They got up and went to work and then came home, even if it wasn't always directly home. "We're working on this case around the clock," a lead detective would state to the press. Well, yes and no. You work at your job twenty-four hours a day, too. You're always thinking about it. You get up at two in the morning for a glass of milk and a piece of cheesecake and think, "Oh, yeah, I should tell Dodd to change those labels." Or soaping your hair in the shower, it occurs to you that, since a Supreme Court decision in 1972, unanimous decisions by a jury are not necessary for conviction in state criminal courts. But only three states paid any attention to the decision and you aren't in one of those states, so it isn't going to affect your client. Who doesn't work around the clock?

But cops usually weren't in any fanatic rush any more than anybody else. Things proceeded, one step at a time. Investigations didn't travel by bullet train; they traveled by bus. Sure the detectives would want to talk to me and to Kate and to Marty. They'd want to talk to dozens of people. But they weren't going to be ringing doorbells at, say, three a.m., I knew that.

"I'm sure they'll get around to it," I told Daisy.

"What's that?" she said.

She was referring to Marty's script, which was rolled and sticking out of a side pocket of my new sports coat. "Something I have to read for a friend of mine."

"You have a stain on your pretty jacket." She licked the tips of a couple of her fingers and brushed at my lapel.

Daisy had white skin, freckled on her upper chest and other places, and thick, coarse, almost wiry red hair that built up like a pyramid from her shoulders to the top her head. She had a broad back that tapered down, some, to her waist. She wasn't too thin or too tall. She was attractive, not a beauty. Neither was I. She chewed a lot of Aspergum, for no reason other than she liked its smell and taste. I once pointed out that the little orange squares complimented the color of her hair and she liked that. She claimed never to have had a sore throat in her life. Was it the gum? I didn't know and neither did she.

She was backed by serious money. Her father owned a company that served as a liaison between those who built skyscrapers and those who manufactured bathroom fixtures and accessories. Daisy was the company's chief representative. She went to dinner with people named Kohler. She knew everything about toilets, bathtubs, sinks, and saunas. She knew all about handles, pipes, bathroom lights, even wiring. Combine that with an MBA from Yale and you had a woman who could handle herself pretty well among architects, contractors, carpenters, and raunchy Italian construction crews.

When I first came to the city, I stayed in an old but well-kept hotel just off Fifth Avenue. Looking at neighborhoods and apartments, I walked all over New York. I met Daisy one day on her block. She was walking her dog, a little white, curly-haired Shih Tzu named Sheila. Sheila broke loose from her leash and ran right for me, God knows why. I reached down and scooped her up. After a brief conversation, Daisy invited me up for coffee. She liked me and I liked her, too.

I called her every week or two. If it was convenient, we'd get together, chat, sleep together, see you next time. We had known each other almost the whole two years I'd been in town. It was fun and easy, but it wasn't deep or complicated. Fine with me. Fine with her.

This particular night, with Patsy murdered only hours before, Daisy and I didn't do anything. She opened a bottle of fruity, white, Spanish wine from the Alella region. So she said. We climbed into her bed with it. Beer, Jim Beam, now wine. I was only thirty-eight, but I'd feel it tomorrow. How did the saying go? Beer on whiskey, very risky. Whiskey on beer, never fear. Okay, but what happens when wine is thrown into the mix?

We snuggled some and talked. She was always interested in hearing about the distant planet known as Kentucky, or its neighbor Tennessee. She listened with an expression on her face that said, "You are talking about far off lands I will never see." Sheila left us alone and I was glad of that. I love dogs, but there's a time and place. And the Shih Tzu wasn't really my breed, I have to say.

Before I left, Daisy turned on the TV again, maybe to get some new information on the murder. We watched a repeat of the report we had heard earlier. I figured the cops had done everything they could for now and were probably home getting a good night's sleep.

Mr. Bluffing wasn't far behind them. Daisy walked me to her door wearing a long, luxurious, silk robe that looked like a number from the 1930's. She never had dressed after her bath. She had her arm around me, around my waist. At the door I kissed her goodnight.

"Are you all right?" she asked.

I had gone from an afternoon high, to an evening of being crocked, to sobering up, back to getting close to drunk on wine. All that on top of shock and sadness. Now I was mostly just nauseated.

"I'm fine." I let my face drift into a slight smile.

She squeezed a handful of silk at her throat. "That poor girl. What did she do to deserve being murdered?"

Chapter 11

About eleven forty-five that night, Marty was jarred awake by the downstairs buzzer. It was the cops. So forget everything I said.

Marty had fallen asleep on his sofa. He sat up, his head a cinder block. After I had left him earlier, he sipped a few more drinks and finally fell out. Not that he remembered any of this as he staggered to the intercom.

"Who is it?" he said, none too politely, as he held in the button.

"Police. Like to talk to you if we could."

"It sent a shiver through me," Marty said, telling me all about it the next day. "I wasn't even conscious enough yet to remember the murder."

He didn't know what time it was, even if it was morning or night. He looked around to make sure this was his apartment. It was. The fog cleared in a second or two. His heart dropped from his throat and fell back into a relatively normal rhythm. He jammed the other button with his thumb to unlock the door downstairs.

Marty opened his door, blinking, still waking up. A muscular man in his forties with slicked back black hair and a thin, graying moustache stood there with his partner, the homicide detective with the crew-cut and splotchy-red face.

"I'm Detective Flannigan," the crew-cut said, drawing out his gold shield from inside his brown jacket. He and Marty were about the same height. Marty glanced at the badge before it vanished. "This is Detective Rivo."

"Come on in," Marty said. They did and Marty eased the door closed.

Rivo, more my height than Marty's, gave the room a cursory survey. Flannigan pulled out his notebook and pen and lit right in. "You're Marty Sequatchee?"

"Yes. You guys want to sit down?"

"Thanks," Flannigan said. He let his head bobble and rubbed the base of his neck as he considered his options. He chose one of the more or less maroon chairs. Rivo took the other one, but not before he circled, glancing into the kitchen, glancing down the short hallway that led to the bedroom, and not before spying himself in the huge mirror and giving himself the once over.

Marty, of course, didn't know how this was going to go. His insides were tight. He realized he was taking short little breaths, almost panting. His hair was matted down where he had been sleeping on it, and the rest of it was wild. His corduroy slacks and cotton shirt looked as if they'd been tied in a ball for a few days, then untied and worn right away. His head felt the same way.

"Sure sorry to bother you so late," one of the men said to Marty.

"It's okay. I fell asleep on the couch after I, uh ...," he referred to the nearly empty Jim Beam bottle and his glass and mine, both with melted ice, "after I'd had a few. I shouldn't drink. My father drank."

"Who knows why I said that?" he would say to me. "Interrupted dream, maybe."

It was true, though, I found out after knowing Marty a couple of years. His father had been a poet, painter, failed businessman, rabid writer of angry letters to newspapers and city officials, and hopeless alcoholic. He was killed on the old highway 11W between Rogersville and Knoxville when Marty was nine. His stepfather, who still lived in Tennessee with Marty's mother, was a mechanical engineer and never touched the firewater.

"I don't guess we have to break the news to you, since you haven't asked why we're here," the bigger detective said.

"Patsy," he said, but he said it so quietly he had to say it again. "Patsy."

"Patsy Holton, yeah," said Flannigan. "You want to throw some water on your face or anything?"

"Why don't I do that?" Marty said. "Why don't I do that and make some coffee?"

"I'll pass on the coffee." But to his partner he said, "You want some coffee, Paul?"

Rivo's one word answer was emphatic and extended. "Noooo," he said, like he'd already had twenty cups this night.

"I'll be right back," Marty said. He left for his bathroom where he didn't like what he saw. The hair, the eyes of blood, the clothes. He used his fingers as a hair brush while he let the water warm up. He plugged the sink and in a moment leaned over and submerged his face, pulled up and exhaled, patted himself dry.

When he returned to the living room, Flannigan said, "Better?"

"Yeah, thanks."

"How'd you find out about it, Marty?"

"About Patsy? Friend of mine told me."

"What's his name?"

"Jay Bluffing."

"He's the one with the sister, right?"

"Kate, yeah."

Marty realized these guys were on top of things. Had they

already talked to Kate? To me, this Bluffing character? Should he ask?

"Have you already talked to Kate and Jay?"

"We're going to be talking to a lot of people," Flannigan said. He wasn't smiling, exactly, when he said it, but there was a sense of "we have a mountain to climb and we will climb it and we will plant our flag." He looked to his partner for affirmation. "Be talking to a lot of people, won't we, Paul?"

Rivo said something like "Whoa," meaning "you bet we will."

"When did you see Patsy last, Marty?"

"This afternoon." Since his question about Kate and me hadn't been answered, Marty realized he'd better get everything straight. These guys could have questioned others earlier and after Marty's answers, they would look for inconsistencies.

In Marty's head, things quickly started to get ridiculous. Did these policemen think him a suspect? It occurred to him because anytime the cops question you, you feel guilty. Okay, maybe, just maybe, you're not guilty of this, but you're guilty of something and we know it.

"You saw her this afternoon?"

"Huh?" Marty was doing more thinking, runaway thinking, than listening. "Yes, downtown, at the theatre. I'm a playwright. She, she, she," he stuttered, "she came to see a rehearsal of a play I'm doing. But she left at the intermission and didn't return."

Rivo perked up some, looked at Marty with eyes a little wider, looked at him like a kid looks at a circus clown before the clown actually breaks into his act. "You write movies, too, don't you?"

Where did he hear that? "I have, yes," Marty said.

"How do you do that?" Rivo said.

"It's a job," Marty said. It must have been funny because Rivo looked at Flannigan who looked up from his scribbling, and they both chuckled for about two seconds. “It’s a job” or “it’s the job” is an expression these cops had spoken many times, Marty figured.

As long as he was looking at Marty anyway, Flannigan continued. “Did you consider Patsy Holton your girlfriend?”

“We had only known each other a couple of weeks. Been together, three or four times.”

“You were intimate?”

Marty wanted to say, “What are you, Masters and Johnson?” He didn’t. He said, “We were intimate, yeah.”

“Know anybody who might have a reason to do her harm?”

“No. But I really don’t know anyone she knew, except Kate and Jay.”

“She ever mention anything about someone being angry with her?”

“Who?”

“No, I’m saying, did she?”

“No.”

“She ever indicate she might be afraid of anybody?”

“No.” Marty paused for a beat, then said, “I mean, it’s New York, so ...”

“So?”

“Everybody’s afraid.”

Flannigan accepted that and jotted something down. Then, in Marty’s bathroom, a plastic bottle of mouthwash fell over, hitting a bottle of rubbing alcohol which, in turn, knocked over two or three other products from Procter and Gamble. When the bathroom door and the bedroom door were both open, you could hear sounds from back there out in the living room. Both Flannigan and Rivo flinched and sat up a little straighter.

“You’ve got company,” Flannigan said. “You should have said something.”

“No, no, it’s my cat. My cat bumps things.”

“She’s clumsy, huh?”

I laughed when Marty recounted that part. In fact, I laughed through a lot of it, how could you not? "People who don't know cats assume they are all female," Marty said to me.

But to the detectives he had said, "No, he's not really clumsy, he's just not careful."

Flannigan and Rivo looked at each other, Rivo shrugged. Flannigan said, "The case of the careless cat, huh, Paul?"

"My daughter used to have a cat," Rivo said.

"Yeah?

"She disappeared. The cat, not my daughter."

Flannigan seemed surprised. "I don't believe you ever told me that."

Out of the blue Rivo said to Marty, "My daughter wants to be an actress. She's giving it a try."

"Oh, yeah?"

"I keep telling her, but she won't listen."

You keep telling her what? Marty was only thinking that, he didn't say it. Because he knew what Rivo meant.

"Twenty-two years old, been to Fordham, could do anything, really. Wants to be a star."

"Beautiful girl," Flannigan chimed in. "Beautiful."

"Well," Rivo said, not denying it.

"You have a picture of her, don't you, Paul?"

Rivo found his wallet, opened it to his daughter's picture, reached the whole wallet out to Marty who took a good long gander at the girl. Yes, she was a beauty even though she was cutting up in the photo. She was dark, like her father, but not much resemblance beyond that, at least as far as Marty could tell. It wasn't a professional photo, just a snapshot taken around the house.

"Wow," Marty said.

"Thanks," Rivo said as Marty returned the wallet. "She's making a face in this picture, acting up. I took it."

Making a face, yeah, but it didn't matter. She was a babe.

"You don't look old enough to have a twenty-two-year-old daughter," Marty said.

"Me?" Rivo pretended to be surprised. "Doctors and cops, we marry young."

Marty had never thought about it. "Why's that?"

"Doctors cause they have too much to do, too much to study, no time to worry about their love life, so they get that out of the way." He looked to his partner.

"Cops because, from the beginning, they see so much violence and chaos," Flannigan said, "have to go home to a family, to some order and comfort."

These guys had talked this out. Maybe they were right. "You don't wear a wedding band," Marty said to Flannigan.

"Very good," Flannigan said, complimenting Marty on his dazzling observation. "Divorced three times. I'll try it again someday. I'm seeing a lady now, little younger than me, might be the right one. She told her mother I've tied the knot three times before, you know, to get her opinion. Her mom says, 'Well, at least he's the marrying kind.' Not that I've met the mother. She's in the old country."

Marty couldn't believe this seasoned homicide detective was opening up like this to a total stranger. Maybe it was pride over the current girlfriend, spilling over.

"What would you tell her?" Rivo asked Marty.

"Excuse me?"

"What would you tell Ellen?"

"Ellen is ...?"

"My daughter," Rivo said. "Her name is Ellen Rivo."

"Oh, your daughter. You mean, advice?"

"Yeah, like advice. Any advice for her, being in the show business yourself?"

"Don't take 'no' for an answer."

Rivo waited. Looked at Flannigan who had stopped writing and looked up from his notebook. Rivo looked at Marty again.

"That's it?" He was clearly disappointed. Surely there was a magic formula.

Marty told me it crossed his mind that if he didn't come up with some smart, specific advice for the girl, Rivo might arrest him for Patsy's murder.

"Tell you what, Detective," Marty said. "There's a coffee shop on the corner. I could meet her there in the morning and tell her everything I know over a cup of coffee."

"What time?" Rivo said it immediately.

"Say ... ten-thirty?" Rehearsals started at eleven. He could squeeze the kid in and be a little late for the theatre.

"She'll be there," Rivo said.

Marty thought of Patsy's body, lying on her parquet floor or on her bed, wherever the killer had left her. Her lifeless body, maybe bent unnaturally, maybe her neck broken. And here was Rivo playing agent for his own daughter. Didn't seem right.

But it did mean one good thing. The murderer, these detectives knew, was not Marty Sequatchee.

Flannigan brought things back to where they belonged. "Anything else you can think of to tell us about Patsy?"

Marty mulled it over. Nothing occurred to him. He shook his head, suddenly distant.

"Well," Flannigan said, putting away his pen and book. Both cops stood and headed for the door. Flannigan reached back, handed a card to Marty. "Call us if you think of anything you think we might like to know."

Marty took the card, looked down at it, looked back up to Flannigan. "I didn't trust her one hundred percent." The instant it was out of his mouth, Marty wished he hadn't said it.

"What do you mean?" Flannigan said.

"Not something you can explain."

"Money missing from your wallet after she was around?"

"No, nothing like that. It's just ... I always had the feeling if something better came along, she'd be gone."

“Oh.” Flannigan lost air. He dropped his chin, touched the back of his neck, then looked up again. “Then I don’t suspect you trust anybody one hundred percent, do you?”

They thanked Marty for his time, apologized again for the hour, for waking him, all that. Then just before Marty closed the door on them, Rivo called back, “Ellen Rivo.”

“Got it,” Marty said.

Chapter 12

The sleeping arrangement in my apartment was like this — my sister got the bedroom. No, she didn't insist on it, didn't even ask for it. But when she came to the city and I realized she was going to be staying for an indefinite period, we made the switch. It was my idea. I talked her into it.

Fortunately, there was an area, a separate little sitting area, off the living room near the big window that looked out onto the street. It was large enough to fit in a single bed and even an oak dresser. That's what I did, I fit them in. I wasn't going to open and close a sofa every day, that's for sure.

Then Kate bought me one of those folding dressing screens that starlets used to change behind in movies like *Forty-Second Street*. It was pale yellow, mostly, I would always remember, an antique. She bought it at a store on MacDougal Street and it was delivered.

Closet space was the real problem. Kate took the bedroom closet, of course, and I used the smaller closet in the hall. A shirt, a bathrobe, a wool sports jacket from Barney's, or all of those and more, could often be seen draped over the screen. Didn't matter. We weren't expecting anybody to pop in from *Better Homes and Gardens*.

A black housekeeper named Tina came once a week and for four hours worked her heart out in that one-bedroom, one-bath apartment. She worked for someone else in the building, too; that's how I had found her. Every week she would make the place spotless in a couple of hours, then spend the rest of the time on a specific project like the walls and woodwork, the appliances, the bathroom tiles, the closets, or something else. She loved Famous Amos for his chocolate chip cookies, and as long as a bag of those was around, there was no stopping her.

Ten minutes after she left, of course, the place was untidy again with dirty dishes, shoes and books out of place, a damp bath towel tossed over the shower rod, a glob of shaving cream in the basin, dappled with flecks of whiskers. But you could eat off the floors for a week.

I now live, all these years later, in a big house on Cherokee Lake outside of Knoxville, Tennessee. It's on about four wooded acres. An old, country hick named Fugut keeps the land a little groomed and a little wild, with the help of about fourteen Mexicans. The housekeeper strolls in twice a week and puts in her time, but she's no Tina.

Coming home from Daisy's that night of Patsy's murder, I let myself in quietly. It was late. Kate would be asleep in her room. I went straight to the kitchen, stood at the fridge drinking cold milk out of the carton for about five minutes. No liquid ever tasted better. I wondered if Patsy had kept her apartment clean and orderly. I doubted it. I had a feeling she was sloppy at home with no housekeeper to whip the place into shape. I imagined she died among dusty furniture, dirty dishes, uncapped skin cream jars, open drawers with stockings hanging halfway out. She, herself, was clean as a whistle. You could see and sense her commitment to personal hygiene and neatness. But after scrubbing each square inch of herself and after brushing, grooming, tweezing, and applying dabs of this and that, my guess was she left behind a mess, a mess of her own making.

A mess of her own making.

I rattled three Bayer aspirins out of their bottle and washed them down with another half-pint of milk. Next thing I knew I was stretched out on my bed by the window. I reached up and turned the wooden rods that closed the slats on the shutters. Some of my clothes were off, and some were hanging over the dressing screen.

On my way down into some black pit, I passed the charred body of a fine Kentucky gentleman, who should have been alive and living out his days on five hundred beautiful acres surrounded by happy horses and blue-green pastures.

Chapter 13

I was dead till after eight the next morning. When I opened my eyes, dull morning light escaped from a cloudy sky and oozed through slits in the shutters. At the foot of my bed, Kate was sitting on the edge of the mattress drinking a cup of hot coffee. She was wearing a years-old pair of Levis that fit her sleek frame like a rubber glove. A flannel shirt, mine, was buttoned most of the way up her front but misaligned.

Early in the twentieth century a French chemist by the name of Schueller developed a commercial hair dye. He was the first one to do it. He named his company the French Harmless Hair Dye Company, but it didn't do well ... not at first. But he hung in there and eventually did better after he changed the company name to L'Oreal. Even today, L'Oreal would pay millions if they could capture the glorious natural straw blonde hair Kate had.

This particular morning it was piled on her head, and her face was scrubbed clean, no makeup. She was a natural beauty, as natural as white on a swan. Her eyes were ultramarine this morning and a little puffy underneath. They blinked at me.

"What happened to you last night? The police were here. Where were you?"

"The police?" I hadn't heard from Marty about his interview yet, of course, so I had no idea what they might have said or asked. Well, I had an idea. It would be pretty standard stuff. I gestured for her cup, she handed it to me. I needed it. I took one sip, then another. Caffeine, the miracle drug, right up there with penicillin. "Do they know anything?"

"If they do, they aren't telling. They wanted to know if I knew anything."

"Well, sure. What'd you tell them?"

"I just told them we were friends. Told them about yesterday afternoon. How she left the theatre to make a call. They weren't here long. To tell you the truth, I was in a daze. I didn't even know if Marty knew. They said they were going to talk to him, said they might want to talk to you."

"I told Marty. I spent some time with him."

"How did he take it?"

"Just like us, except add he was sleeping with her and enjoying it a lot."

She stared at me, and her eyes widened one millimeter.

"You buttoned your shirt wrong."

She looked down, realized her error, undid all the buttons and tried it again. As she did so she said, "Homicide detectives Flannigan and Rivo," no verb. "I didn't know where you were."

"Daisy's."

"Oh," with no enthusiasm.

Kate and Daisy had met only once. It was the time Daisy had come over to my place one afternoon about six months before, April it was. Kate had been in town a couple of weeks. She had decided just a few days before to stay awhile.

Daisy had wanted to see where, how, I lived. She didn't leave the East Side too often. Fifth to York, uptown and not too far down, was her domain. The West Side was more or less Kentucky to her. If she did venture to the likes of Columbus Avenue or Amsterdam, it was to have a meeting inside a high-rise under construction. When the meeting was over and after she'd spot-checked the bathtubs, vanities, and toilets, she'd step out, probably escorted by a foreman, hop back into her Lincoln Town Car or cab, and zip back to the land of Bloomingdale's and Sutton Place.

She was looking over my apartment that day, as reserved and suspicious as a prospective buyer. Kate came home, excited about just having attended her first acting class. She even mentioned a young woman named Patsy she had met and liked.

Kate and Daisy said hello, but it wasn't a glorious event. They didn't click. Daisy probably thought Kate was too pretty, especially to be my sister, and Kate probably thought Daisy was too educated and successful. I didn't know for sure because none of us ever really talked about it.

Kate asked, "Is she for you?" and not much else. Here was the Kentucky blonde who looked and sounded as if she'd bucked plenty of hay in her time and the East Side Jewish executive who could convince you in about ten minutes why the Rosenbergs shouldn't have been executed. Her mother's father had been a famous poet and had even won the Bollingen Prize from the Yale University Library in the 1950's.

My young sister had dropped out of UK after two years and married a guy named Roy, a third-string lineman for the Wildcats until he broke his collarbone in practice and quit. He turned out to be a slouch and just generally no good. His real love was shoplifting. I defended him once, suspended sentence. The merchandise from Parks-Belk was recovered. Next time he was caught, Kate left him and so did I. She had never found what she wanted to do in life. A catering business she started with a friend back home had failed quickly. She drifted in and out of other jobs, even answered the phone in my office for a while, but nothing seemed to be for her. Maybe show business was the answer.

She was insecure, certainly. Daisy wasn't. That would be another reason why they didn't jive. Kate never inquired about Daisy. I wasn't even sure Daisy remembered the two had met.

Anyhow, I left it alone. If circumstances changed someday and I had a chance at Becky Norse from Marty's play, I'd grab her like she was the ripcord on my parachute and I'd been free-falling for six thousand feet. Kate had liked Becky when we were all around the table at the bar. Didn't she? Come to think of it, I hadn't asked her. It didn't matter.

"Jay, what do you think happened?" Still sitting on the bed, Kate took her coffee back and finished it with a gulp.

"To Patsy? I have no idea."

I threw off the sheet, swung my feet to the floor, sat in my boxer shorts. "Is there more joe?"

Kate stood up, disappeared around the screen. I headed for the bathroom. We met in the kitchen a couple of minutes later, and she had coffee for both of us.

"Did the police say it was a break-in?"

"I asked. They wouldn't tell me. But it must have been, don't you think? She probably came home, right there in the middle of the afternoon, and somebody was burglarizing her apartment. And they killed her."

"Most people are killed by someone they know."

"What does that mean?"

"It's a statistic, that's all. Do you know a lot of people who knew her?"

"Yeah, they asked me that. Not really. I mean, the people in our acting class."

"What about guys?"

"She was private about that. Before Marty came along, I'd asked her if she was seeing anybody. She generally said, 'Not really.' I have a suspicion, though. I think she was seeing her boss, Preston Hondonada, maybe, you know, sometimes."

"What makes you think so?"

"The one time I visited her at work, at the TV station, months ago. The way they looked at each other as we were leaving. There seemed to be something going on."

"Why didn't you ask her?"

"I started to. I said, 'He's sort of cute.' She looked at me quickly, then looked away. 'He's not cute and you know it,' she said, 'he's just on television. And he's married.' Funny, though. I felt that was more of a warning to me than a worry of hers. Anyhow, I dropped it."

"Hmmm. Cops'll have fun with him."

"Jay, it could have been me. Here, in our apartment. It could have been me."

"Honey, every female in the city is thinking that. Say, I meant to ask you ..."

"What?"

"That girl we met yesterday, the one in Marty's play?"

"Which one?"

"The funny one. I mean, the one with the sense of humor."

"The goofy one?"

"Becky," I said, sharply. "What was goofy about her?" And I realized my back was up. Kate's casual dismissal of her upset me.

"Oh," Kate said, "you like her?"

"I thought she was fun."

"Did you ask her out?"

"No." I left Kate in the kitchen and headed for the shower. The phone caught me on the way, and Marty said, "Two detectives worked me over last night."

He painted the whole picture, right down to Flannigan's blowzy face and three-wife history, to Rivo's aspiring daughter and Bob the cat. I remembered Kate muttering, "... detectives Flannigan and Rivo."

"Okay, thanks, I'm sure I'll be next," I said.

We hung up the phone, and I finally made it to the shower. Then I planned to go to breakfast and start reading that movie script Marty had given me. Why not?

Chapter 14

What Marty Sequatchee thought he would be was an engineer. As far back as the eighth grade, he had that notion. Probably because he built an electric motor for his science project that year, more or less from things around the house and from the construction site of a new Sears a half-mile away. It was a powerful little series motor for its size, to hear him tell it.

He made the whole thing himself. He attached copper strips to an empty spool from his mother's sewing box. Well, the spool wasn't empty at first, but that part was easy. The spool became the commutator. He made the armature and field coils, electromagnets, by wrapping copper wire around two pieces of scrap iron, which he bent into two perfectly shaped brackets. The armature itself was a metal rod he found in the trash bin where they were building the Sears. He hack-sawed it to length. The brushes on either side of the spool were made from thin pieces of springy brass. He put a drop of solder here and there and so forth. The whole unit was mounted on a wood base and hooked up to his old Lionel train transformer, and it actually worked.

He soldered a two-inch pulley to one end of the armature, then built a miniature amusement park ride out of toothpicks and ice cream sticks and hooked it to the pulley by a thick, flat rubber band. The ride was one of his own design, although it was very much like The Roundup, except Marty's just went round and round and didn't lift to a diagonal or anything like that.

All this completed, he had to write a description of his project, what he had done and how he had done it, explaining how an electric motor works, basically the attract-repel principle. His teacher preferred the reports accompanying the projects to be typed. Marty didn't know how to type, but he found a book in the library that promised to teach him in twenty-four hours. He figured if he took the book home one particular afternoon, he'd be typing by the next.

Sounded logical but it didn't quite work that way. Nevertheless, he learned the home keys and stuck with it and eventually pounded out his two pages on a manual Royal which once belonged to his mother. He won an Honorable Mention for his efforts. Apparently, the top prizes went to experimental projects. *The Effects of Gamma Rays on Man in the Moon Marigolds* projects, not minor feats of electrical engineering.

What he really took away from the experience was the ability to type. It eventually led him to writing plays for the stage and movies for the big screen.

The adorable and perky young lady sat on her side of the coffee shop booth and listened to Marty's chronicle, riveted. I was there in the next booth, not riveted, but hearing, whether I liked it or not. I was eating breakfast and trying to read that movie script. Marty had wanted me to join them, of course, when he came in and saw me, but I begged off and let them conduct their business.

I knew from Marty's call they would be there, so, no, I wasn't there by accident. Sure, I was curious.

Ellen Rivo was dressed up in an autumn outfit of brown and speckled orange. Her accessories matched perfectly, right down to little pumpkin earrings. She had an orange silk scarf tied around her neck, the knot at her lovely throat. Her hair was perfectly coiffed and sprayed, and she must have been up half the night applying her makeup. She looked rather stunning, really, just overdone for the Greek coffee shop. You might see a woman who looked like this, except she'd be about forty-four, running a medium-sized company on Sixth Avenue, a modeling agency, maybe, or a casting agency for mainly television commercials.

In the late 1800's a society fly named Ward McAllister said there were only about 400 important members of New York Society. Maybe Ellen was supposed to be made up to be one of The Four Hundred.

Most of the show people that I noticed, male or female, young or older, slouched around in loose, comfortable attire. If they were caught in a suit, it was because the part called for it and the curtain was up. Twenty-two-year-old Ellen Rivo had it wrong, but that was okay. She just didn't know. She was obviously trying to impress Marty, and there was something sweet about it.

All she had asked was, "How did you get into writing plays and movies?" Marty, made a little nervous by the young Ms. Rivo, answered her question by starting in the eighth grade.

To his credit, though, after the electric motor story, he jumped quickly to college, to a few novels and plays that opened his eyes, to one English professor who inspired him. On he went to his drive to New York City in his '65 Chevy, finally getting to his first (disastrous) theatrical production. Did he ever regret not becoming an engineer? Yes, sometimes, because engineers can actually do something. Ask a writer of movies and plays to do something practical and see what you get.

When she first sat down, she handed Marty her eight-by-ten glossy. Man, what a doll. Those big, moist Italian eyes. Marty instinctively turned it over on the back, but she had no resumé.

"I haven't done anything," she said. "I'm green as a pickle. I played Humpty-Dumpty in second grade and sat on a painted refrigerator box wearing a pillowcase until I jumped down on cue." She made a dumb face, probably the one she was making in the photograph her dad carried. It was sort of endearing, especially juxtaposed against her outfit. "That's the extent of my acting experience. I wasn't going to lie, so there's no resumé."

She folded her arms on the table top, leaned in a little and said, "I'm sorry about the death of your friend."

"Thanks," Marty said. "I'd only known her a couple of weeks." He made that clear because I know he honestly felt there were others, Patsy's parents for instance, who more deserved the sympathy.

He decided to have some scrambled eggs and rye toast, but Ellen settled for her coffee, one cup only, black, and really didn't say much more about herself at all. She wanted to talk about Marty. She loved his movies, loved his movies, and had loved the two plays of his she had seen. They talked about all that. She particularly liked Marty's first movie, *Learning the Body*. "It almost made me want to become a doctor," she said.

"Some people thought it was a ripoff of *Men in White*, but I didn't mean for it to be. Problem is, there are only so many stories."

"*Men in White*?" Not surprising she wouldn't know the flick, it was from 1934 and adapted from a Sidney Kingsley play. Marty told her but she'd never heard of Sidney Kingsley. Neither had I, by the way.

"My major was psychology," she said. "Marty, forgive me for not being knowledgeable in the theatre. But the art of acting, thc craft, the art and craft of acting, I think I can do it."

"Are you an existentialist?" he asked her. "Man is what he makes of himself?" Marty didn't go around talking that way, like he was Woody Allen, for crying out loud. He was just having some fun with her. Nobody would believe he was Woody Allen.

"Existentialism. That's philosophy, isn't it? I was psychology."

"But psychology was originally a branch of philosophy, wasn't it? I was just trying to get at your roots."

She paid the check. They had a minor squabble about it, but she absolutely was going to pay the check, period. Why was it so important she pay? "My dad told me to," she said, "but I would have anyway. It's only right."

We all left the smoky place at the same moment, about 11:45 that morning. Ellen and I walked out but Marty Sequatchee was in her pocket, I could tell.

Marty introduced me to Ellen before she headed off down the street. Ellen Rivo. We watched her walk away.

"An engineer, huh?" I said.

"Yeah, I know, I talk too much."

"I liked the existentialist part."

He went on to say he had found it interesting that Ellen did not blister his ears with tales about her own interests, abilities, talents, boyfriends, hopes, and dreams. She and Marty both knew why they were there, sure, to meet, to chat. Maybe he could give her a clue, point her in one direction or another, maybe give her the name of a person to call. An agent, producer, something or someone like that. So it made sense he would do most of the talking. But it was Marty's experience with young actors and actresses who sought advice, that that's not usually how it worked.

Usually, the young talent would talk, talk, talk, talk, never thinking for a moment Marty might know a little more than she or he. Talk, talk, talk, trying to impress the veteran, not realizing they were cutting their own throats, as far as Marty was concerned. "You know everything, kid. You don't need me," Marty would think.

Not this one. And he didn't think she was faking it. "Do you think she was faking it?" he asked me.

To me she seemed honestly interested in him, in his story. She didn't push but inquired. And she listened. She didn't yawn or look at her watch. Maybe she was playing him for a sucker, trying to get him to extend himself for her, to go the extra mile. Maybe so he would walk away so charmed he would get on the horn to every professional contact he had and say, "You absolutely have to see this girl!"

Or maybe she was just a good kid, raised right. Was that so hard to believe? After all, her dad was a homicide detective. It seemed to me Paul Rivo had instilled some values in his daughter, values like a sincere interest in others and, gulp, respect for your elders.

"What are you doing? Wanna go down and watch some rehearsal?"

He seemed to know I had some free time. He flagged a taxi and we climbed in. "Sheridan Square, please," he told the driver, and we took off in one of those big, lumbering Chevys.

When we walked into the back of the theatre at a quarter past twelve, Marty expected to see the rehearsal in progress. It wasn't. The cast, except for one member, was sitting around on the stage taking a break, running lines, smoking, teasing, chatting, my agent says this or that. I tried through telekinesis to make Becky Norse's head turn toward me. It didn't work.

Wayne, the director, came in behind us, and Marty turned to him. "How's it going, Wayne?" Wayne flattened his hand at his eyebrows, slid it up his high forehead as though he had enough hair to push back, which he didn't. It was either just a quirky habit, or he did it to wipe off perspiration, in which case, please, use a damn handkerchief.

"Come on out a minute," he said, turning and leaving the theatre. We followed him.

Chapter 15

Wayne led us through the downstairs lobby, up the stairs to the other one. He turned around and said, brusquely, "I thought you were going to be here today at the start of rehearsal, Marty." He had ignored me so far and didn't deviate from that behavior. I hung back and tried to be a piece of furniture.

"The girl who was murdered yesterday afternoon on the Upper West Side was a friend of mine," Marty said, in his own defense.

"You're kidding?"

"Patsy Holton, Wayne. She auditioned for us."

"She did?" His tone had softened.

"The beautiful brunette ... who ... wasn't very good?"

He remembered. "That was her? What a shame."

"She was here yesterday. She saw the run-through, or half of it."

"I had no idea."

Marty had given Wayne the impression his tardiness this morning was tied to Patsy's death. Well, it was. Because of her murder there was Detective Rivo, and because of Rivo, there was his daughter.

"I'd only known her since her audition, but it was a shock."

"I'm sure sorry, Marty."

"Anyhow, what's going on here?"

"Louise walked out on us."

"You mean she quit the show?"

"Quit the show. Walked out on us."

"Why?"

"She was unhappy with the character. You kept cutting her lines, and that just confused her more."

"Let's be fair, Wayne. Every line of hers I cut was your idea."

"The play was too wordy. It still is."

"I'm working on it."

"Are we going to stand here and argue about cuts or figure out how we're going to replace Louise?" The palm of his hand jumped to his forehead and held there as if he were testing himself for fever. After a two-second pause, the hand continued on up and over his head. His face began to cloud over, and he looked like he might throw up. He went over to the men's room and went in.

"Replacing a twenty-two-year-old actress in New York sounds easy, doesn't it?" Marty said to me after he looked around and found me pretending to be a lamp. "Thousands of them, right? You bet. But that doesn't mean they're any good. For Louise MacArthur's role, we auditioned dozens of young hopefuls. Louise was the only one who came close to getting the part. Now she's gone, and the show opens in just under two weeks."

Wayne came out of the john, patting his face with a paper towel. Some color had returned to his face.

"Can she do this? Just leave like this?" Marty said.

After all, there were rules. Rules of ethics and union rules, for that matter. You didn't walk without some kind of notice.

"I let her go," Wayne said. "We're going to keep her if she doesn't want to be here? Leave, I told her, get out, go. And she did."

"Let me get this straight," Marty said. "Are you telling me

she was considering leaving, threatening to leave, and you said go ahead?"

"It got heated."

"It got heated, and you boiled over?"

"I may have."

"Wayne, she was very good."

"She was unhappy."

"She had the smallest part in the play. Of course she was unhappy. Besides, I didn't even think she was unhappy. You boiled over and fired her."

"If you had been here, maybe you could have diffused the situation. You weren't here."

The ASM, the kid with the hooded eyes with not enough space between them, came from somewhere with a handful of eight-by-ten photos. "Here they are," he said, handing them to Wayne.

Wayne jerked them away from the kid and started shuffling through them like they were baseball playing cards. Got him, got him, got him ...

"Does the rest of the cast know?"

"Sure, they know. That's why they're sitting in there on their bums." Having finished rifling through the photos of possible replacements, he handed them to Marty.

"We better pick one and see if we can get her. And we better be quick about it."

Marty flipped through the eight-by-tens. Okay, it was the smallest part in the play, but that didn't matter. Every actor had to be the best, the best you could find. A successful production of a new play was so tenuous, Marty would tell you, you couldn't open saying to yourself about one of the performers, "Not what we wanted, but she'll do." Would an artist painting an oil refer to an undeveloped background detail and say, "Oh, that's not the focus of the picture. It doesn't matter"? Plus, the character had only three scenes, true, but they were difficult, important scenes.

"I don't know, Wayne," Marty said, having gone through the stack twice. "But I have a hunch."

"All right."

"I met someone this morning I'd like to audition for the role."

"Marty, we can't start auditioning again. We just don't have time. Less than two weeks."

"Just one girl. I have a feeling she might be excellent, might be as good or better than Louise."

Wayne walked away, a short distance away, shaking his head and pampering it with his hand. He paced back and forth for a few seconds and then said, "Okay, get her down here."

"I've got her eight-by-ten." Marty was still carrying his soft leather briefcase. He found a chair to set it on and dug in for the photo. He pulled it out, dealt it to Wayne who took a long gander.

"All right, she's cute and the age is about right." But he shrugged because that meant almost nothing. He snapped the photo over to the back. "Where's her resumé?"

"Yeah. I don't have her resumé." If Marty said the girl had never worked in the business a day in her life, Wayne would hit the ceiling.

"Call her. Get her down here right now. I'll go back downstairs and do some scene work till she gets here."

Marty took the picture back, looked at it again, turned it over on the back again, realizing something important was missing.

"Damn."

"What?"

"I don't have her phone number."

"Who's her agent?"

"Her agent? I don't know." She was as far from having an agent as Marty was from delivering an Oscar acceptance speech.

"Call Equity. Or look her up in the book." Equity, the actor's union, might put Marty in touch with her or have her call Marty. The only problem was, Equity wouldn't know she existed.

"I know how to reach her," Marty said.

"What's her name?"

"Ellen Rivo," Marty said.

If I had been a lamp, I might have started flickering S.O.S.

Chapter 16

In one of the cramped administration offices, Marty stood at a desk so cluttered with scripts, papers, magazines, letters, books, and junk, he had to hunt for the telephone like clawing through earthquake rubble looking for a possible survivor. He bumped a green glass ashtray and a dozen cigarette butts flipped out onto the desk, dragging plenty of ash with them.

Mumbling to me, he found the phone, picked up another pile of play scripts from the chair, balanced them on a corner of the desk, making a two-foot-high stack three feet high. He sat down, reached for his wallet, searched through it for something he knew he had stuck in there last night. He found it. It was the card Flannigan had given him.

Marty dialed the number on the card and listened to it ring a couple of times before a deep, gruff voice answered. "Homicide, Detective Masgrove."

"Is Detective Flannigan there, please?"

"He's not here. What's the message?"

"Oh. Uh ..."

"What's the message?" The voice was impatient and loud enough for me to catch some of it.

"How about Detective Rivo?"

"He's not here either. What's the message?"

"My name is Marty Sequatchee."

"What?"

"Marty Sequatchee. Sequatc — "

"Wai, wai, wait ..." You'd think he'd have a pencil handy, but we could feel him looking around for one. "Sasquatch?"

"Sequatchee." And he spelled it out for Masgrove and put a phone number with it. "If Detective Rivo could call me here as soon as possible, I'd really appreciate it."

"All right."

"Thanks," but it sounded like Masgrove was gone already.

Marty leaned back in the old wooden office chair. The coiled steel spring in the rear of it squeaked a little. I found an inch of desk space and hiked the underside of one thigh and part of my butt onto it.

A figure passed by the open door. "Oh, Rita," Marty said. The woman, Rita Wauller, took a step back, into the doorway. She peered in at us. She was one of those rather unattractive women with huge breasts and slightly rounded shoulders because of it. Because, I guessed, she had spent so many years trying to hide the enormity of her boobs. If she knew anything at all about make-up, she could apply some here and there and look thirty-five instead of forty-five. She worked at the theatre in some administrative capacity. She had a position that almost sounded important, but I don't remember the meaningless title Marty said she held. She seemed to be the only staff person around this afternoon. Or maybe the chubby girl with dirty hair, her name was Dori somebody said, was in the box office.

"I'm expecting a phone call on 06," he said, pointing to the black phone in front of him.

"Aren't you lucky?" Rita said, her mind on other things.

"I'm just saying, I'm here. I'll get it."

Rita vanished from the doorway again. Marty leaned forward, put his elbows on the table, clasped his hands together, rested his chin on this thumbs. He looked at me, but I didn't say a word.

You could read his mind. This was nuts. Ellen Rivo. Psychology major. Never been on a stage. Experience, zero. He glanced down at the photos of the girls who had tried out for the part. The one on top of the heap, a smiling little pixie of a thing, stared back at him. "What about me?" she seemed to say. "I'd be good. I don't audition well, but I'd be great in that part, given the chance." It made a lot more sense than what he was doing.

"Here's a chilling thought," he said. "What's going to happen after we audition Ellen, and she turns out to be awful, an embarrassment? Will I get a call from Detective Rivo asking what the hell the problem was? Will he want me, on second thought, to 'come downtown and let's talk about Patsy Holton under a sweat light for about sixteen hours.' Will the press get hold of that and wonder if I'm a suspect in the murder? Will it hit the papers and ruin my career?"

"Make the best of your time in Attica," I told him. "Form a theatre group."

The phone rang. He picked it up and held it away from his ear this time to make sure I could hear both sides of the conversation. After all, I was a lawyer. "TASSQ, this is Marty."

"Marty," the cheery voice said, "Detective Flannigan. You wanted to talk to me?"

"Oh." Masgrove got it wrong. "Actually, Detective, I wanted to talk to Detective Rivo."

"You can tell me, Marty," Flannigan said.

"No, no," Marty said, "it's nothing like that."

"Like what?"

Marty realized Flannigan thought Marty had a new thought about Patsy, an important, thus far undiscovered piece of information concerning her murder. The clue that would crack the case. Or maybe Flannigan thought Marty was going to confess. "I wanted to get in touch with Detective Rivo's daughter, Ellen. I don't have her phone number."

On the other end of the line, nothing. There was muffled murmuring in the background, but Flannigan was quiet. He was probably sitting behind some cheap metal desk, maybe uncapping a tube of some topical steroid cream to rub into those florid cheeks I'd heard about.

"Detective?" Marty said.

"Yeah, I'm here, Marty. Just going through Paul's Rolodex."

"Oh," Marty said.

Flannigan read the phone number and Marty wrote it down. "You're going to give her a call, huh?"

"Yeah, we want her to come down to the theatre where I'm working."

"I thought you were to see her this morning?" Personable, friendly. Was that just a coating, masking a suspicion of some kind?

"I did. We had a breakfast meeting."

"Right."

"But something's opened up at the theatre, and we wanted to talk to her about it."

"Call her up."

"That's what I'm going to do. Detective Rivo won't mind your giving me her number, will he?"

"Why? Why should he?"

Marty could get flustered. He was usually smooth and in control, but sometimes he'd lose all confidence, start to stammer and free-fall.

"It's just that she forgot about her number, to, to, to give it to me, her number." It wasn't her fault. She was nervous, inexperienced, she didn't know. Marty was supposed to be the pro here.

"Call her up," Flannigan repeated. He sounded refreshed today. After he finally finished up last night with Marty, maybe he had a good time with prospective wife number four.

"Oh, I will, sure thing. Uh ... anything new on Patsy's death?"

Just the hint of a pause. "We have some leads."

Marty waited for Flannigan to review the case with him, fill him in on everything they had so far, and tell him where the investigation was headed. But he didn't. "Some leads," is all he said.

Wait a minute. These cops did know, didn't they, that Marty didn't have anything to do with Patsy's death? That he really cared for her, never had a cross word with her? Yesterday afternoon, he was at the theatre when Patsy left. Marty came uptown much later. Then he walked west from the subway station at 72nd and Broadway. Patsy was dead by then, right? If she weren't, Marty could have turned right, walked up to 74th, turned right again, gone into Patsy's apartment, killed her, then hurried out, over to Riverside to see his old friend. Ridiculous. And these detectives knew it. Otherwise, they wouldn't be setting him up with Ellen Rivo. Unless ... unless they were using her as a decoy ...

I laughed, spontaneously, loud enough to be heard through the phone, laughed at the way my mind had raced through those nonsensical thoughts, all of them, in about a half second.

"You all right?" Flannigan asked Marty.

"Yeah!" Marty said, clearing his throat and frowning at me. "Thanks for the number."

"Okay," Flannigan said. "You keep my phone number now, in case you want to call me about anything else."

"Sure will. Thanks again. Bye."

Marty depressed the receiver buttons with his index and middle fingers.

"What are you laughing at?"

"Nothing."

He released the buttons, dialed, and waited. "Ellen, this is Marty Sequatchee."

"Hi, Marty."

"Listen, I don't know how this is going to sound, but I'm down here at the theatre, the TASSQ ..."

Chapter 17

After Marty had his first play produced, way back when, and after the mourning period, he went on to his second play. It was done in a reputable off-off Broadway theatre uptown. The woman who ran the theatre was a Northwestern graduate, smart as they come, and destined for theatrical greatness in the producing realm. She saw something in his writing, a gritty realism, a bold attempt to get at Truth. He was trying to be facetious when he told me that, but it's probably exactly what she saw.

The play was scheduled for a limited run, four weeks. That's the way those non-profit outfits worked, apparently. They would schedule and produce a season of six or seven new plays. While one was in production, the next was in the wings, casting or in rehearsal.

But when this second show of Marty's opened to better than expected notices and sold out immediately, the play was extended for two weeks. It was something rarely done in those days because the theatres had their schedules to stick to, more or less. The extension sold out, too, and the word of mouth and extra performances helped the fledgling playwright get a bit of a name for himself. Sequatchee was the name and people, at least people in the business, would remember it. For awhile.

But it wasn't quite as easy as it sounds. When the play

opened and the good reviews hit the papers, the cast partied and all was well. Then, at the end of the celebration that opening night, the female in the play — there was only one — told the director she was leaving the show, immediately. She had a chance to work on a new play by Edward Albee and she wasn't going to pass it up.

Edward Albee of Pulitzer Prize and Broadway fame, well, who would even try to stand in her way? "My play was an itsy-bitsy, non-commercial hit," Marty said. "Crumbs compared to an Albee gourmet feast. So the girl had to be replaced, post haste."

The director, with Marty's consent, hired the daughter of one of that particular theatre's major patrons. She had auditioned and was simply terrible. At the time of her audition, Marty and the director had told her how wonderful she was, but that the coloring and general physicality of the other girl was the reason they were going in that direction. But now, after the first girl had dropped out, they were in a bind. Since the theatre itself survived on the annual donation from the rejected girl's father, the pressure to hire her was overwhelming.

She learned the part practically overnight. Not literally overnight. A couple of performances had to be cancelled, then rescheduled at the end of the run. But the point was, she did the job. She came in with no hard feelings and threw herself into the part and the play.

And ruined the show. The poor thing was so devoid of talent, she didn't just hinder what was going on up there on the stage, she absolutely destroyed it.

Marty may have exaggerated when he talked to me about her inability to perform, however, because, after all, the show was extended two whole weeks. Or maybe he wasn't exaggerating at all, and the play itself was so good it stayed afloat despite an actress torpedoing it every night. Then again, maybe not. The play ended its six-week run and has hardly been seen or heard of since.

We came out of the deli across the street from the TASSQ with hot coffee in cardboard cups as Marty finished telling me about that production from years before. He couldn't hire Ellen Rivo just because her dad was a homicide detective or because she had charmed him at breakfast.

A cab pulled up at the curb across the street and dropped her off. The taxi rolled away.

"Ellen!"

She looked back over her shoulder, waved and smiled. She wore the same long, brown, cloth coat she had worn to their morning meeting, but it wasn't that cold. I wondered what she had on underneath because on the phone, just before he hung up, Marty had said to her, "You can dress casually."

Even from across the street you could tell she'd changed her footwear. She had on cowboy boots now, fancy ones. We dodged angry vehicles and crossed over to her.

"How many cups of coffee have you had today, Marty?"

"Five or six."

"Wow." She said it like someone with a one-cup limit. She barely acknowledged me and didn't seem to care if I was overdosing on caffeine.

Marty guided her into the theatre with his open hand centered at the base of her spine. Inside, he pulled out three script pages from his back pocket and unfolded them. "Why don't you take these upstairs and read them over. You'll be reading Annabel. It's self-explanatory, but she's twenty-one, southern, can't get along with her stepfather who resents her."

Ellen took the pages but stared at Marty. "He resents her, or is he really sexually attracted to her? He can't do anything about it, so it's expressed as resentment."

Marty stood there looking back at her. He glanced at me, but I was no help. "Well ... why don't you just go up and have a seat, take your coat off, get yourself together, and read the pages over? We'll be with you in a few minutes."

We watched her climb the first few steps. Then I said, "I think I better get going."

"No, no, stick around. This should be interesting. What else do you have to do?"

Anytime somebody used that line on me, they usually had me.

We went into "the house" to get Wayne. The director was on stage doing what he was supposed to be doing, directing. I stayed in the back. Marty strode down the aisle and stood with his arms folded, defensively, and waited. After a couple of minutes, Wayne finished with some instructions, turned, and saw Marty.

"Ten minutes, people," Wayne said and hopped off the stage.

Walking back up the aisle, Marty said, "Uh, Wayne, I have to tell you, she doesn't have a resumé."

"Didn't bring a resumé?"

"Right. Because she doesn't have one."

"What?" Wayne said. They went through the double doors, out into the downstairs lobby, and I trailed behind like a lamb.

"Shhh," Marty said. "Don't get excited. She hasn't had much experience, but I think she'll be good." Of course, he didn't think that at all. In fact, at this point he was just hoping she wouldn't humiliate herself and him, and I was hoping the same thing. "Look," Marty went on, "it's ten minutes. It's not going to wreck the schedule, and she might be the one."

Wayne was annoyed and you couldn't blame him. He preferred to work with pros, if that was all right with Marty. But they'd come this far, so why not hear the girl read?

"Is she ready?" Wayne asked, starting up the steps.

"Wait. Let's give her a minute."

Wayne shook his head, so negative. "I'm going to get a coffee. Bring you one?"

Before Marty could answer, the voice of the dirty-haired girl in the cage that was the box office spoke up. “Marty?”

Marty held up his mostly empty cup to Wayne, who was going out the door. You couldn’t tell if that meant, no, I’m covered or yes, bring me a coffee. He left, and Marty took the few steps over to the box office.

Me, I’d had enough coffee, thanks, anyway, Wayne. The girl reached the handset out to Marty. “For you.”

“Thanks.” Marty took the phone. “Hello?” Nothing. “Hello,” he said again, “this is Marty.” He looked at the ticket girl, speaking to her as though it were her fault. “There’s nobody on the line.” He dropped the receiver into the money tray below the bars.

“Oh,” she said. She was reading again; I couldn’t see what. She put her book in her lap and pulled the phone back in like a fishing net.

“Do you know who it was?”

“No.”

“Anytime anybody calls me, please ask who it is.”

“I’ll try, but I’m not your secretary, Marty.”

There was a shaker-style wooden bench against a wall, and I was using it. Marty sat down beside me. You can sit here, the bench said, but don’t get comfortable. Either go into the theatre or leave.

He covered his mouth and said to me quietly, “If she were my secretary, she’d wash her hair or find a new job.”

“Another of the calls, huh?”

“They have my home number, and they know I’m working here.”

The door opened, and Wayne returned with a coffee for himself, period. “Okay?”

We stood and traipsed up the stairs. “Are you sure?” I said to Marty. “Should I be in on this?”

"My friend Jay's going to watch the audition, okay, Wayne?"

"Fine," he said, without even looking at me.

Casual to Ellen Rivo meant something like a salmon-colored neck scarf tied with the knot off to the side like Dale Evans. She sported a blue silk blouse tucked into pressed Jordache jeans which were tucked into the pointy western boots, also salmon, with twirly designs and rhinestones on the sides. She hadn't changed her hair; it was still starched. She sat, legs crossed carefully, on a well-worn loveseat reading over the pages. She stood when we arrived. If I had been furniture before, now I was wallpaper.

Ellen didn't have any taste. No, the clothing wasn't tasteless. That wasn't right at all. She just didn't know how to dress appropriately. No big deal, I thought. If a miracle happens and she does the role, they can dress her, can't they?

Wayne didn't react to her appearance, and Marty was grateful for that, I could tell. Wayne, in his sweatshirt, old Wranglers, and low-cut, once-white Converse sneakers walked up to her and introduced himself. The three of them had about twelve seconds of palaver. Then Wayne said, "Okay, any questions about the character before you read?"

"Why don't I just dive in? If I don't give you what you want, you can give me some adjustments, and I'll try it again?"

At least she knew something. She knew what adjustments were, and that's more than I knew.

"I'm going to read with you, okay?" Marty said, and he pulled another set of the same pages he had given her out of his pocket. "I'll be the other two."

"You're going to be both of the other people?"

It seemed to throw her. So although she knew some, it wasn't much. Marty sat down on the loveseat, so she sat down beside him. Wayne found a folded wooden chair against a water cooler. He opened it quickly with a "clack" by holding the top, extending his arm, then jerking his arm back quickly. He flipped the chair around and sat in it backwards but facing Ellen and Marty.

"Anytime you're ready," he said.

Chapter 18

When I got home that day, I pulled out the movie script again and sank into the sofa. I'm no critic, but I didn't think it was very good. But then I knew before I opened it, it needed work, otherwise it wouldn't have come to Marty in the first place. The characters were asinine, and the story was trite. How do you rewrite this and make it into something more than scratch paper? I was fifty or sixty pages into the text, and that was my budding opinion.

In the early afternoon, just before I fell asleep reading, I decided to go out and buy an afternoon edition of the *Post* to see what their latest was on Patsy's murder. I also needed to drop off my new jacket at the cleaners. Walking down the block, I thought more about the script.

Hard to follow? No. Tricky terminology and funny margins? Yes, but not exactly baffling. I caught on, I got it, just like the maid at the Motel Six would soon enough.

It was a romantic comedy. A guy is moving to New York from Los Angeles to be with his girlfriend. A girl is moving to Los Angeles from New York to be with her boyfriend. Okay, you're already ahead of it. They meet in the middle of the country and fall in love. But there's complications. For example, they don't know they love each other. Circumstances, all contrived, keep them together in Kansas City for a few days, but eventually they go their separate ways until they get together, of course, again and for good. It doesn't sound too terrible, maybe, stated briefly. But the two main characters were so flat and uninteresting, who cared if they stayed together or moved on to their respective, and unfortunate, partners?

And the words written for them to say? Nobody talks like that, stiff and stuffy. If they did, somebody out there in gun-toting America would shoot them for sure. Of course, that was one reason Marty was being called in, to make the dialogue "dazzling and quirky." So maybe I was being too critical. Could be I just didn't understand the process, the steps these movies go through. For all I knew, Marty could turn the script into the next *It Happened One Night*.

I left the cleaners, stopped at the corner and bought the paper. Patsy's murder was front page. I read as I walked. I didn't read anything I didn't know until it was disclosed there was no break-in, and nothing seemed to have been taken from the body or the apartment. It led the police to believe the victim knew her killer.

That would be comforting news to millions. All those women who last night were saying, "It could have been me," were now breathing a deep sigh of relief. "It couldn't have been me," they're saying. "She knew him, but I don't know him."

Before I knew it, I was on Broadway outside Pauline's Dream, the combination clothing and head shop where Kate worked, off and on. I went in and saw Kate folding jeans in the back. She smiled when she saw me coming. A seafood market next door made Pauline's Dream reek of fish. More sticks of incense burned in the shop than Bic lighters at a rock concert, but it didn't help much.

"It was somebody she knew, apparently," I said, offering her the *Post* if she wanted it. She didn't.

"I know. Just like you said."

"Take you to lunch?"

"I can't go to lunch today," she said. "Herb needs me. I have to stay here. I'm always running out on him."

Herb Leech was the sweet, nervous little guy, who owned Pauline's Dream. Why it wasn't called Herb's Dream was a question I kept meaning to ask but forgetting to. Maybe Pauline was Herb's sister.

Kate didn't have to work. She knew I would take care of her, but she wanted a job so she could contribute to the household. I took care of the rent, phone, and Con Ed, and she bought most of the groceries. Sometimes I slipped her some extra pocket money.

"What are you going to do this afternoon, Jay?"

"There's always something to do."

How true it was. A museum, a movie, a bookstore. But my favorite thing in decent weather was to walk around town. I must have walked a thousand miles in two years. I knew this carefree life, this floating on the city's constant waves of energy, culture, and curiosity wouldn't go on forever. There would come a day the bon vivant, the flâneur, would work again. Cases, clients, briefs, courtrooms. Not necessarily for the money, but for the structure, the sense of purpose. And the money. Otherwise, you wilt. I knew that. I was okay for now, though.

Ah, face it, I thought — I'm adrift in the Sea of Manhattan.

A young woman interrupted Kate and me. She wanted to know if Kate worked there. We had to look up to see the woman's face. It was a long, shallow face. Kate asked what she could do for the woman, and the woman said she needed a pair of jeans with a twenty-six-inch waist and a thirty-six-inch inseam. Damn, that chick was tall. And thin. I waved to Kate and walked away as she was telling the customer she might possibly find jeans that size at a family-run store farther uptown. Yes, you could get anything and everything in New York, but you had to know where to go to find it.

Outside Pauline's Dream, the sun was shining. It was brisk,

and I thought of Louisville and Knoxville, thinking both were probably ten degrees warmer this day. But I was glad to be right where I was.

Twenty minutes later I was on the Upper East Side, strolling south. I knew, vaguely, where I was going, although I hadn't admitted it to myself. No, I wasn't headed for Daisy's place. I would never do that without calling, and I'd never call her in the middle of the day. Some people worked for a living.

As I ambled down Second Avenue, I had a thought. Why couldn't the guy be from the West Side and the girl be from the East Side and they meet going through the park? His bus is stuck in traffic going east. Her cab is stuck going west. They both get out at the same time and run into each other. It would be a more manageable and much less expensive story, wouldn't it? Just a thought.

I was headed for the exclusive McNoel Hotel where Don Toswell's wife sometimes, allegedly, rendezvoused with her boss.

Chapter 19

I stood across the street from the inconspicuous McNoel and stared at the main entrance. This was one upscale little hotel. The building itself was old, but the exterior had been sand-blasted or renewed in some other fashion. It retained its charm but looked fresh and inviting. Well, inviting if you knew it was a hotel. Because there was no sign out front, no markings to identify it, just a plaque with three brass numbers, the street address. You came to this place because you were in the know.

It wouldn't have occurred to me that illicit afternoon affairs took place here. Until I thought about it for two seconds. Why not? If you have money, and there were people in New York City with more of it than an infinite number of monkeys could count, why not check into the best? Or maybe Susan Toswell's boss had an apartment here, a pied-à-terre.

A handsome gentleman in a tailored suit (he looked like Richard Gere looked in those days) stood off to the side of the door, his hands behind his back. He looked around, up the block and down. He looked across the street. He even looked at me for half a second. He could have been waiting for someone, but I didn't think so. He looked more like the Secret Service. I guessed the security at a hotel like this was more than anyone knew.

A doorman came out and quietly hailed a cab. The doorman,

too, looked as if he could have been in the movies. And he wasn't dressed like he belonged on the label of a gin bottle. He wore a uniform, but it was gray, also tailored, and tasteful. His hat wasn't tilted, and it didn't press down and fold an ear or anything.

When the taxi slowed and stopped at the curb, the doorman pulled the back door open. A blond sophisticate with skinny legs below a short skirt and waist-length fur came out of the hotel and slid into the cab like a wet bar of soap. The doorman gently closed the door, and the taxi sped away. I was standing across the street thinking, "I wonder if that was Don's wife?"

"Sure it was," I said to myself. Except it wasn't to myself, I had actually uttered the words. Standing there, alone, on the corner, talking to no one. I made eye contact with a big man in a turtleneck and open cashmere topcoat who passed by and looked at me with disdain. He had obviously heard my remark. He hurried on past before I asked him for a quarter.

What was I doing there? I didn't know what Don's wife looked like. Never met her, never saw a picture of her, never heard Don describe her. Or what if I did know her on sight, so what? Was I expecting to see her come out of the hotel, her hair mussed, her makeup smeared, her blouse buttoned incorrectly as Kate's had been that morning? Maybe I was hoping to see her boss. Hey, that guy looks like he might be him! Right. Jay, you have too much time on your hands.

I checked my watch. It was after two. If I was going to see anything, which I wasn't because I couldn't because I didn't know anybody, I was going to see them go in, not come out. Or maybe it was a lunchtime deal. I didn't really care. Then I had an idea, smiled, and crossed the street.

The Gere guy, his hands still behind his back, regarded me politely as the doorman smiled and opened the heavy glass and brass door. "Good afternoon, sir, welcome," he said.

"Good afternoon."

Now *there* was a doorman. I walked into a serene, plush lobby. Subtle grays, dark blues, and black. It was the era for that and how classy it was. The color that off-set the muted tones came from a thousand dollars worth of gorgeous flowers. Everything that was supposed to gleam did. The carpet looked and felt brand spanking new. Maybe Tina worked here, too, when she wasn't cleaning Upper West Side apartments.

The lighting was recessed and as soft and inviting as butterscotch pudding. You couldn't tell if it was morning, noon, or night. In here it was always twilight in spring. Off to the right through an archway was a beckoning bar, dimly lit.

Behind the front desk were two Nordic beauties, also in gray suits that could have been designed by, well, okay, Yves Saint Laurent. They smiled at me, too. A concierge at a spotless black desk off to the side, looked up and smiled. He was another blonde and looked like a Swedish soccer player.

Another secret service agent in a black suit and spit-shined shoes came silently out of an unmarked door and walked across the stone-colored carpet. He paid no attention to the lone customer in the lobby, some guy named Bluffing. I didn't mind; I had started to feel conspicuous. The man went to the elevators, there were only two or three of them, and one of them opened immediately as if it were afraid not to. He stepped in, and the doors erased him.

I was dressed rather well. Casual but well. Dark flannel slacks, a warm, wool sweater, good shoes. But I wished I were wearing my new jacket from Barney's.

"May I help you, sir?" I had moved over to the front desk, and the question had come from no dumb blonde. Smooth and efficient, she exuded confidence and courtesy, grace, style, intelligence. If I had shown her a mathematical diagram and asked her to explain the slope tangent relationship to the change of the curve direction, I had a feeling she would have, and gladly. I smiled at her. It seemed like the thing to do.

"I'd like a room, please."

"Do you have a reservation, sir?"

"No, I don't."

"One moment, please." She tapped her computer keys.

I glanced at the goddess working the other computer. She sensed my eyes on her, looked up and ... smiled.

"How long would you be staying, sir?"

"Just one night."

"I do have a suite available, sir."

"A suite?"

"All our accommodations are suites, sir."

"Perfect." I tried to act nonchalant.

She did some more clicking at her keyboard. Being from Kentucky, I almost asked a question that just about anybody from down there would ask. No, not "Does it have a bathroom?" What I almost asked was, "How much is it?" But I didn't. I kept the hayseed in check. It was going to be pricey, and I didn't care.

I checked-in using my gold AmEx card. I didn't have any luggage. Perfectly fine. I was given a few general instructions, ever so politely, and then I walked to the elevators.

Another young woman and a young man were standing over near the elevators now, talking quietly to each other. Both were in tailored, gray attire. In unison they smiled at me and said, "Good afternoon, sir."

"Good afternoon," I said.

These were staffers, but what kind of staff? Bellhops? You're kidding me. The young man quickly preceded me to the elevators and pressed a button with a long, manicured index finger. A guest at the McNoel, apparently, shouldn't have to undertake the arduous task of pressing a button.

I waited a full two seconds for the elevator doors. They opened, I entered, and rode, slowly, to the third floor. The inside of the elevator was mirrored and trimmed in polished brass. Or maybe it was gold. I still didn't know the price of my suite, but I felt its price going up.

They must have gutted and renovated this hotel yesterday because everything in the suite seemed brand new, too. There was a compact but full kitchen, separate from the other rooms, of course. It had state-of-the-art appliances, and if anybody ever so much as made a pot of coffee in it, I would have been surprised. The Corleones never cooked a spaghetti dinner here for the family, that's for certain. Unless ... unless their housekeepers were nothing less than extraordinary. Everything, immaculate. I started thinking Tina was overpaid.

The sitting room was perfect, the bedroom and bathroom, exquisite. I took off my shoes, pulled back the bed covers, flopped and stretched out, sank into endless yards of Irish linen, crisp and cool. I thought maybe I'd lie there for a minute, then call housekeeping to come up and change the sheets. Certainly, they would do it with a smile.

Instead, I reached over for the phone. With an outside line, I called Daisy Leiber. That's right, the one I never called during the day. Machine. I left a message. "Call me at this number," I said, and dashed off the digits printed on the phone, "as soon as you get this message."

Every time I was with Daisy, it was at her apartment. She never came to my place. Even if I could have coaxed her to the West Side for a night of debauchery, I wasn't going to entertain her and bed her with my sister living there, knowing she might come home any minute. Anyhow, my bed behind the screen was made for one.

Surely Daisy checked her messages during the day, everybody did. She'd call me. Meanwhile, I hadn't had any lunch. There was probably a room service menu somewhere, but I didn't really need it. If I ordered something, they'd have it. What did I want? Now there was a good question. What did I want?

While I was thinking about that monumental question, I dozed off and took a short nap.

Chapter 20

Just before Daisy arrived at the hotel, I started to phone Kate to tell her I wouldn't be home that night. But I decided not to. I didn't make it home every single night, and she didn't worry about me. If I called, I'd have to tell her where I was, and I didn't feel like explaining my sudden urge to check into a luxury boutique hotel.

I made use of the McNoel. Daisy and I did. She got there about four-thirty, and we didn't leave the suite, going our separate ways, until nine or so the next morning. We frolicked like wanton, decadent fools, took four or five baths and several showers. We laughed and splashed and whooped it up like high school kids in a fun house, prom king and queen. We were royalty, and our subjects be damned.

"How did you find this place?" she wanted to know. She'd lived in New York City all her life, not counting her college years in New Haven, and her current apartment was less than twenty blocks away. But she'd never heard of this prize package hidden in plain sight.

"Friend of mine told me about it," I said.

We played, in bed and out. We watched parts of a couple of movies, made fun of them. We did everything but cook. I talked to her about Saul Bellow's *Humboldt's Gift*, after she happened to bring it up. A giant of a book from a brilliant novelist. We both had read it back in the 70's.

Is that who Marty Sequatchee longed to be, I wondered? A young Von Humboldt Fleisher, the bold, brazen, boundless intellectual, savage teacher, master poet? Well, Marty could long for it all he wanted, but that wasn't who he was. Or if there were a Humboldt trapped inside the playwright, he would never get out.

Daisy turned on the stereo at one point and tuned in to an opera, Verdi's *La Traviata*. Uh-oh. She danced around the sitting room in a tiny pink teddy or negligee, whatever you call it, and said, "We are Alfredo and Violette living in our country house outside Paris!" I had gotten lucky with the Bellow book, but with opera, I was lost. She realized it and tuned in the Stones. Jagger pleaded, not wanting to be a "Beast of Burden," and baby, we were rocking.

We ordered room service four or five times. One order was for champagne and just before I hung up, Daisy said, "And some Aspergum." I looked at her like, "You don't mean it," but she gestured at me, meaning, "Go ahead, Aspergum."

I asked tentatively, because I must have forgotten for a moment where I was. I might as well have been asking for an extra towel. When the bottle arrived, a Laurent Perrier, there beside it on the polished silver tray was an orange box of Aspergum on top of a white linen napkin.

Daisy ordered breakfast in the morning. "You need some Jew food," she said, and that's what we had, but she threw in some bacon and eggs with the lox and herring and onions and bagels, and she made sure we had plain butter along with the cream cheese. She was just being safe. She didn't want me to freak out.

She left before I did, she had to go to work. She gave me a long, tender kiss at the door and looked me in the eyes so deeply I thought she was staring at the back of my head. "I loved this," she said, and then she left. I stood there a moment, wondering if our relationship had been kicked up a notch by some guy we didn't even know, a guy named McNoel.

I finished dressing, checked the rooms over for anything possibly left behind, then headed out. In the elevator I guessed what the total charge would be. When I actually saw the bill, it was three times the generous figure I had settled on. I acted like it didn't hurt. I returned everybody's morning smile and put a little extra jaunt in my step as I left. Before I was out the door, three different female employees asked me to please come stay with them again. Or they could have been three Miss Universe contestants in gray suits, I wasn't sure.

A different doorman from yesterday opened the door for me, and, following me out to the sidewalk, he, too, encouraged me to return soon to the McNoel. It sounded like a swell idea. What an amazing, thrilling experience it had been. I'd be back, I thought, soon as I make my next couple of million.

The sidewalk. Here was the city again. Here was reality. I had rolled out of the fun house, into the light and the world. As I walked west, turned onto Second Avenue, and headed north, another thought hit me and hard. We couldn't do that again, Daisy and I. It could never be the same again, never that spontaneous, surprising, and new. Would trying it again sometime be fun? Sure it would. But it would never be the same. What we had for fifteen or sixteen hours, well, that was why the expression existed, "once in a lifetime."

I trekked along, continuing my mildly depressing thought. I guessed I was heading home, if I was headed anywhere. No, it could never be the same again at the great McNoel.

But a block or two later I wasn't thinking about Daisy or the hotel or any of it. Curiously, I was thinking about Becky Norse and her laugh and how she had both slapped and comforted my thigh the other day at the table at that bar. There we had been in all our ease and comfort, drinking pitchers of beer, while Patsy Holton was being murdered.

Chapter 21

It was about two weeks later Marty's show opened at the TASSQ. Two of the butts-in-seats on opening night were mine and Kate's. Of course, we would be there. Marty had trimmed about ten minutes out of the play, and it made a big difference. I thought it was sharp and tight and had come a long way in a couple of weeks. I thoroughly enjoyed it, and so did Kate.

The critics, the important ones, had come a few nights before. Kate knew how it worked and enlightened me. The theatre announced the date of the official opening. Usually in these pint-sized theatres it would be after only five or six performances or previews. The reviewers would call up and make a reservation to see one of these previews so that some days later, on the morning after "The Opening," their notice could appear in the paper. To get the kinks out, a Broadway play might preview for six weeks before the official night, and maybe play out of town for weeks or even months before that. The TASSQ and all the other little, struggling theatres like it didn't have that luxury. Even *The New York Times*, represented by Frank Rich or Mel Gussow, could be in the house on the very first night of its run.

"Fortunately," Marty once commented to me, "theatre critics are so astute, so educated, knowledgeable, and open-minded, they cannot only see a play and its production for what it is at the moment, but their intellectual and imaginative prowess is such that they can determine what it will become as it evolves in performance over time. Theatre critics are geniuses and should be worshipped, for we are all pagans and they are the sun."

The TASSQ couldn't really afford to advertise. If a play and its production were good, subscribers to the theatre would provide a substantial base audience, and those people telling other people about the show sold more tickets. So you'd be all right for your first performances, maybe even the whole first week. Then came the reviews. If the papers trashed you, especially *The New York Times*, you ran night after night in front of more empty seats than occupied ones. Those who did drag themselves to your play came predisposed to hate it. The show would begin and immediately step into quicksand. By the end of the night, it was up to its chin.

That usually didn't happen with Marty's plays; the critics were generally favorable toward him. No review ever set a play of his on its way to the Pulitzer Prize or to Broadway, but he did have a couple of commercial transfers to larger theatres over the years on the heels of such quotes as "A joyous evening!" or "A play often bursting with brilliance."

Usually his reviews were along the lines of the ones for his new play at the TASSQ. At the party after the opening night — it was held right there in the theatre, on the stage and in the house — everyone anxiously anticipated what *The Times*, and others, would say. Sometime after midnight the first copy of the paper made its way into the theatre. Marty and Wayne read it together, at the same time. Marty looked up, stepped back, and said, "He liked it!" Then, after a contemplative pause, "Didn't he?"

Sometimes, I suppose, you couldn't really tell. But this time, the review was more than favorable. The actors came out unscathed, the director was complimented, the designers mentioned, and the play itself was deemed worthy. So there it was. Some reviews were better, some a little worse. But all and all they came out very well. In a playwright's mind, of course, anything less than a total, foaming-at-the-mouth rave was disappointing.

The news burned through the party like a firecracker fuse. If it wasn't all they had hoped for, you couldn't tell it. Nobody's spirit was dampened by it.

When the word officially hit, I was sitting with Ellen Rivo in the middle of the house, drinking cheap white wine out of a plastic cocktail glass. She had been cast in the role vacated by the short-haired Louise MacArthur. Ellen had done a fine job, and I told her so. "You were so real," I said, "so natural."

"There's a reason for that," she said. "I didn't know what I was doing, so I didn't try to act." It worked. She sparkled in her role.

At least 150 people attended the opening night party. The cast, designers, and crew, of course. There was the theatre staff, a few patrons and other supporters of the TASSQ, and innumerable friends, well-wishers, and general audience members. Many subscribers who had seen the show that night had stuck around for the frivolities, the wine, the cheese, and the bowl of shrimp on ice, which sat in the middle of a plate of crudités. In a vague coincidence I alone could register, The Rolling Stones blared through the sound system, that same old song, "Beast of Burden."

I camc to be sitting beside Ellen Rivo only because I happened to move to get out of someone's way and sat down in the aisle seat, which I just happened to bump. There was Ellen, next to me. I reintroduced myself, reminded her we had met outside the coffee shop and that I had watched her audition. We exchanged our few words. She was dressed to the nines and too formally for the occasion and didn't at all resemble the character she played. I noticed she was staring down at the stage where Marty and Becky Norse were sitting on the apron, stage right, their legs dangling over the drop-off.

Marty and Becky were close together, talking. I didn't have to find them through Ellen; I was aware of them, all right. I wanted to be down there instead of Marty, sitting with Becky, especially since her boyfriend wasn't in sight. I had been working my way in that direction when by accident, I'd taken the seat beside Ellen.

Becky wasn't happy. She wasn't the free, funny (goofy), thigh-slapping, good-time girl she had been a couple of weeks ago in the bar. Her shoulders were slumped, she looked dour, and there was none of the fun energy that had whirled around her. She hadn't been singled out and slammed by any review I had heard about, so what was the problem?

Marty put his arm around her, squeezed her, whispered in her ear. That did it. "Excuse me," I said to Ellen. I stood up and worked my way down the aisle.

I had congratulated Marty as soon as I could find him after the curtain came down (a figure of speech because there was no actual curtain), but this was the first time I'd been close to Becky. "Hi guys," I said.

Marty reeled in his arm, first mission accomplished, and both of them sat up a little straighter. Becky looked at me, blankly, and blinked a few times. "You were outstanding," I said to her. "I couldn't take my eyes off you," I went on, not really lying.

"Thank you very much," she said quietly, but the remark didn't seem to improve her mood.

"The guy from *The Times* paid you quite a compliment." He had written that she was "fresh and frisky," "drawing the audience to her, and into her, with surprising ease." (He had written almost the same thing, in different words, about the rookie, Ellen Rivo.)

"Yeah, thanks," Becky said. But there was nothing fresh or frisky about her at the moment.

"Where's Kate?" Marty said.

"Oh, she had to go, Marty, but she loved the play." Kate had slipped out right after the show was over.

Marty's sly smile said, "Loved it, huh?" Maybe he was thinking, "She couldn't take two seconds to tell me herself?"

"Is everything all right?" I said to Marty.

"Sure, yeah, we're fine," he said. Becky had looked away but was now looking at me again. Marty said to her, "You remember my friend Jay Bluffing, don't you?"

"Oh, gosh," she said, trying to pull up the sides of her mouth with the appropriate facial muscles. I didn't know what "oh, gosh" meant. "Oh, gosh, of course I remember him," or "Oh, gosh, I'd forgotten."

I wanted to jump up there onto the edge of the stage, sit beside her and put my own arm around her, maybe say, "Tell me what's wrong, talk to me, I'll take care of it, I'll fix it."

I nearly did it, too. I figured if it backfired and blew up in my face, I could always scoot away saying, "Just kidding." I was inhaling a final breath of courage when we were interrupted by a man I didn't know.

"Marty?" the man said. The man was just below average height, solid, with black hair, short and combed with too much mousse, and a very trimmed, graying moustache, and I could guess who he was.

"Detective Rivo," Marty said, and they shook hands.

Okay.

"I loved it," Rivo said, slapping Marty on the back. "You know what I loved most about it?"

"Your daughter?" Marty said.

"Well, yeah, but besides her. What you wrote, it's touching and clean. You go to the movies or the theatre today, you don't know what kind of deviancy you're going to encounter, am I right?" He looked at Becky, then me, to see if we agreed. We seemed to.

Marty introduced Rivo to Becky Norse, and Rivo said, "You're a real pro," subtly distinguishing her from his daughter. Then Marty said, "This is my friend, Jay Bluffing."

I shook hands with the man as the title "detective" still reverbed in my head. I told him I had spoken with Ellen and told her she was excellent. Rivo liked hearing that and beamed.

"You're investigating Patsy Holton's murder?"

"Yeah, but not at the moment," Rivo said. There was a touch of "give me a break, will ya?" in his tone.

"Jay knew Patsy, too," Marty offered.

"Yeah?" Rivo said, forcing fake-surprise into his voice.

"She and my sister were good friends," I said. I knew I wasn't telling Rivo something he didn't know.

"Oh, that's right," Rivo said.

Or, maybe the investigation had become so widespread and complicated that Rivo didn't remember every single person on the periphery of Patsy's life. Not a chance.

"I expected you'd want to talk to me," I said.

"Nobody's talked to you?" Rivo said, again with that, "Really? No kidding?" inflection.

"Jay's a lawyer," Marty said for no good reason.

"Oh, yeah?" Rivo's eyebrows went up as he stared at me. "Maybe that's why nobody wants to talk to you."

Okay, it was mildly amusing, I gave him that. Rivo glanced up the aisle, through the mingling crowd, and picked out his daughter still sitting where I had left her. She was looking at us. No, not at us, at Marty. Still.

"I want to thank you for giving Ellen a chance," Rivo said to Marty. "Really appreciate it."

"We wouldn't have done it if she hadn't deserved it. She's a natural."

"At everything she's ever tried," Rivo said, proud of his baby.

Except maybe at dressing appropriately for most any occasion.

"Good night now," Rivo said. He offered a loose salute and Marty instinctively returned it.

"Leaving already?"

"The music's too loud for me. I guess I'm past it."

Marty and I thought the same thing at the same time — too loud? Past it? Rivo was only seven or eight years beyond the playwright and me. You mean it's that short a time before ... it's over?

Rivo headed off, up the aisle.

"I thought at first he was probably your agent, but then your agent's a woman, right?"

"Yes," Marty said, "and she didn't make it tonight. She wants to give the play a chance to breathe and find itself."

"What does that mean, exactly?"

"That she was thinking, 'I just can't go to another stupid play, not tonight.'"

"Excuse me," Becky said, hopping off the stage. "Be back."

She was half-spun around by somebody as she hit the floor. She turned herself in the other direction and walked away, her eyes angled toward the floor.

"Broke up with her boyfriend the other day. She's a little bummed about it."

I wasn't. I looked off in the direction she had gone, thinking maybe I could follow her. "She broke up with him, or he broke up with her?"

"Huh?"

"Her doing or Harry's? I just wondered." I could tell Marty was surprised I remembered the guy's name.

"Mutual."

"Then why is she depressed?"

He looked disappointed he had to explain. "The ending," he said. "Lots of situations are sad when they end, even if everybody knows they have to."

Come on, I knew that. What was I, a moron? Someday,

maybe soon, I would stop seeing Daisy. It would happen. It would melt away like an April snow. And it would be sad.

"Yeah," I said. Then I took a deep breath and blew it out. I realized I was, at least temporarily, inwardly hostile toward Marty because he had had his arm around Becky. Had he already moved in on her?

Before I dealt with that I said, "Ellen's almost as good as the other girl."

"Almost," Marty said. "I had to call Louise. She cried on the phone. That little part in this little play in this little theatre. More people will see tonight's episode of "Night Court" than will ever see every play now running in New York.

"It was important to her."

"Yes, it was, and God bless her for it. You ever finish that movie script?"

"Oh, sure."

"I have to get into it tomorrow. Why don't I pick it up from you in the morning and read it? Then we can grab some lunch. You can tell me in depth what you thought of it."

"Let me ask you something." I had to. "Are you seeing her now?"

"Who?" Marty was way past Becky. He was looking through the house, recognizing some people, not knowing others. He kept time to "Miss You" with his foot.

"Becky. Are you seeing Becky now?"

Marty refocused on me and let the Stones go on without him. I had a feeling the answer to his question was going to be very important to me.

Chapter 22

As soon as the applause had died down that night, Kate slipped out. She had said earlier she was leaving right after the show to meet a friend, and I let it go at that. Kate had gone to Patsy's funeral in Pennsylvania a week or so before, and ever since her return, she'd acted differently. I'd made a couple of gentle inquiries but she brushed them off. I was asleep in bed behind my screen that night after the show, but I heard her come in. I usually programmed myself not to conk too deeply until I knew she was home, unless I knew she was staying out all night. Baby sister.

Marty had decided at the last possible moment to go to the funeral, too, even though it was just days before his show opened and he was still cutting, rewriting, and shaping the play. He had planned to fly to Pennsylvania for the service and return right away. I'm not sure why I didn't go. Maybe I was paying Patsy back because she never showed the faintest romantic interest in me. Don't go to her funeral, that'll teach her.

Marty was running late and told the cabbie so. But somewhere uptown on the Roosevelt Parkway, in a chilly, relentless rain, they blew a tire. The cabbie got out to change it, but it was going to take forever. Especially since he had no jack.

Marty tried to find another taxi, couldn't, ended up walking west to First Avenue, still no luck. By then it was too late. He wasn't going to make the flight. He silently apologized to Patsy and kept walking west. Finally, soaked, he climbed onto a cross-town bus and went home. I told him he would have been on the same plane with Kate, same return flight, too, but it never happened.

I took the film script up to him that morning following the opening, instead of making him come to me. I handed it over and we firmed up the lunch. Before I left, I said, "Kate really did love the show. I want you to know that. I'm sure she'll call to tell you."

Marty laughed and put his hand on my shoulder. "Have you been worrying about that all night?"

"No, but I was thinking about it and came to the conclusion it was rude of her to leave without at least giving a thumbs up."

"People have lives," he said. A simple, true thing that spoke volumes.

We met later at a place on Columbus called Lucille's Café. Lucille's made a fabulous warm Grecian chicken salad, served in a bowl the size of the Capitol dome. I had that. We sat at a table by the window where you could eat, talk, and watch Westsiders flow by, some of them with destinations and others, like me, looking for one.

Marty had a roast beef sandwich, the beef the color of his living room chairs. It was stacked so high it would have made Philippe Petite dizzy. Petite once walked a tightrope between the towers of the World Trade Center but probably never ordered one of these sandwiches — too scary. I was beginning to understand why I was in New York. The hotels and the food.

"You call her yet?" Marty said.

"No, not yet." He had given me her number the night before. It was on a contact sheet that had the phone number and address of every member of the cast and crew. I had folded it carefully and put it in my wallet where it remained.

"You're going to, aren't you?"

"Yes. Today, maybe. Maybe this afternoon."

"You should call her."

"I'm going to, Marty." There was a little "don't push me" built in.

We were talking, of course, about Becky Norse. At the edge of the stage the night before, Marty had answered the question quickly and directly, "No." My sigh of relief had been enormous and audible.

Marty doctored his sandwich with pepper and too much salt. "I must be blind," he said. "You're really attracted to her, aren't you?"

"I like her. I can't deny it." I ate a bite of white chicken and a piece of lettuce. Whatever the rich, creamy dressing was on this salad, it was superb.

"I should have seen it a couple of weeks ago at the bar," Marty said, reflecting.

"Naw ...," I waved at the air between us.

"Or you should have told me."

"She left to meet Harry, remember?"

"Oh, yeah. But you can't ever let something like that stop you, if your little heart's going pitter-pat."

"I told my little heart to shut up unless things changed."

"Well, now they have. Still, you hesitate."

"She's low, she's sad, as you said last night. Maybe it's the worst possible time. If I had asked her out for a cup of coffee while she was still with Harry, it might have been better timing."

"So what are you going to do, wait another two weeks? Somebody else could gobble her up by then." Marty was eating his sandwich. He had to start at the top and eat into it and down. It was like demolishing a red brick building.

"I'm going to give her a call."

"If you haven't called her by this evening, I'm going to say something to her."

"What? Say what?"

"I'm going to tell her you want to ask her out," he said. "I'm going to ask her if it's something that would interest her, or if the very thought of it conjures such revulsion she'd rather hang herself than even get the call." Marty held up his nearly empty beer glass to our waitress as she passed. "Could I get another one of these?"

"Me, too," I said.

She winked at Marty. In her pink shirt and black bowtie, she zipped away like a hummingbird. Marty thought for a second, then said, "Goofy Becky."

"What?" I leaned back a little, and my knees involuntarily rose up and bumped the table.

"No, no, no, don't misunderstand. That's a compliment. She's good goofy. Becky is a sweetheart. I'm crazy about her."

I realized something. Marty had worked with her, endless hours, for four weeks or more, in the closed, tight environment of a theatrical production. Becky was now bringing to life a character Marty had created from the depths of his own soul. He probably felt very close to, and for that matter, protective of, her and everyone in the cast.

The guy must have read my mind. "Jay," he said, "putting on a new play in New York with limited time and limited funds, everybody giving everything, everybody with the single goal of creating a living piece of art to breathe and move and talk on a postage stamp stage for a few weeks, to try to express a thought, a philosophy, to try to entertain, even educate, it's an exhilarating time. While you're working on getting it up, it's like everybody's trapped in an elevator together."

I started to mention Louise, who had fallen down the elevator shaft, but I didn't. Marty was serious, and I didn't feel like making a joke. What I said was, "You get to know everybody pretty well."

"Pretty well, yeah," he said. "You certainly get to know if

a person is a good person or not. I can tell you: Becky is a good person. Fun and silly and ...," he stopped.

"Goofy." I let him off the hook.

"I was going to say daffy. But everybody loves her for it."

A fresh Amstel in a frosty glass was set in front of each of us, the empties removed. We faked a toast and sipped the foam off the top. We kept eating.

Goofy, daffy, whatever. I knew what they meant, they being Marty and Kate. The way she touched people, sort of clawing affectionately. The way she let her feet splay out sometimes, like a duck. The way she laughed, loudly, then covered her mouth with her hand as if to say, "What have I done?" I hardly knew her, didn't know her, but I knew that much. I remembered those things that for some reason got to me.

Marty ate his way through the bottom floor, and I did everything but lick the salad bowl. The woman behind Marty was having a cigarette, and gray smoke from her table drifted up and, of course, back toward us. Marty fanned it away.

"Say something to her," I suggested.

"Naw," he said quietly. "Let her enjoy it. I smoked once."

I looked at Marty's hands, but they weren't trembling, so that was good. He took another sip of beer, pushed his empty plate away from him. "Speaking of your sister ..."

"Yes?" I said as I looked up at the waitress snatching Marty's plate, then my own. She didn't do any winking at me. "What about Kate?"

"How come she's so beautiful and you're so ugly?"

"And I was going to buy your lunch," I said.

Marty hid his smile and said, "Tell me what you thought of that script."

"Wait, wait, wait." I took a swig of beer and wiped my mouth. There was a question I had wanted to ask for a month and this was the perfect moment. "I'm curious about something, I have to ask you. The day you met Kate and Patsy, at the audition. You must have noticed Kate was interested in you. Or ... was certainly willing to become interested. Right?"

He wasn't going to admit to it. I didn't expect him to. But he knew what I meant and knew it was true. He shrugged – it was almost imperceptible – and looked around the café.

"You had Patsy's attention, too, certainly. But ...," now that I was in the middle of it, it seemed like an improper subject, even a silly question.

"Are you going to ask the question, or do we sit here till dinner?"

"She'd kill me if she knew I was bringing this up," I said, picking up a spoon, turning it over, and tapping it on the tablecloth.

Marty gave up and jumped in. He knew what I was trying to say. "I asked Patsy out instead of Kate because of you."

"Me?"

"Sure. You ask me to do your sister a favor, then I move in on her? I don't think so."

"She's twenty-eight years old, Marty. She's her own woman. She goes her own way. I would never try to give her advice on men," I said, trying to sound as if I meant it.

"I start seeing her, get involved with her, but then when I faced you, I'd have a funny feeling. You'd be thinking, 'Anything else I can do for you, Pal?'"

I knew what he was saying, why deny it? "Okay," I said.

"You introduced me to two luscious babes. Frankly, with Patsy, I thought I was stepping into the less complicated situation. Maybe I wasn't. Now, you know, now or sometime down the road, our friendship secure and the time being more proper, sure, I'd love to take Kate out. Are you kidding me?"

I shook the spoon at him. "Stay away from my sister, you bastard."

Then we talked about that lousy script. I was blatantly honest about it; I had no reason not to be. I gave the story a

C-plus, the characters a C-minus, the dialogue a D. Marty let me talk before saying anything, except he did find a remark or two I made somewhat humorous. When I sprang the idea about the couple meeting in the park instead of in Missouri, he completely broke up, and his chest heaved up and down.

"What's so funny about it?"

"No, it's not that it's so funny. In fact, it's a good idea. I was just thinking: what if the bus he's taking across the park hits and kills a guy, and it turns out to be the guy who wrote the movie in the first place."

A couple of diners that were also lingering turned to see what was so hilarious. Marty's laugh struck our neighbors, and they laughed without even knowing why. "Justice prevails," Marty continued, spitting the words out through guffaws.

Maybe it was the beer, we'd had a few. I laughed a little myself.

Chapter 23

At home after lunch, I went straight to the phone. I took the contact sheet out of my wallet, unfolded it, and called her.

Her message machine picked up and said, "I'm out but only for a few minutes. I had to go to the paint store. So tell me who you are, and I'll call you. Bye." I panicked and hung up.

No, I didn't panic. But I didn't want to leave a message. I wanted to talk to her. What was I going to say? "I'm that guy you've met a couple of times but never remember my name. I want to take you out, so call me."

I had a better idea. She lived way up on 116th just west of Broadway. There was a paint store on Amsterdam somewhere about 101st or 102nd Street. That had to be where she was going. I brushed my teeth and bounced out again. I grabbed a cab, took it up to 96th, and hopped out. I moseyed on up Amsterdam looking for that paint store. And there it was.

I started in as she was coming out. It's a good thing I was there, too, because she was loaded down. She had a gallon of interior latex swinging in each hand and a bag of brushes, thinner, and other goodies under her arm.

She didn't recognize me. She looked at me and knew she knew me, but not exactly from where. But it only took a second.

"Hi there," I said, sounding amazed I had run into her. What a phony.

"Hi," she said, and by that time she had placed me.

I held the door for her, but instead of going into the store myself, I came back out onto the sidewalk with her. "You're not going to believe this, but I was just thinking about you."

"You were?"

"Well, the play last night and all."

"Oh, gosh."

"No, but when I think about the play, I think about you. You're the best thing in it."

"That's so kind of you."

"The truth."

She stood there in a huge navy blue pea coat. She wore dark, baggy slacks with her heels together, her feet sticking out to form a funnel. She flexed at the knees a time or two, and I wondered if she might launch into a full Charlie Chaplin routine, but she didn't.

"Can I help you with those cans?"

"No, thanks, I'm just going to get a cab." She stepped over to the curb and set down the paint. Now she flexed her arms and grimaced. She seemed mildly surprised I had followed her to the curb. "My boyfriend and I split up. The apartment's mine. I'm going to paint it."

I'd better say something and fast or look like a fool. I couldn't speak. I just looked at her. She was looking at me. Then she looked away, looked about a mile down the street.

I had the remembrance, peculiar for the moment, that Patsy Holton was murdered by someone she knew. I wondered if that's what Becky was thinking as she looked past me. Was she longing to be as far away from me as she could get because I sent the chill of suspicion down her spine? Should I say, "Becky, I'm not a murderer, if that's what you're worried about." I didn't say it.

"I knew you had a boyfriend. Then I knew you broke up. That's why I'm here."

She had just started to raise her hand at the street. She lowered it. "Huh?"

"That's why I'm here."

"Where?"

"I called you and heard the paint store message. I came up here hoping to bump into you. And literally did." My mind raced to find a reason why I shouldn't be telling her the truth, but I couldn't come up with one.

First, she blinked at me. I didn't know what was next. She smiled, slapped my chest with her open hand, then laughed and covered her mouth with the same hand she'd just hit me with. I loved it. That was the girl at the bar that afternoon who had such a good time rubbing against and beating on my thigh and digging through the Barney's bag. "You did not," she said.

"Sure did. Because I want to ask you out. I'd like to take you to dinner. How about tonight?"

"Well, there's the show."

"How about after the show? Do you ever eat late?"

"I have eaten a meal as late as midnight. I once had a pop tart at three a.m."

"It occurred to me a minute ago that," and I paused to giggle like an idiot, "that since there's a murderer loose somewhere on the Upper West Side, a guy moving in on you on the street might make you nervous."

"You're a friend of Marty's, aren't you?"

"Yes."

"Did he put a contract out on me?"

"I'm not a killer."

"Whew," she said.

I ended up walking her home, lugging the paint for her. I didn't mind. In fact, I was glad there wasn't a cab handy. This was our first one-on-one time together, and the walk gave us an opportunity to chat, a warm-up before dinner. A chance meeting (well, sort of) was the best way to come upon a young lady, anyhow. Especially outdoors. Loose, free, either one of you could run if you wanted to. And her with the paint, perfect. The paint and other paraphernalia gave us a focal point we could use to anchor the situation. Much like Daisy's dog had done the day I first met her on the street a couple of years before.

I used to see cigarettes do that. A guy would stand there, hoping to get something going. "Cigarette?" he'd say, offering her the pack. "Thanks," she'd say, taking one. He'd light hers, then his. Now they had something between them. Neither Daisy nor Becky nor I smoked, but it didn't matter. There was the dog and the paint.

On the stroll uptown, Becky really brightened. Gone was her dark aura from the night before. Was I responsible? Was I allowing her to put her ex- out of her mind? She laughed, talking about the color she had chosen for her studio apartment. Powder blue.

"I was going to paint it yellow," she said, "but then I said, 'No, don't be a coward, a yellow-bellied coward. Paint it powder blue, be a cloud!'"

"Good choice. Except ..."

"Huh?" she said, leaving her mouth open after she said it and looking at me with the innocence of a little girl.

"Clouds are white. The sky is blue."

She clamped her jaw shut as that registered. "You're right," she said, and laughed and laughed. "I had it backwards!"

"And generally speaking, the sky is sky blue, not powder blue," I said, swinging the paint cans by their half-moon, metal handles.

"I'm retarded, Jaybird, retarded," she said, and I loved it when she called me that. And it didn't stop there. She didn't seem capable of simply calling me Jay from that point on. She called me everything she could think of with a "J" in it. I was J.P. Morgan, Jay Rockefeller, and Jay and the Americans, by the time we hit 116th Street. Annoying? Not when she said it. I ate it up.

We arrived at her building. I hauled the paint up her front steps. She opened the outer door for us, we stepped into the vestibule, and she dug out her keys.

"You can't come in," she said, quietly, her head lowered.

"Okay."

"You can't come in because it's a mess. I'd be embarrassed." She unlocked the door, held it open an inch with her back.

"No, no," I said, "I don't have time." I set down the two gallons of paint but let my shoulders droop and my upper limbs hang as straight and low as possible. "I have to go get my arms shortened."

Her reaction gave me every reason to believe it was the funniest line ever uttered in English. She howled and slapped at my chest with both her hands. "Your arms shortened," she repeated, and then she actually kicked me. Not hard, but she raised her leg and kneed me right in the outer thigh.

"Ouch," I said.

"Oh, I'm so sorry, Jay Gatsby!" she said, covering her mouth while she laughed about it. It had been one of those spontaneous, involuntary kicks. What a goofball.

"I'll pick you up at the theatre after the show."

"Great. I'll be looking forward to it."

"Me, too." I reached down, grabbed the paint again and put a gallon in each of her hands. I made sure her bag of other supplies was tucked securely under one arm.

"You are so sweet," she said, "and not a murderer like some people." She leaned in and kissed my cheek. A simple little peck like that and J. Alfred Prufrock blushed and shuffled like Lou Costello.

I was still swooning when she disappeared inside. I danced down the outside steps like Fred Astaire and glided home by way of parasail. Maybe I was calling the wrong person a goof.

Chapter 24

Marty had gone home after lunch and started reading and marking up the movie script. The assignment could pull him up out of financial hell, I would eventually learn, so he had to get cracking. As I suspected, he worked in his bedroom.

He'd been poring over the pages for an hour or so when someone buzzed him. He came out to the intercom and pressed the appropriate button. "Who is it?" he said with annoyance. Not so much because his work was interrupted, but because buzzing somebody in the middle of the day in Manhattan, no call first, no warning, well, it just isn't done.

Marty entertained me with this information and with a recap of the agonizing events that followed. I heard it all on a day when he was sick with aches and fever. His condition didn't keep him from talking, and he wanted to tell me about this visit from Ellen ... and her dad.

It couldn't be a friend buzzing him, a friend would know better. Couldn't be the super; he'd just knock on the door. So who was buzzing him? Maybe a delivery man who wanted to leave a package inside and was getting no response from the recipient, so he was trying other tenants. Or wait, maybe it was a package for him.

He asked who it was, and the voice came back, "Marty?

It's Ellen." This wasn't good. He knew it, knew it, knew it, this wasn't good.

It couldn't be good. A red flag came out and waved in front of him as if his apartment were suddenly the Bristol International Speedway, and the NASCAR race in progress needed to be stopped immediately because of a horrible accident.

"Ellen?" he said, stalling.

"Ellen Rivo."

He pointed a finger at the door release button but hesitated before he pressed it. But what could he do?

He opened his door and heard her coming up the wooden stairs. In a doorman building, this wouldn't have to happen. You come home as Marty had done this afternoon, the doorman greets you, and you say, "Charlie, I'm not home this afternoon."

Charlie says, "Yes, sir, Mr. Sequatchee," and that's the end of that. But unless he nailed this writing assignment and some sudden cash, Marty's only move would be down and out, not up.

Ellen came down the corridor wearing a plaid suit, burnt sienna, with a dark green blouse. It all seemed to fit her well enough, except the sleeves of the jacket might have been a little short. Or maybe that was a style. The sound of the heels on her stodgy leather shoes, Vandyke brown Marty called them, was deadened by the strip of industrial carpet lining the hall. The outfit didn't work. Not on her, it didn't. Not on this twenty-two-year-old kid. What was wrong with her? Couldn't she look around and see what people wore, what young people her age were wearing? Then there was her hair. She had shaped it a little differently, but it was still fancy and probably sticky. Was she trying to be older? Why would she try to be older?

She was wearing enough eau de cologne to freshen up that German port city and the rest of Europe, and the scent preceded her down the hall.

"Hi," she said with a big, disarming smile. Marty had come

to his senses and climbed out of her pocket right after she was hired, but he knew she was an admirer, a fan, and who's not thankful, and forgiving, for that?

"Hi, Ellen. Is something wrong?"

"Wrong? No, nothing's really wrong. Except some guy outside just gave me the willies. Some big, tanned, muscular, blond dude. He smelled like whiskey, even from ten feet away, and he looked mean."

"What did he do?"

"Just watched me. Watched me come into your building. I'll tell my dad about him."

"He worried you that much?"

"What's the use of having a father who's a homicide detective if you can't sic him on people?"

They stood facing each other for a second or two until Marty realized she wasn't going to offer any explanation for ringing his bell out of the blue.

"Come on in," he said, opening his door wider.

"Thanks," and she went in ahead of him.

Marty stepped into his living room, watching her look the place over. "Lovely apartment," she said.

"Please ... have a seat."

She chose one of the cherry-cream chairs and politely sat, knees together, gently tugging down on the hem of her plaid skirt.

"Can I get you something to drink?"

"Let's split a soda."

"All right." Marty went into the kitchen. He opened a can of Coke, divided it into two tall glasses, plunked in some ice. No nodding this time, he was shaking his head. Couldn't figure it.

He came back and handed her a glass. She had kicked her shoes off, but that was nothing. Women do that all the time, don't they, even under the table in first class restaurants?

She had also unbuttoned her suit jacket and the three buttons that secured her blouse up high around her neck. The blouse looked like it could have been worn by a rock star during the British invasion in 1964 or '65.

She sipped her Coke as she watched Marty over the rim of her glass with those two huge, oval pieces of Italian marble she used for eyes.

"Let me guess," Marty said, easing himself down into the companion chair. "You're having a problem with one of your three scenes. Let me guess which one." He took a drink and thought about it. "Probably the last one. And I know why. Your situation is not resolved. We hear about your problem, see you working on it, but we don't see you have a catharsis, a climax, a resolution. Let me tell you why," he said, knowing he was sounding defensive. "Not everything should be tied up in a neat little bow. That's boring. We don't want to send every character on his, or her, merry way. In this show, your character is left up in the air. That's good; it's interesting. Did any of the critics rip us for it? No. They liked it. What you have to do as an actress is complete your character's story. Make it up. Maybe she jumps off the Tallahatchie Bridge. Maybe she goes west and drowns in the mighty Mississip'. Anything you say, that's what happens to her."

By this time Ellen's jacket was off and folded on an arm of the chair, and several more buttons of her blouse were unhooked.

Listening as hard as I could to Marty bleed out every detail, I shifted in my seat and said, "Yeah, yeah, keep going."

He was having another sip of soda when she stood up, undid her skirt, and let it fall to the floor.

He gagged on the Coke, choked, spit some of it out à la Albert Brooks and some of it went down the wrong pipe. He stood up and held onto his chair until his coughing fit subsided. By this time, her blouse was off. This was another one of those times he wasn't such an old smoothie.

"What are you doing, Ellen? Don't do what you're doing," he told her.

He should have said that garments ago, because she was standing before him now in bra and panties, hands on her hips, one hip jutted out to the side, and it doesn't really get any sexier than how she looked.

"We're not going to play games, are we, Marty? Let's just play and not play games. Thanks to you, our minds have met. Now it's time for our bodies to meet, to explore the relationship between our minds and our bodies. Let's get metaphysical."

The knock on the door was a gentle rap. Marty looked at the door, then at Ellen who had her hands between her breasts at the front fastener to her bra.

"No, no, no," Marty said, quietly. "Put, put, put ..."

She gathered up all her clothes and her Coke and sauntered off to the bedroom in no great rush. Marty went to the door. What now? Who now? Had to be the super or a neighbor in the building. He opened the door to Detective Paul Rivo and froze.

"Marty. How you doing? My daughter up here?"

"Uh ...," Marty looked around at the empty room to see if maybe she was there and he hadn't realized it.

"I talked to her a while ago. She said she was coming over to your place this afternoon, you two were going down to the theatre together tonight."

"Uh ..."

"Oh, another tenant was coming out as I was about to hit your buzzer, so I just came on in. All right? My partner's waiting for me downstairs."

"Finnegan."

"Flannigan."

"Huh? Right."

"We've been over to the Holton girl's apartment again down on 74th. Felt like walking through it one more time."

"Uh ... I was out to lunch, so ...," Marty paused to phrase it so as not to lie, exactly. "It's possible she could have come by while I was out, then when I came back she would have been, of course, gone. Since I wouldn't, wouldn't have been here," he stammered.

"Women, huh?" Rivo said.

"Yes, sir, you're right about that."

"You couldn't spare a glass of water, could you?"

"Huh? No. I mean, no, sure, come on in."

Rivo stepped in, and Marty headed for the kitchen, leaving his apartment door open. Rivo turned to the door and pushed it closed. He took a blue and white packet out of his pocket and waited for Marty.

When he returned with the water and handed it to the detective, Marty's hand was trembling slightly. Rivo tore open the Alka-Seltzer foil, plopped the two tablets into the water. "Hey, you're shaking. It's over, Marty, you can relax."

"Over? What's over?"

"The opening," he said. "And you did well, you did well." Rivo looked down into the glass, then back at Marty. "Heartburn and acid indigestion," he said. He sounded like the guy on TV who used that phrase relentlessly while hawking Alka-Seltzer, Tums, or Rolaids. "Dyspepsia, doctor calls it." The term "acid reflux" had not yet entered the lexicon.

"Poor eating habits, that's all. Used to be certain foods I couldn't eat. Nowadays, there's certain things I can eat." They waited while the water finished fizzing. Then Rivo gulped the drink as a minor eruption came from, apparently, the bathroom. Two or three drugstore items fell into porcelain. Both men looked toward the hall that led to the bedroom and bathroom. Marty was ready to say, "She's here, she's naked, arrest me," but Rivo smiled and said, "That's a careless cat."

As I continued to take all this in, my mouth open a good inch and a half, I thought of *Double Indemnity*, of the scene, almost unbearably tense, when Fred McMurray talks to Edward

G. Robinson while Barbara Stanwyck hides behind the door. There was a movie. Maybe Marty could write a script like that someday. The soft version, of course.

Now Barbara was in the bedroom, but Fred still needed to get rid of Edward G.

"I'll take that," Marty said to Rivo, and the cop handed Marty the empty glass.

"Thanks much," Rivo said, just standing there.

"Sure, it was just water."

Rivo looked at the glass. "I hope that's all it was."

Why didn't the guy leave? What if he started wandering again and wandered over to where Ellen had been sitting? The scent of her cologne would surely be lingering.

The phone rang. "Excuse me," Marty said and moved to take it in the kitchen. He set Rivo's glass in the sink and picked up the wall phone. He'd deal with the call, and Rivo would be gone when he came back out. Wouldn't he? Meanwhile, please, Ellen, don't come out of that bedroom.

"Hello?"

Nothing. He could hear someone breathing, barely, on the other end of the line, but that stopped quickly, the person must have covered the speaker part.

"Keep calling. I'll figure it out," Marty said, into the phone. He replaced the handset and stepped back into the living room. Since Rivo was still standing there, Marty decided to make the best of it.

"Somebody keeps calling me and doesn't say anything. They're on the line, I know, but they never say a word." Then, remembering Ellen's entrance, he said, "You didn't see some unsavory looking blond guy outside, did you?"

"No, I didn't."

"Maybe I've hurt some actor's feelings."

"How many times has the person called?"

"A bunch. I haven't counted."

"When did the calls start?"

"Uh ... a month ago, maybe?"

"Before Patsy Holton was killed?"

"Before ... yeah, before. In fact ..."

"What's that?"

Marty thought a second, to make sure. "She was here the night I got the first call. We were in ...," he stopped short again, deciding not to say "in bed." "We were in the bedroom."

"So the party calls day and night?"

"Yeah, you never know. Are you thinking the calls might have something to do with Patsy ... or her death?"

"You might want to jot it down every time you get a call."

"Jot it down."

"Yeah, to have a record of when each call came and how many there were."

"Okay."

And finally he started to leave. Marty couldn't get the door open fast enough. Rivo half-turned again to Marty. "Will you tell Ellen something for me?" Marty's esophagus tightened. "Tell her her mother got the room down the hall she's been wanting. She's pleased about it. Ellen will be, too."

"Room down the hall?"

"That's what I stopped off to tell Ellen in the first place. Her mother. Just say her mother's in the room she's been wanting."

"Okay." Curious as he was, this conversation had to end before Ellen couldn't take it anymore, walked in and said, "Hi, Daddy, yes, I'm here and, look, I'm nude."

Rivo left, Marty closed the door and let himself breathe. Now what in the world was he going to find in the bedroom?

In the retelling, Marty paused. "Well," I said to him, "What in God's name did you find in the bedroom?"

I think he loved drawing it out. Of course he would. Drama was his profession. He took a long swig of orange juice and coughed weakly, a wounded cowboy just before dying.

Chapter 25

Marty took a deep breath and proceeded with caution back into his bedroom that afternoon.

Ellen was sitting at his desk, stark naked, reading the movie script, with Bob spread out on his back, his partially white underside completely exposed as his legs went in four different directions like the ties of a trapeze net.

"No, no, no," he said, and Bob rolled, jumped down, and fled. Marty, however, had not been talking to Bob. In his bathroom, he grabbed his robe, came out and threw it over Ellen and the chair from behind.

She kept her eyes on the script and said, "Here's an idea. What if they're both disabled. Like, she has a clubfoot and he's, I don't know, semi-retarded."

"It's a comedy," he said. "Put the robe on, please."

"Physical deformities and retardation can be funny, don't you think? Or they could be, couldn't they? Cause I've only read about twenty pages, but this script seems to need some oomph."

This was a decade before a couple of guys known as the Farrelly brothers would come out with movies like *There's Something About Mary* and prove Ellen right.

"Put the robe on," he said again.

She sighed, stood, climbed into the robe. It swallowed her.

She tied the sash around her waist and yards of cotton seemed to gather at her front. "Everyone says you're such a ladies' man. Is it not true?"

"Do you know your father was just here?"

"I heard him. He knew I was coming here."

"Yes, he knew you were supposed to come here."

"He knew I was here."

"He knew you said you were coming here."

"He knew I was here, Marty. What do you think, he's Inspector Clouseau?"

"Good grief. This is embarrassing."

"Marty, I'm twenty-two years old."

"That's the other thing. I'm close to your dad's age."

"Oh, you are not."

"Well, I will be!" A line that made no sense, but Marty Sequatchee was rattled.

"You just don't find me attractive."

"I find you more than attractive. You're gorgeous. You're a little more aggressive than I like them, but lack of physical beauty is not one of your problems. But I'm not going to get into a sexual relationship with you, not now, not like this."

"What do you think my father's going to do, shoot you?"

"Don't you see how it looks? I put you in my play, you who have no experience, who is young, maybe a little naïve. I snap my fingers and you're naked in my apartment."

"You didn't snap your fingers."

"Of course I didn't."

"I guess I thought that after our days of rehearsal and all, I mean, it was so intense and you were so wonderful and helpful ... I thought you wouldn't mind my coming here."

"You could have asked. You could have said, 'Could I come over to your place and sleep with you?'"

She looked down at the floor. "Sorry," she said, stretching the word out about as far as it would go.

"I'm flattered, it's just that ... it's not the thing to do, not the proper thing to do."

"What did my dad want, anyhow?"

"Your mother."

She reacted to that, anxiously. "What about her?"

"He said to tell you she's moved into a different room, into the room she wanted."

"Oh, good," she said, breathing again.

"What does it mean? Where is your mother?"

"She's in an institution out at Long Beach." Long Beach, on Long Island, was known for its retirement homes, rest homes ... old folks homes, really. That's not what she meant by institution. Her mother would be much too young.

"An institution?" Marty said.

"A sanitarium."

Okay, they'd have a sanitarium or two out there, sure.

"She's had her nineteenth nervous breakdown." A figure of speech, of course. The Stones had performed "Nineteenth Nervous Breakdown" at the party the night before, Marty reminded me, but yes, I remembered.

"I'm very sorry," Marty said to Ellen, quietly.

"Yeah. It's rather sad. She's had problems ...," and she made her index finger run circles around her ear, "... for a long time, ever since I was little. Maybe she didn't want me."

"I can't believe that."

"My dad wanted me, I know. Not so sure about her. It could happen to me, you know? I could fall into her footsteps. I could turn out to be a loony."

Marty felt he'd stepped into an Ibsen play, not that I knew which one. I wouldn't know an Ibsen play if Ibsen's ghost read one to me aloud.

Ellen moved over to a dresser where she'd set her carefully folded clothes. She undid the robe, stepped out of it. Marty turned away.

"I'll be out here," he said, pointing. He left for the living room.

He sat out there slumped in one of his soft chairs, his cheek like modeling clay in his hand. He stared at the floor and had a few thoughts. One in particular. Ellen came out shortly, all zipped and buttoned and proper, carrying her coat. "When did you start wearing your mother's clothes?" Marty said.

She looked down at herself, then quickly at Marty again. "She's my size. She's built just like me. She's young, too, my mother. She's only forty-four. All she wears is housecoats, even when she comes home from time to time, you know, before her next one. She hardly ever leaves the house. So if she dresses at all, it's in old jeans and a pullover. She has a couple of pairs of almost-new designer jeans? They're mine now."

"Whose idea was it you wear her things?"

"It just happened over about a year's time, I guess. I used to go into her room and rummage through her wardrobe. I'd slip on this or that. Pretty soon, it's all I wore. There was once a time she bought lots of clothes and looked like a million dollars."

"Why do you ...?" he gestured toward her with a loose hand.

"What?"

"Why do you spray your hair with that stuff?"

She reached up, not quite touching her hair. "I've been thinking about that. Maybe I'll change my hair style and wear it like I do in the show."

Not a bad idea.

"Val suggested I do." Val was the costume designer for the theatre. He also darted around like Tinkerbell, advising on hair and make-up. "I started wearing it this way because it's the way Mother used to wear her hair. I thought it went with the outfits. You think I should change it, too, huh?"

"Yeah."

"Okay. I think you and Val are right." She had her coat over her arm and now went to put it on. Marty stood, helped her.

“What does your mother think about you wearing her clothes?”

“Well, you’d have to know my mother. She doesn’t respond to very much, one way or the other. Just sort of drifts along.”

“You’re the psychologist. What exactly is wrong with her?”

“I’m not a psychologist. I said I studied psychology. What I really did was take a couple of psychology classes. I never graduated from college, Marty, it was all too much. I only went a couple of years. That’s why you kind of threw me when you started talking about existentialism.”

“Ah, I was just kidding.”

“No, I know. It’s all right.”

“I wondered why your mother didn’t come to the play last night with your dad, but I didn’t want to ask.”

“Yeah, it’s awfully hard on him. He tried to talk her into coming. He could have arranged everything, but she didn’t feel like it.”

“Another time.”

“Maybe when I’m on Broadway. Or in one of your movies. Oh, that movie script in there — you seem to be working on it, but it says it was written by somebody else.”

“I may do a rewrite on it. You noticed it could use some work.”

“I did not think it was excellent, as much as I read.”

“I agree with you.”

She paused, made sure she had her purse, her mother’s purse. Then, before heading for the door she said, “Now you think I’m a slut.”

“No, no, no, I don’t.”

“Promise?”

“Promise. I don’t think you’re a slut.”

“I did what I did because ... because I thought it would be all right.”

“It is all right. It never happened.”

"I'm going down to the theatre. I know it's early, but I want to walk around on the stage and say my lines."

"Good."

"Will you be watching the play again tonight?"

As an aside during his meticulous relating of the Ellen episode, he let me in on a little secret. He had never seen any of his plays all the way through, top to bottom, in one sitting, with an actual, authentic, paying audience. Or had never seen any of them in one standing, as it were, because he was generally on his feet at the back of whatever theatre. There he paced back and forth, silently slipping out into the lobby when a line was "dropped," the pacing was off, a funny line fell flat, or the entire audience was bored into the REM phase of sleep. Or, if there was no room for pacing, he would leave the building and down a shot and a beer at the nearest bar, returning to the back of the theatre just in time to hear, usually, some waking audience member yawn loudly over the best line in the whole play. Or something like that. Anyhow, he never sat through performances of his plays. He just couldn't. He did, however, pride himself on the fact that never during a performance of any of his shows had he ever puked.

"You'll be watching the play again tonight, won't you?"

"Actually, Ellen, I wasn't planning to come down to the theatre tonight."

"Really? Why not?"

"I've done my job. The play's open. The reviews are out. I won't be coming down every night, just from time to time."

He motioned to the door and followed her to it. She said, "Do you realize if that girl had not been murdered, none of this would have happened? I wouldn't have met you through my dad or anything."

"I guess that's right."

"I hate she had to die for me. Were you in love with her?"

Ask me in thirty years, Marty thought. "I was very fond of Patsy," he said. He reached down and opened the door.

"I went to her funeral."

"You did?" It really shocked him.

"Yeah. I went with my dad, so he wouldn't have to go by himself. Don't you remember? It was the one day I couldn't rehearse."

"Yes, I remember, but you didn't tell us why."

"Because I thought you would be there, too, at the funeral. I thought I would surprise you."

So it was Rivo who represented the NYPD in Latrobe. Someone would have, of course, just to look around at the faces, to ask some subtle questions. Patsy knew her killer, that was key. That person could have been standing right there at the gravesite, or he could have been conspicuous by his absence.

"Her mother and father were so sad. But they went through the whole thing with their heads up and were kind to everybody. At the grave they held hands, even though I heard he lives in Asia somewhere, and they hadn't even seen each other for seven or eight years."

"I'll walk you down and get you a cab," Marty said.

"No, that's okay. I'm just going to the subway." But, just like her dad a few minutes before, she wasn't going anywhere. Marty stood there with the door open. He wanted to say, "Aren't you getting hot in that coat?" But he didn't.

"You know who was there? At the funeral? Preston Hondonada, the television personality."

"Patsy worked for him."

"I know. Dad told me. I'm a complete sucker for the stars. I was a little disappointed in him, though."

"Why?"

"The way he was checking out all the women. It was a little slimy. He's not really very attractive, but maybe he thinks he can get away with anything just because he's important."

Chapter 26

I walked into the downstairs lobby of the TASSQ that night just before ten o'clock. I went in quietly because the show was still in progress, but I wasn't in there two minutes before the applause popped like a busted water pipe and spewed forth all during the curtain call.

The ASM hurried down the steps from the second floor. He opened the thick and black doors at the rear of the theatre, and shortly the audience began to file out. The applause had been enthusiastic, and the faces I glimpsed as they left were satisfied ones. Some wore wry, enigmatic smiles, a few eyes were leaking tears. I surmised it had been a good performance.

Instead of standing there in everybody's way, I snaked my way to the stairs and headed up. The dressing rooms were up there, down a long corridor off the upstairs lobby. The cast would come out that way, and I could meet Becky there.

I had made us a reservation at a popular restaurant in the theatre district. It would be crowded and buzzing with the after-Broadway-show crowd, actors and actresses, maybe even celebrities and stars. I hoped Becky would like it, would feel comfortable "around her own," as it were.

I sauntered around the upstairs lobby for a couple of minutes, examined a few show posters in frames on the walls, checking my reflection in the glass of one of them to see if

I looked all right. The dashing Jay Bluffing. Then I sat in a wooden folding chair and waited.

Several other people, friends, drifted up the stairs to greet a member of the cast. The actors began to come out in their street clothes. They poked out one at a time or in pairs. I spoke to any of them that were interested. Most weren't. They looked around to see who, if anyone, was there to see them. They seemed to have a post-performance glow about them, a natural high. I thought I might see Marty, but so far I hadn't.

Ellen Rivo emerged, buttoning up her long brown coat, a coat which fit her, literally speaking, but which didn't fit in the figurative sense. It was too old for her. She seemed to recognize me and said hello very quietly. I opened my mouth to ask, "How did it go tonight?" but she hurried on by, down the stairs and the question never came out. Maybe she was embarrassed, thinking I knew something I didn't know. But I hadn't yet heard the story of her visit and her dad's, to Marty's apartment earlier in the day, so I didn't eye her any differently.

After fifteen or twenty minutes, I was still waiting. The whole cast had come and gone, except for Becky. It made me a little nervous. Then I realized what was up — we were going out to dinner, our first date. Of course it was going to take her a little extra time to get ready.

So I waited another ten minutes. By now the ASM was running around shutting things down, turning out bathroom lights, checking to see if doors were locked. I heard and felt the heat go off. Then she came out. I stood and lit up like a birthday cake.

She came over to me, smiling weakly. Something was wrong, but I pretended not to notice. Hey, it's me, I thought, J.C. Penney. Whatever the problem, I knew I could cheer her up.

"Harry's here," she said.

"Who?" I said immediately. But I wasn't kidding anybody, I knew who Harry was.

"My boyfriend's here, Jaycee. He's in my dressing room. I feel terrible. I don't know what to do."

I didn't say what I was thinking. Being a lawyer, it wouldn't have been terribly difficult for me to make a case for myself. But I didn't feel like it. I just wanted to take her out, I didn't want to present a brief. "What do you want to do, Becky?"

"I want to go to dinner with you."

"Then ...," I held my palms up in front of me.

"Oh, it's not that simple. So much history. He brings up our history, and it freezes me."

"So ... I should leave?"

"You're never going to forgive me for this, are you?"

"I don't know. But I'm not going to paint your apartment."

"You were going to do that?"

I decided to let her wonder. "Don't worry about this, okay?" I heaved sincerity into the words.

She closed her eyes and said, "Gosh, I feel rotten."

"You should. You should feel rotten." No, I didn't say it. She was in a spot, and instead of resenting her and blathering something selfish and nasty, I just said, "Maybe some other time. Good luck, kid." I still liked her. Besides, I'm the one who practically cornered her, pushed her into making the date. I should have given her some time. Marty. He's the one. "Call her. Call her. When are you going to call her!"

I turned and left. I hurried down the stairs and out of the theatre, my gaze on the toes of my buffed and swanky shoes.

Chapter 27

A busload of detectives was working Patsy's case, but Flannigan and Rivo had caught it that fateful afternoon and, surely, they considered it their baby. It had a lot of press and heat. You could get stabbed in Harlem, shot in Queens, beaten to death in Brooklyn for the change in your pocket. But this was the strangulation of a beautiful young actress in her own apartment on the hip, up and coming Upper West Side of Manhattan in the middle of the afternoon, for reasons unknown. Everybody but the mayor himself, I suppose, was examining her apartment with a magnifying glass and interviewing people.

Of course, nobody had talked to me. They hadn't gotten around to that yet. Everybody knew the first hours after a murder, certainly the first day or two, were the most crucial in solving the case. But the fact was, everything couldn't be done at once. Investigators listed their priorities and went down the list. I would be near the bottom. Kate, understandably, they got to right away. Me? No hurry.

Unless I had killed Patsy, which I hadn't. They knew that. In those days, when the cops didn't know yet who committed a murder, they'd announce, "Everybody's a suspect." Wasn't true, though. They always had suspects, and they never included "everybody."

It was late morning, the morning after Becky broke our date. I had been up for a while but was lying in bed again when the phone rang. When Kate didn't pick it up by the third ring, I bounced up and answered it. It was Detective Rivo from a couple of nights ago. Did I remember him? Yes, I did.

They came over, came in, and we exchanged the usual inanities. Flannigan winced and tilted his head like his neck was killing him. Rivo dabbed at a trace of white residue at the side of his mouth and tapped at his upper chest with a balled-up hand. I had the feeling they'd just had a bite to eat.

"You want to talk about heartburn?" Flannigan said to Rivo. "I'd trade you this pinched nerve at the base of my neck for your heartburn."

"No, you wouldn't."

"Yes, I would. All these aspirin I have to take to get rid of the pain?"

"You're not getting rid of the pain."

"I know that," said Flannigan, giving me a quick glance. They were, I guess, continuing a conversation begun before they arrived.

"No, I mean, aspirin is an analgesic. Analgesics impair the perception of pain."

"What?"

"The pain is still there after you take a couple of aspirin. You just can't feel it. But the pain is always there."

"The pain is always there?" It was a suggestion that made Flannigan, and me for that matter, stop and think. The pain is always there.

"You should take ibuprofen," Rivo went on.

"Why?"

"Ibuprofen reduces inflammation, which can actually help reduce the pain. Or get a massage, couple of times a week. Which would you rather have, a massage a couple of times a week or a pack of Tums?"

I was standing awkwardly listening to all this. Was it supposed to be funny? Was I supposed to laugh? I didn't know, so I didn't do anything but listen. Then Rivo turned to me and asked what kind of law I had practiced in Kentucky.

"A little bit of everything," I told them.

"Criminal law?" Flannigan said.

"Some. Mostly I put deals together. I helped my brother-in-law out of a minor jam once. It might not have made *The Times*. Some other cases, you know."

"Your brother-in-law?" Rivo said with mild surprise. "I understood your sister's not married."

I marveled at how thorough these guys were. They knew Kate wasn't married, but further, they knew I had only one sister.

"She's divorced from a guy who liked to go shopping with maxed-out credit cards and no checks or cash."

"Is your sister here, by the way?" Rivo wanted to know.

"No, she's not, I don't know where she is."

"Let's talk about Patsy Holton," Flannigan said.

"Sure." About time.

Flannigan pulled out his handy notebook and pen. He started writing immediately. Date and time first, I'd say, and then on from there. The guy seemed to love to write.

But since I didn't know much, I didn't give him volumes. I started at the beginning, telling them about the first time I met her, through Kate, of course. Told them about the occasion or two when I sat and talked to her when she was over visiting Kate. No, I had never been to her apartment. Told about the day after the football game when I sat with her and Kate at brunch. Told about the audition, the night at Sandolino's, and brought them on up to the rehearsal, to the intermission when she left. The only thing I didn't mention was that slight feeling of distrust I had toward Patsy. I couldn't articulate it, certainly couldn't substantiate it, so I decided not to stir it up.

Flannigan stopped writing and put his pad and pen away. No, I wasn't exactly spouting a mother lode of startling information. I wondered why he wrote down anything at all of what I said. Rivo was up and wandering around. He even peeked behind my screen.

"She didn't say who she was going out to call that day?" Flannigan said when I took a breath.

"No, she didn't."

"Do you know Preston Hondonada?"

"The TV guy? I know who he is."

"Did you know Patsy worked for him?"

"Yes."

"You never met him?"

"No."

"Does your sister know him?" Flannigan said.

Okay, that was a trick question, and I knew it. Why would he ask that? They had interviewed Kate right after the murder. It had to have been in the top three or four questions they asked her. I took a second or so to mull this over, and Flannigan jumped on it.

"She know him or not?"

"I believe she visited Patsy at work once and saw him there. I don't know if they were actually introduced or not. You'd have to ask Kate."

I stared right at Flannigan with the "ask Kate" part, and it was one of those I-knew-and-he-knew-I-knew moments. What I didn't know was why it would matter if Kate knew Hondonada or not. Then I realized it mattered because Patsy was murdered by someone she knew. Did Kate know the same person?

Preston Hondonada. Now there would be a suspect. Patsy's boss, a TV celebrity, probably an egomaniac, and married. Kate had suspected there was possibly something between him and Patsy. Could Patsy have been putting pressure on him, that old routine? I could have said, "Did Hondonada kill her?" But they wouldn't have answered with anything but jive, so why bother?

Flannigan looked down at his too-wide necktie, moistened his index finger, brushed at what appeared to be an orange soda stain. I could recommend a good dry cleaners on Columbus but didn't.

"Didn't make it to the funeral, huh?" Rivo said, jarring me back to the moment.

"No. My sister went." Like they didn't know that, too. They knew who attended the funeral, are you kidding?

Flannigan lugged himself onto his feet. He rolled his head back and forth on his neck a few times like Stevie Wonder. "Appreciate your time," he said. He handed me a card with writing on it.

"I wish I could help," I said, looking at the card.

I opened the door for them, and they left. There was no reason for me to get all teary-eyed. I'd see them both again.

PART II

Chapter 28

In 1996, I believe it was, I saw a TV show about a girl who was murdered and the actress looked like Patsy Holton. Some. She looked like her a little bit. Enough to make me think of Patsy, anyhow. In the TV drama, we learned an awfully lot about the victim. Watching the program I realized how little I had known about Patsy, and Marty hadn't known much about her either. There were written accounts of the case, some of which revealed shades of her character that may have surprised us. But I suddenly had the urge to know more. Or maybe I just wanted to be in my thirties again instead of nearly fifty.

I didn't sleep well that night. I was up early and on the road by six. I drove from my house on the lake in Tennessee to Latrobe, Pennsylvania, and looked up Patsy's mother. She was defensive at first but I ended up spending hours with her. She opened up to me about her only daughter.

She even called Patsy's best friend from high school, who still lived in the neighborhood. She had been close to Patsy until the murder. I visited with her after leaving Eileen, Patsy's mom, and her perky mother just loved to talk. When I headed south again the next day, I knew enough about Patsy to lay out in my head a whole storyboard of her life, at least from her teenage years on.

Patricia Suzanne Holton was a high school cheerleader but never should have been. She didn't have enough school spirit. She went through the motions, often slightly out of step or one step behind, and she encouraged the fans to "stand up, sit down, fight, fight, fight," by yelling at them through a red and white megaphone almost as big as she was.

But, alas, her heart wasn't in it. She cared nothing whatsoever about football, less about basketball, forget baseball and all the fancy sports like soccer and lacrosse.

No, she never should have made cheerleader, except for one thing — she was beautiful. So all through high school she got just about everything she wanted, including grades, because she was, well, she was Patricia Holton. Not that she was a slouch or a dummy, she wasn't. But if there was an American history test, all essay questions, and one question asked her to discuss briefly the Fourteenth Amendment, she might write, "It was passed to protect the freed blacks and to punish the South politically and economically." Period. Okay, that would be essentially correct, but you couldn't really call that a brief discussion. Not even a mention of Andrew Johnson or Thaddeus Stevens. She would answer all questions that way, seldom being wrong but seldom providing any depth or real sense of understanding. But when the teacher went to put the grade at the top of the page, he would hesitate before he wrote C and, invariably, write B. Or, once in a blue moon, if the teacher was old Miss Grindgear, D. But Patsy usually avoided the Miss Grindgears and sailed along.

Patsy resigned from the cheerleading squad after her junior year. What a relief for her and everyone else, except for the high school boys who could no longer watch her do the splits at mid-court or balance precariously at the top of a ten-girl pyramid.

Why would she get the coveted top-stone slot with all the other girls under her feet? Because the angel goes at the top of the Christmas tree, that's why.

In February of her senior year she was asked by a kid in the

Thespian Club to try out for the play they were going to perform in the spring. At first reluctant, she decided to do it. The play was *Bus Stop* (by William Inge), and she beat out three blondes for the part of Cherie. The kid who had nervously asked her to try out was a gawky, wide-eyed, forty-watt bulb named Tad Arnett. He played the role of Bo Decker. They rehearsed for eight weeks and performed the play twice. Forty-six people saw it the first night and twelve the next.

There were two results of consequence. Patsy caught the acting bug, and Tad was bitten by the love bug.

When she graduated that June, Patsy worked the summer at Phillips' Grocery, a friendly store on its way out. It wasn't a convenience store, exactly, but yet it wasn't a supermarket either, and it had seen its day. It hung on that summer, word was, because it had a gorgeous new check-out girl.

Patsy daydreamed about her future. She had no plans beyond Phillips'. Sometime in late July she decided she'd go to Slocum Junior College northwest of Latrobe. Penn State wasn't too far away but it was out of the question. Her mother thought Slocum was a good idea and promised to help her financially and maybe Patsy's father would, too, if he could be found and asked.

She applied to the school, was accepted, and started classes in September. She would have continued, part-time, at Phillips', but it closed its doors for good after Labor Day.

There was no formal theatre program at Slocum, but Patsy took literature classes and read plays. She discovered Raymond Carver's short stories. She felt like some character in his stark, middle class world and wanted to escape.

She found a course on Shakespeare and studied Hamlet, the greatest play ever written according to her instructor, with whom she had a brief affair. The greatest play ever written? He never convinced her. Too complicated and too long.

But the instructor did convince a friend of his who owned a local heating and cooling firm to give her a job answering the phone. It was a decision the teacher no doubt regretted when he found out Patsy was sleeping with his friend.

She went a full two years at Slocum, came out with an associate degree in English. That meant she could probably teach high school English ... if she transferred to a real school for another two years and got her teaching certificate.

She was still living at home. It was easy and cheap, and her mother left her alone. So did her father. He left them both alone. Occasionally he would drop in, always unexpectedly. He and Patsy would exchange a few pleasantries. Then Patsy would leave. Because very soon the quarreling between her mother and father would begin, and she just couldn't bear to listen to it.

About every two or three months Patsy would get a call from Tad. He'd want to get together with her, take her out, meet her somewhere, anything. She always found an excuse not to see him, and he always called back. More than once he used Bo Decker's first act curtain line on her, "Well, I ... I just never realized ... a gal might not ... love me." It didn't work.

She was civil to him. Civil and reserved. But Patsy was looking for bigger fish. Then one evening she and her mother were sitting at the kitchen table, talking, smoking. They smoked the Marlboro 100's that came in the gold pack, each cigarette as long as a soda straw. The phone rang, it was Tad, and Patsy rolled her eyes to the ceiling and back again.

"Just called to tell you I'm leaving town," he said, "I'm going to the big city."

Patsy wondered what he was going to do in Pittsburgh.

"Pittsburgh? I'm going to New York, Cherry, New York City." He always called her Cherry, ever since *Bus Stop*. Not Cherie but Cherry, just like Bo in the play.

"What are you going to do there?"

"Well, if you had ever given me the chance, I would have told you. I'm going to be a playwright."

"A what?" she said. She knew what a playwright was but was so surprised to hear him say it.

"A playwright. I'm going to New York to be a playwright. I've written three plays already."

"You have?"

"Sure I have. Three whole plays."

Tad had not gone to college. He took a job out of high school at a bookstore in Latrobe and had worked there all this time.

"When are you going?" Patsy wanted to know.

"I'm pulling out tomorrow morning, Cherry. I'm going to New York City tomorrow morning. The Big Apple, baby."

Then Patsy uttered the words that would change her life and, in about five years or so, end it. "Take me with you."

They came across Pennsylvania on Interstate 78, got lost in Jersey City for a while, finally made it into Manhattan and downtown. They sat in Tad's 1979 Ford Grenada in front of the building on Avenue A where they were going to live. They peered out the car window and looked suspiciously at the five-story structure. Tad had finagled a sublet from a burned-out, would-be novelist that frequented the bookstore in Latrobe.

The stairs leading up to the top floor were off-kilter, slanted to one side. The apartment itself, one long room, was a dump. It had a toilet and sink at one end and a bathtub, the kind on rusted-metal legs, at the other end in the filthy kitchen. In the middle of this railroad flat was an unmade bed with yellow sheets that were supposed to be white.

Patsy and Tad stood speechless looking the place over. Somebody turned on the water in an adjoining apartment, and iron clanked in the walls.

"We can fix it up," Tad said.

Now, at twenty-three, Patsy had lost the just-picked-apple freshness of the Bus Stop star, but she was still only twenty-three, and the contrast of this lovely creature against this slum apartment was depressing and laughable at the same time.

"We'll clean it up and fix it up," Tad said.

Chapter 29

Cocktail waitress, receptionist, drug store cashier, diner waitress. These were some of the jobs Patsy wandered through during her first years in the Apple. Her official residence, according to her mother and her long-time girlfriend back in Latrobe, remained, for four years, the slum on Avenue A. Not that she was ever there. The fact is, she never slept there more than eight or ten times, and two of those times were the first two nights she was in town. Because as soon as she landed her first job, that of serving drinks at a club on 8th Street, there was always some man or another and she made sure he had a respectable apartment, preferably with a clean bathroom.

But it wasn't as bad as it sounds. She did not turn into a wandering tramp who would sleep with any guy for a warm bed and a roof in a decent neighborhood. Often, she would go home with a fellow and not even let him touch her. They would dine, talk, drink, have a good time, maybe even sleep in the same bed (she often relegated him to the sofa). She could talk her way out of sex easily by playing the "good girl," and asking the guy to respect her for it. Sometimes a man was upset, but usually not. He'd just think to himself, this girl is a prize. Maybe she is The One.

Of course, they would probably never see her again, not in their apartments, anyhow. If they came by where she was working and pressed her, she would, as politely as possible, dismiss them. They would trail away, never even suspecting they had been used.

Or she could get mildly interested in someone and have a brief affair. She lived with one guy for six months, unofficially that is, because she never really brought in any belongings other than clothes, and she never paid any of the rent. Not that she was asked to. He was a middle-range, middle-aged executive at CBS, divorced, and had a lovely one-bedroom in a fine old building on West 79th off the Park. It was Patsy's first real exposure to the Upper West Side.

She hoped he was up and coming and might become the head of programming for CBS, or at least, a prominent vice-president. When he came home one evening, ashen and suddenly older, she knew before he said a word. They had canned him. Patsy packed her couple of cheap suitcases with all she had and left.

She checked in on Tad, which she did occasionally. He still loved her, he always would, but he was reconciled to the fact that she was never going to be his. To wit, she never let him touch her, ever.

By this time, Patsy had started taking acting lessons from David Roscoe, a pretentious, egomaniacal, cape-wearing, forty-five-year-old cad whose claim to fame was a TONY nomination years before, his only Broadway appearance. And now that she was free of the turkey from CBS, Patsy could have the affair with Roscoe that he'd been wanting for several months.

Patsy was slinky, coordinated, and graceful when she wanted to be, and at twenty-five, still ripe. If the city had nibbled at her or taken a bite or two, it didn't show. But no one would say she had acting talent. You're born with it or you are not, and she wasn't. There is only so much that instruction and training can do, even when conducted by a genius like David Roscoe. Classes and scene work with other students cannot instill the magic; nothing can. So even though she needed only to walk down the street or into a room to evoke admiring comments and create a nearly magical air, the same, paradoxically, was not the case when she tried to play a part.

It may have been, incidentally, the main reason she and Tad remained friends, because he, too, (in the field of writing) did not have the gift. Though he sat for endless hours at an electric typewriter, making miles of words appear and turning out more plays than George M. Cohan, each and every one he wrote was alarmingly bad. This lack of inborn ability can bond two people, each seeing something of themselves in the other, even if they can't quite put their finger on what it is.

Patsy began going to "open calls," auditions where the world was invited to try out for a particular show. Also known as cattle calls. Besides the fact her talent-tank warning light was on, there was another problem — she brought to these auditions the same enthusiasm she had given to cheerleading. What she really wanted was for the head of the Schubert organization to see her buying a sundae at the Haagen-Daz shop, take her by the hand, and say, "Come along, dear. I'm going to make you a star."

After a year of rejections outside the classroom, Roscoe had an idea. The annual automobile show was coming to the New York Coliseum at Columbus Circle. The huge and fairly ugly Coliseum no longer exists, but for years it was used for trade shows and exhibits of all kinds. Sexy young women were hired to stand in front of new Oldsmobiles or Volvos and, by way of a memorized spiel, sing the vehicles' praises.

Patsy was chosen to stand on a platform in a long, low-cut gown and heels and exalt the qualities of the latest BMW 750iL, a German panzer which came with a factory-installed telephone in the console between the two front seats.

David Roscoe told her he arranged the job for her, but the truth probably was she got it on her looks, along with her ability to memorize the shtick. It was a popular exhibit.

Her third day on the job a particular gentleman caught her eye. He was about forty or so and not too unattractive. He had a large head with plenty of black, wavy hair. He had broad shoulders and a powerful looking chest. His waist was the diameter of a Cheerio, and his legs were too short for the upper part of his body. He was shaped somewhat like Brutus in the Popeye cartoons but without the belly. His big face was clean-shaven and he had interesting, piercing eyes, Patsy noticed, when he removed his sunglasses to get a better look at her.

Because she had caught his attention as well. He smiled at her, revealing less than perfect teeth. She returned the smile, lowered her head slightly, looked at him through the tops of her eyes. It was a sexy look, almost hypnotizing. The man edged closer to the platform, close enough for him to kiss her thin, smooth ankle, which is exactly what he wanted to do.

Now, she looked down at him. No, he wasn't the most handsome man she had seen in the last three days, nor was he the first to come on silently to her. But there was something special about this one, and it interested her. She stooped to him and offered her hand. "Hello," she said.

He shook her hand. "Hello to you," he said, "I'm Preston Hondonada."

"I know," she said.

Chapter 30

During 1918 and 1919, 21 million people died worldwide from influenza. They called it the Spanish flu, but it had probably originated in Hong Kong. It doesn't matter where it came from. It spread like crazy because of all the World War I troops dispersing and going home. They carried the virus (a bird virus, we now know) to the cities, towns, and rural areas everywhere. Well over half a million people died in the U.S. alone. Half a million.

A long time had passed since 1919, and medical science had come a long way. Nevertheless, Marty Sequatchee was going to die of the flu. He knew it. His hope was that death would come sooner rather than later and so stop his suffering.

It was the first weekend of his new play, and he hadn't been back to the theatre since opening night. Ordinarily, he would have checked in by Friday night, just to see how it was going, but this time he hadn't because he didn't want to see Ellen Rivo. Sure, they had talked it out and everything seemed fine, but still, he preferred to avoid her for another day or so.

Friday afternoon his agent called and said the producer of the romantic comedy script was in town again from Beverly Hills. Not Los Angeles, Beverly Hills. He was in town, and he wanted to see Marty's play at the Sunday matinee, and maybe they could talk afterwards.

This was wonderful news. First, it meant he, Marty, probably didn't have to trek out to Los Angeles over this job. Second, he would be meeting the guy in Manhattan, where Marty would be comfortable and, more or less, relaxed. And third, the play was running. This was important because it showed Marty was active, busy, getting produced in the New York theatre. Those Hollywood types were always impressed with that. The theatre sat only a hundred and fifty people, but it didn't matter; it still had snob appeal.

So the agent set it up. Marty was to be at the theatre before the three o'clock show on Sunday. He would meet the producer, the agent and producer would see the play, and the three of them would pow wow over drinks and maybe an early dinner afterwards. Perfect.

But Saturday morning, Marty woke up with a chill. By afternoon, he had a fever and could hardly stand. By six p.m. he was in bed under forty blankets, freezing. When I called him around seven to see if he was going to play football the next morning — sunny skies predicted, fifty-five degrees! — he was near death.

"What can I do for you?" I said.

"Kill me. If there's a drop of compassion in you."

"Anything else?"

"I do need a few things, but I hate to ask you."

"I'm offering, what do you need?"

Forty-five minutes later Marty opened the door and my question was, "Don't you have any other friends?"

"None of my other friends would be stupid enough to come over here today."

Marty wore a sweatshirt, sweatpants, socks and slippers, and was wrapped in blankets like a giant enchilada. He had a wool watch cap pulled over his head and down past his ears. There were two dark holes in his head where eyes were supposed to be. His cheeks were concave, and he hadn't shaved. His whole face looked sticky, moist. His nose looked as if somebody had squeezed it for several hours, on and off, with a set of pliers. A low groan emanated from him, sounding like the distant wails of a thousand prisoners chained in a dungeon under his apartment building. For the first time since I had met him, he looked forty. Or fifty.

"Get away from me," I said.

Marty retreated, suppressing a cough so it came out as a half-dozen little pathetic coughs. I took the bag of supplies into the kitchen with the patient following but not too closely. I had brought grapefruit and orange juice, honey, lemon, Kleenex, aspirin, and a box of Aspergum. Marty picked up the box and looked at it. It was the one item he hadn't asked for.

There was also chicken noodle soup, cream of chicken soup, chicken and rice soup, and chicken broth — Marty had requested chicken soup but had not been specific. I had grabbed the things from the Korean deli on Columbus between 85th and 86th.

Marty pulled out a mug and proceeded to make a concoction of water, honey, and lemon while he said, "Have you gotten together with Becky yet?"

"Yeah ... no. We've talked about it."

"You're in negotiations?"

"Something like that." I didn't want to tell him negotiations had broken off and I had walked away from the table. He stirred the beverage, popped it into the microwave, stood there and watched it go around.

"Why don't you go back to bed? I'll bring it in to you."

Marty didn't argue. "Thanks, Florence." And he left.

When the drink was near boiling, I took it out, stirred it again and took it into the bedroom. Marty was back in bed, propped up, and surprisingly, still alive. Opposite the bed were Marty's books, hundreds of them, filling the wall of built-in shelves. Reference books, history books, poetry, novels. But mostly, plays. If he didn't have every play ever written, name one he didn't have. Half a dozen of them, by Sam Shepard, David Mamet, and Lanford Wilson, were scattered around him. I handed him the mug, at arm's length, and stepped away. He put his lips to it and tested it like a bird.

He nodded toward his desk and said, "Sit down. Let me tell you about a visit I had from Ellen Rivo."

When he finished reliving it for me, I just sat there looking at him. "She should see you now. She might not find you so irresistible."

The mini-coughs came again and he nearly spilled what was left of the drink. "I can't find my lovely agent," he said.

"What do you need her for?"

"I've been asking myself that for years."

He told me about the meeting at the theatre the next afternoon and how he had tried to call his agent at home, no luck. "I've left her a message," he said, "but I'm afraid she's away and won't get it. I don't think I'm going to be able to get down to the theatre tomorrow," he said, blowing his nose and coughing for emphasis.

"No, I don't think you'll make it."

"I wonder if I have pneumonia. That's what usually kills you, you know, when you have the flu. Pneumonia."

"Oh, I'm sure you do," I said.

"I can't stand up this producer. I don't know what to do."

"If you don't get in touch with your agent, I'll go down there tomorrow afternoon, meet them and explain."

"I don't know. Maybe I can just suck it up and go down myself. I don't have to leave the apartment until two o'clock tomorrow. I could be well by then, right?"

"No. And even if you feel marginally better, what do you want to do, infect the whole cast?"

"You're right. If there were some way I could just infect

my agent." He raised the hot drink an inch or two. "You want some of this?"

I smiled and turned to go. "Call me if you want me to take you to the hospital."

"Naw, that's for sissies."

Thinking maybe he had spoken with his agent or that his illness could be a twenty-four hour bug, I called him the next day, Sunday, at noon. I woke him up.

"Hello," Marty said, into the phone, but the subtext was, "The end is near."

"Well, I take it we're not jogging around the reservoir this afternoon?"

"No, I did that this morning," cough, cough, "and played football for two hours. Where were you?"

"Did you reach your agent?"

"Not a word from her. She's been away, I'm sure, and is probably driving in from Connecticut right now to pick up Mr. Beverly Hills."

Car phones have come and gone, but when we were having this conversation, the revolutionary devices were on the horizon, soon to be mass installed, but it hadn't happened yet.

"Don't worry about it. I'll be there when they arrive, I'll take care of it."

"Apologize but don't overdo it. Don't go on and on about it. Marty's sorry, the flu, couldn't be helped, was looking forward to talking about the project. Tell my agent I tried to call, all that, tell her to call me. Ask how long the guy's going to be in town, because I really am very interested in the assignment. Or I will go to L.A. if necessary."

"Shut up," I said.

"Make sure you somehow let the producer know you're a lawyer."

"Why?"

"It'll impress him."

Yeah, I was a darling of a friend to do this. The truth is I had a hidden agenda — as long as I would be there at the theatre on official business, why not say hello to Rebecca as she showed up for the performance? I could let her know there were no hard feelings and, just out of curiosity, see if she remembered my name.

Or if she happened to slip by me before the show, maybe I'd buy a ticket and sit through it again. I could stand it a third time. I could certainly stand seeing her, even if it were as some made-up character on a stage.

Chapter 31

My afternoon schedule was light that Sunday, so I was at the TASSQ by two-ten. Marty was supposed to meet his agent, Stassie, and the producer in front of the theatre at ten till three. Okay. Marty had described her, I shouldn't have any trouble spotting her. If I did, we had joked, I could just wander around on the sidewalk outside the front doors saying, "Stassie? Oh, Stassie?" What kind of a name was it? Marty didn't know. He'd never cared enough to ask. It probably stood for Stephanie, who went by Stephie until her little brother tried to say it and it came out Stassie, and Stassie stuck. As good a guess as any. What the producer looked like, we didn't really know.

I went into the lobby, up to the ticket window. The girl, the Faulkner fan, was at her post again.

"I'd like one ticket, please, for the matinee."

She gave a brief snicker. "We're sold out. There's a waiting list if you'd likc to give me your name, but I have to tell you, it doesn't look good." Her snicker must have meant, "Don't you know anything?"

"Oh." It never occurred to me that all one hundred and fifty seats would be taken for a Sunday matinee. "I'll see it another time." I heard the snicker again as I turned away. I wanted to turn to her again and say, "Look, Marty Sequatchee is a friend of mine, okay? He'll get me in anytime I want." But I didn't.

I went outside and stood. I knew the actors came in that way, the front way, same as the customers. That's the way it was with a lot of those shoebox theatres. Forget the stage door entrance; you're thinking about Broadway.

Sure enough, I watched most of them arrive. I stayed out of the way. Actors. Actresses. You don't hear the word "actress" as you did in the old days. They're all actors now. Political correctness. Humankind is constantly evolving.

Anyhow, some of them wanted to be seen, noticed, as they made their entrance into the theatre. They looked around, heads high, as if waiting for the flash bulbs to burst. Others, just the opposite. Heads lowered, usually under a concealing hat, they would appear at the door and slip inside like mice. Then there was Ellen Rivo, who came down the street and walked into the theatre like an ordinary person.

In fact, she looked more ordinary than she had the last time I saw her. She wore an old pair of khaki pants and a plain pullover sweater under a faded jean jacket. And her hair looked more like it did when she was on stage, instead of like she was trying to be Jane Russell circa 1957. Marty and Val had obviously gotten through to her.

At a quarter of three, Becky had still not arrived. Was something wrong? I knew the performers had to be at the theatre thirty minutes before the show. "Half-hour," it was cleverly called. There was a crowd milling around now. One hundred and fifty people can seem like a thousand in front of a miniature theatre, in the lobby, and filing into the house itself.

I went back inside, and this time waited in line at the window while people paid and picked up tickets. When it was my turn, I said, "Is Becky Norse here?"

The girl stared out at me. Maybe she was trying to remember where she had seen me before. "What?" she said. "Of course she's here."

"Okay, I just didn't see her come in."

"She always comes early." She was busy and looked past me to the next customer in line.

I almost said, "I'm a lawyer," but caught myself. I didn't think the dirty-haired girl would be impressed.

I went back out onto the street, looked around for Stassie and company. It was two-fifty, the appointed time, but they weren't around.

But coming toward me from down the street was Detective Rivo. He arrived, saw me, and stopped. "Back again, huh?"

"You, too."

Rivo grabbed the door handle. "Waiting for someone?"

"Yeah, I have to deliver a message."

The detective opened the door and went in. I thought to myself, "That's a good dad."

I stood there and surveyed Sheridan Square. At two-fifty-five they still hadn't arrived. I peeked inside to see if they had slipped past me and were waiting in the lobby. They weren't. I made eye contact with one lady standing by herself. She vaguely fit the characteristics I was told to look for in Stassie. Stassie was to be about thirty, tiny and skinny, much of her face resembling a mule's. Her hair would be black, long, and straight like Cher's in 1976. The woman I was looking at was thin with dark hair, but other particulars didn't match. Plus, this female appeared to have lips as opposed to a thin, red, horizontal line, slightly down-turned at each end, near the bottom of her face. I didn't even ask.

But I did go on in and up to the box office one more time. There was no one in front of me. Even the wait-listed customers had been seated or had left. The girl was counting and organizing money and credit card slips. She glanced up, saw me, and gave the slightest little shake of her head which I read to mean, "What is your problem?"

"Excuse me? Did you have two tickets for Stassie Simmons? Or they could have been in Marty's name, Sequatchee."

She didn't hesitate. "Simmons and Friend didn't show. But her seats are gone." What a bust. No Becky, no agent, no nothing.

I left and walked over to that neighborhood bar, the purlieu for the people of the TASSQ. I ordered a draft beer before I went to the phone booth, the old-fashioned sit-down kind, and called Marty.

"I guess she called you."

"Who?" he said, weakly, as he turned down the volume on the Giants-Redskins game.

"Your agent."

"No, she didn't call me. Why?"

"Well, she never showed. I waited till three, then checked with the box office."

"What a miserable excuse for a human," Marty said.

"I can't believe she would just not show up. What if you had dragged yourself down here?"

"What if I had?"

"Pretty inconsiderate, I'd say."

Marty tried to laugh a little but a coughing spasm got in the way. "And if you think that's bad, try Hollywood."

"I don't think I will."

"But this sounds like a joint effort between the two coasts."

"What do you mean?"

"Probably a power play. The producer, cementing his Big Man status, cancels when my agent gets to the hotel to pick him up. Stassie, now angry because she had come back from Connecticut early just for this, turns around and takes it out on me by not calling to let me know."

"Come on ...," I said, doubting him.

"I'm telling you, Jay. That's the way it works."

He thanked me and apologized, even though it certainly wasn't his fault. I hung up and headed back to the bar. My beer was waiting. On the stool next to it was Detective Rivo, testing a cup of coffee and waiting for the Alka-Seltzer in his glass of water to finish fizzing.

I climbed onto the seat beside him. "I thought you were seeing the show?"

"No, I just had to see someone upstairs in the office."

"Oh." I sipped the beer. So he was here on police business. And the only police business that would bring him here was Patsy Holton's murder. He wasn't here because someone connected with the theatre hadn't paid a parking ticket.

"I thought you were here to see the show," he said.

"No, just doing a favor for Marty, Marty Sequatchee."

"How is Marty?" he asked.

"Sick. The flu."

"I'm sorry to hear that."

We drank various beverages for a moment or two. I noticed an antique wooden sign hanging from the frame of the mirror behind the bartender. I hadn't noticed it the last time I was in the place, too busy noticing Becky. It read, "Theatricals Must Use Rear Entrance." I took another sip of beer and a stream somehow missed my mouth and bombed the front of my jacket.

"Damnit!" I said, brushing at my lapel. "It's a new jacket. I've already had to clean it once."

I looked at Rivo again, but if the cop was sympathetic it was undetectable. I blurted out another question, figuring I had nothing to lose.

"Who?"

"Say again?"

"I was wondering who you came down here to see?"

He was surprised I would be so impertinent. He looked at my beer for a second. Maybe the alcohol was doing the talking. He could have easily said it was none of my business. Or, he could have innocently given a name. He didn't do either. He grinned, wryly, and said, "Come on now, lawyer, why would I want to tell you that?"

He gulped the rest of his not-very-good, not-very-hot coffee and left. I would have to wait. The case would be solved. I felt sure of it. I'd wait.

Meanwhile, what was I going to do that day? I was a block away from Becky Norse. Should I hang around down there in the Village for a couple of hours and just happen to be at the theatre when she came out? I could tell her I was there on business, Marty was sick, and I was helping him out. Would she buy it? Who cares? It was the truth. To a point.

Of course, I ran the risk of her thinking, "You poor, lonely sap." And if Harry should show up to meet her after the play, he would, of course, think the same thing.

I didn't even have another Bud. I left the bar, hailed a cab on Seventh Avenue, and went straight home. Maybe I could catch the end of the Giants' game.

Chapter 32

I went over Monday morning to check on Marty. It looked as though he was going to amaze medical science and pull through.

He had expected his agent to call him that morning, but she didn't. He started to call her several different times, but couldn't jab more than four or five numbers before anger would overcome him, and he'd slam down the receiver.

He dragged himself downstairs for his mail. He wouldn't let me get it for him. It was mostly junk, but one official and fateful letter announced that the last of the six limited partnerships into which he had invested many thousands had gone belly up. Not that he told me that at the time. But I could see from his expression he had received bad news. If the rewrite assignment didn't come through, and quickly, he might actually have to get a real job, something he hadn't had in many years. But what was he going to do, step into a job that gave him a hundred thousand dollars up front? Because that's about what he needed. I could have offered my expert counsel if I'd known.

I was about to leave when Stassie called. She had a loud and whiney voice that came through the phone and rattled the room. She apologized profusely. When she had arrived at the King of Motion Pictures' hotel just after two o'clock the day before, there had been a note for her saying the producer had to "rush back to L.A."

"He must really have been in a hurry," Marty said, "since he didn't even write Hollywood or Beverly Hills, just L.A."

"What?" Stassie said on the other end of the line. Apparently, she wasn't listening.

"Never mind," Marty said. "Is he still interested in my doing the re-write or not?" He could have continued and said, "Because the IRS may knock on my door any minute and take me away in chains and shackles."

"Absolutely," Stassie said. "Bottom of the note he wrote, 'I still want to meet with Sequatchee.'"

"I guess this means I'll have to go out there after all."

"Why wouldn't you want to go to California for a day or two? First class all the way, any hotel you want, everything paid for. A meeting, you give your take on the script, you lounge by the pool, before you know it you're sitting in seat 1A again with a mimosa and *The New York Times.* What's so horrible?"

"Okay, look. I need this job. Let's just say I'll do it."

"Of course, you'll do it. And don't sound so desperate. You've made a fortune and you're not even forty." Stassie didn't know about his troubles anymore than I did.

Then she said something like, "Are you all right, Marty? You sound a little congested."

Marty had neglected to mention he was recovering from the flu and had not actually been at the theatre Sunday himself. Let the woman feel some guilt (if that was possible) for two or three seconds.

"I'm fine," he said.

"I still plan to see the play, Marty. I'm really looking forward to it."

Chapter 33

Tuesday morning I was browsing through a bookstore on Broadway. In the literary section, I ran across the Faulkner collection and, remembering the chubby, dirty-haired girl in the ticket booth, I picked up a copy of *As I Lay Dying*. It's a movie now, but it wasn't back then. I stood there and read the first chapter. It wasn't exactly Harold Robbins, someone I'd read in high school. I still remembered *The Dream Merchants*, a Robbins' novel about the early days of Hollywood. I backed up and found the Saul Bellow oeuvre. There was *Humboldt's Gift*. Every hedonistic moment at the McNoel raced across my mind in about three seconds.

I found my way to the entertainment section and picked up a book of capsule movie reviews. Out of curiosity, I looked up the title *Learning the Body* and read the blurb. It didn't sound awful. The guy had given it two and a half stars out of four. I didn't know the titles of any other of Marty's movies. I flipped back to the index. You could look up actors' (or actresses') names and find the movies they had appeared in, and you could look up directors and see what movies they had directed. But there was no index of writers, and I didn't think that was fair.

I ended up buying three or four paperbacks, which I would never read. I strolled on down Broadway and went into the video store I generally rented from, when I rented. I wasn't big on movies. Kate brought cassettes home every once in awhile. I usually wasn't interested. This particular Tuesday I had another one of my bright ideas all of a sudden, and so I said to a clerk behind the counter, "How do I find movies written by Marty Sequatchee?"

He looked Marty up in a Writers' Guild of America Membership Directory, and I walked out with six video cassettes, the three Sequatchee originals and the three on which he had shared credit. I guessed these were his previous rewrite jobs.

I headed home, thinking how foolish I was. What was I going to do, sit down and watch six movies, one right after the other so I could return them all the next day? Yes, rental rules have changed. Back then, you brought the cassette tape back the next day, or you paid full price for it again and again until you did return it.

I saw a fortune in late charges in my future. I couldn't sit down and watch last year's Oscar winner for best picture without pausing it twelve times for snacks, bathroom, telephone, or boredom. Maybe the fact that I knew Marty would be a help. I could sit there and say to myself, "That's Marty saying that. That's Marty who wrote that. That's what Marty thinks." Exactly what I was told not to do.

I returned to the apartment with the goods. I called Kate's name to see if she were home, but she wasn't. She had phoned the night before to say she was staying out. She had done that a couple of times lately. When she and her boyfriend had been together, she'd stay over with him two or three nights a week. But since she ditched him, she was in every night. Now, there must be someone new. I hoped she'd tell me about it because I didn't want to ask. So far she hadn't opened up. Fine with me, as long as she was safe. Twenty-eight, divorced, she knew her way around. I wasn't going to pry. I went into the kitchen and nuked a bag of popcorn.

She could take care of herself. Couldn't she? The question led me back to the thought that Kate might be acquainted with the person who murdered Patsy. Could Kate, unsuspectingly, let the killer into this apartment? I stood in the middle of the living room, considering it. Who did Patsy know that Kate knew? Or, turn it around, who does Kate know that Patsy knew? Shouldn't an extensive list be made and cross-checked?

I came out of the kitchen with a bowl of corn and a Coke and noticed the red dot blinking on the phone machine. "Jay, call me when you get in," Marty's voice said. "I want to ask you about something Patsy said one time."

I called him, and he picked up right away.

"This is probably nothing," he said, "but ... what if it isn't? What if it's ... significant?"

"I'm listening."

"The night we ate at Sandolino's," Marty said, "remember the amethyst ring?" Marty was having an energy surge, as he often did when he got excited, and I could feel it through the wire.

"The ring. She gave it to the waitress."

"Yes. Remember, Patsy said it was given to her by someone who had left town."

"Okay."

"Well ...?"

"What?"

"Who was that person? Someone she knew who left town."

"And left for good, if I recall. Didn't she say something like, 'He's gone, baby, he's gone'?"

"Yes, she did, because she didn't want my feelings to be hurt. But people come and go. The cops probably haven't talked to him, whoever he is."

I was quiet for a moment. A possible suspect? Sure, I guessed, why not?

"Jay?"

"Yes, I'm here," I said, "just rolling it over."

The front door unlocked, opened, and Kate came in. She banged the door behind her. She saw me on the phone and waved.

I spoke above the receiver, "Good morning."

Marty heard the minor commotion. "Do you have to go?"

"No, Kate just came home." She skipped off into the bedroom.

"Should I call Rivo? I mean, I don't want to waste their time," Marty said.

"No, you wouldn't be doing that. Sometimes the smallest detail ...," and I didn't finish the sentence. "What made you think of the ring?"

"A piece in the paper about Tibet. It mentioned Buddha and the particular quartz used to make rosaries."

"What?"

"In Tibet, the belief is that amethyst is sacred to Buddha," he said. "So I read that and thought of the ring, that's all."

"Are you feeling better today, or are you completely delirious?"

"Better. I woke up feeling fine. I've lost ten pounds, but the bug is gone. Went out to breakfast, even. Ran across the Tibet article in *The Times*."

I hung up and stood there, wondering. Kate came back into the room, rubbing lotion into and all over her hands as though she were cooking up a mischievous scheme of some sort. She smiled, glowed, looked like a summer sunrise. I smiled back at her.

"How are you?"

"Good!" she said brightly. "You?"

"I'm fine." She saw the plastic bag of books and videos and dug in to have a look. "Oh, Marty's movies. That'll be fun."

"I thought maybe I'd watch that *Learning the Body*."

"Uh-huh."

"I'm curious how a movie about medical students in the 1930's plays today. In my head I see a gritty black-and-white film with Cagney and Bogart, maybe as competing surgeons, one with a new technique which the other thought would never work. You know."

I was just talking to fill time before she would say, "Jay, I want you to know I've met a great guy and I'm spending a good deal of time with him. I want you to meet him." But she didn't. Instead she held up the newly purchased copy of *As I Lay Dying* and said, "Do you think you'll actually read this?"

"Kate?"

"Hmmm?"

"Who is he?" I said.

Chapter 34

As long as I had asked, she gave me an earful.

Her seat had been exactly in the middle of the plane, she told me, for her US Air flight back to LaGuardia after Patsy's funeral. She was crammed into the window seat with a giant in the aisle seat beside her. One of his legs stretched down the aisle nearly to the cockpit door, it seemed, and the other one folded and angled out so the knee was practically under Kate's chin. She hugged the window. The knee, needing the additional room, followed her.

It had been a long day, and it wasn't over. She closed her eyes and went through the steps required before it would end. She would nap for the hour or so they were in the air, take a taxi home, tell her brother about the funeral ("not much to tell"), soak in a hot bath for an hour, order Chinese food, watch a movie in bed, and be asleep by ten. Maybe sooner.

The jet rose through ten thousand feet and kept climbing. Before it had leveled off, Kate was snoozing. Shortly, before the beverage cart was rolled out and blocked all passage, the southern voice of a young flight attendant woke her.

"Kate? Kate?"

She opened her eyes with minor alarm. The flight attendant, ignoring the redwood tree in the aisle seat, said, "Kate? Why don't you come with me? Someone up front wants to see you."

"Me?" she said.

"Sir, could you let her out, please?" the flight attendant said, more of an order than a request. Maybe because the airline employee in her blue uniform and red scarf was short, too short. The height requirement for the job must have been waived in her case, and every day she probably battled the fact.

The big guy didn't like it, but he moved into the aisle, bent about forty-five degrees at the waist. Kate gathered her shoulder bag, scooted into the aisle, and followed the young woman forward.

"Is everything all right?" Kate said.

"Oh, sure, honey."

At the third row the flight attendant stopped, turned to Kate, smiled, gestured with her hand. Kate looked to the two seats. Comfortable by the window was Preston Hondonada. His tray table was down, and he had a glass half-full of either club soda or vodka on ice. It wasn't club soda.

He said, "Kate, sit, sit, sit ..." Kate eyeballed the wide leather seat, then took it. "I wanted to say something to you at the chapel and then again at the gravesite, but I couldn't find the right moment. Then at the airport I was in the club until just before boarding. You better buckle up. Here, let me help you."

Kate looked down at her lap while Hondonada clicked the two pieces of metal together. She took note of something. It was something Marty took note of when he first talked with Detective Flannigan — no wedding ring.

Hondonada removed his hands from the seatbelt buckle. He and Kate looked at each other for half a second until Hondonada, thinking the unthinkable may be happening, said, "I'm Preston Hondonada."

"Oh, I know," Kate said.

He was relieved. "We were never formally introduced, were we?"

"No."

"I remember that day you came to the studio to visit Patsy."

"You do?"

"What can we get you to drink?" He wiggled a finger toward the same attendant, and she carried her smile back to Row 3.

"She'll have a ...," and he looked to Kate.

"Oh, uh, I'll have a club soda."

"Are you sure?" Hondonada touched her forearm. "It's after five."

"Okay, make it a white wine."

"Sure," the young woman said, "and another for you, Mr. Hondonada?"

"Please."

The attendant slipped away to get the drinks, and Kate looked at Hondonada. "Can I sit here?"

"Of course, you can. It's taken care of." Implied but not repeated was, "I'm Preston Hondonada."

They talked surprisingly little about Patsy during the flight. It was sad; they missed her. She was such a sweet person. When will they catch the killer?

Kate asked him what his next show would be about. He told her he was preparing a one-hour special for the network on the staggering number of rats in New York City.

Mostly they talked about Kate because Hondonada asked her lots of questions, wanted to know all about her. And he said, "I like your accent. You sound so fresh and open."

"I should lose it."

"No, no, no, it's adorable," said Hondonada, his every word ever so slightly garbled from natural causes.

"But if I want to act."

The time went quickly. As they taxied to the gate, it was decided Kate would ride into Manhattan with him. His car and driver would be waiting at the curb.

At first Hondonada told the driver to take her home, and Kate leaned forward and gave him the address. But halfway across the Triboro Bridge, Hondonada suggested they have dinner, if she didn't have plans or wasn't too tired.

They dined at a fabulous restaurant on Third Avenue called Hafferty's. It wasn't exactly a dive. The chef had garnered more stars than any of Marty's movies, that's for sure. They each had a thick, tender New York strip steak, medium rare, with potatoes, broccoli, and a couple of bottles of a fine merlot. They ate and talked and giggled. At some point in the middle of the evening, her inhibitions tempered, Kate made a statement that was, really, more of a question. And, to her, an important one. "You're not wearing a wedding ring," she said.

"Separated," Hondonada said, and with a final sip finished off their first bottle of wine.

"Oh. I'm sorry," Kate said.

"No, no, don't be sorry. Best thing. Had to be."

"Is ... is she all right?"

He moved his empty glass away and stared at Kate. He tapped the white linen tablecloth with four fingers. "That tells me a lot about you."

"What does?"

"That you would ask that question. That you would be concerned about Karen. I said it was the best thing; it had to be. You could have said, 'Congratulations, let's drink to that.' But you didn't, you were concerned about her."

"I just wondered."

"It was considerate; it was sweet. She's fine. She's up in Connecticut in the house on the lake. She has plenty of friends, plenty of money, and I believe she's even seeing someone. I hope so. I did the leaving, true, but I didn't break her heart."

"Good. Where are you living now?"

"For the time being I've taken a suite at an intimate hotel off Second. The McNoel."

When Kate told me that part, she noticed a change in my expression, I guess. “What?” she said to me.

“Nothing. I’m familiar with the McNoel, is all.”

Chapter 35

When Kate finished enthralling me with the Hondonada story, she kissed my forehead, held my shoulders and said, "It's all right, Jay," and left the room. I didn't think it was all right, and she knew it. I didn't know why, but I felt it was all wrong.

Then the phone rang and guess who? It was Becky Norse with an invitation just for me. It was a bit of a shocker because I thought the old boyfriend was back on her team, and my option had not been picked up. Yet in another way, it wasn't a surprise. Why? Because Becky Norse was not the type to kick people in the teeth. I knew that. She was a struggling young woman in New York City, trying to succeed in her chosen profession and be a little happy while she was at it. Trying to find a stable relationship, trying to do her best, and trying, certainly, not to step on any toes. Even mine.

"If you would forgive me," she said on the phone, "I would take you to dinncr. Or lunch."

"You don't have to do that," I said.

"I'd like to, J.B.," she said, "I really would. Okay, okay. Where were we going to go to dinner last week?"

I told her, the hip place in the theatre district.

"Okay, okay, that's where we'll go. Whenever you say."

"Uh ... forgive me for asking, but what about Harry? Or will he be joining us?" I bit my tongue as soon as I said it. Now

I was going to be snide? Now I was going to make her squirm? I had been so gracious, so magnanimous, and here I had to go and spoil it.

But she was great. Becky said, "No, Jay hawk, he won't be joining us. It's over. It really is over. That's why I'm calling you, see?"

"Instead of dinner, how about lunch?"

"Well, okay. When?" she wanted to know.

"How about today?" None of this, "How's your Thursday shaping up?"

"Today?"

It was almost eleven as we were talking.

"Gosh," she said, "Sure, but ...," I waited and let her say it like she meant it. "Only reason I'm hesitating is ... I'm in a mess over here, and I'm a mess, too."

"Let me guess, you're painting."

"You're right! I wish I'd never taken it on. I'm overwhelmed. I've never liked painting, never been good at it. Some people have the knack. I don't. You look at the walls and say, 'Gosh, this'll be easy.' What you forget about are the angles and corners and stuff. This apartment has more nooks and crannies than a miniature golf course. When you were little, could you color and keep it inside the lines? I couldn't. And shelves. The shelves have to come out and be painted separately. Okay. I guess if I stop now and clean up, I could meet you somewhere at, say, one-thirty?"

We agreed on how lunch would be handled, and as soon as I hung up, the phone rang again. Marty this time.

"The theatre just called. Somebody's destroyed the set."

"Destroyed it? How?"

Rita Wauller had phoned and said, too loudly and hurried, that vandals had broken into the theatre the previous night and done a number on the stage. She had gone on to say the evening's performance would have to be cancelled and who knew how many more? She was usually the stalwart type, just what was needed around a theatre where panic and hysteria could set in at a moment's notice, and someone with a clear head and two feet on the ground was a godsend. But this morning she was flustered, even frenzied. I knew who Rita Wauller was and envisioned her on the other end of the line. Well, in a sense I did. What I saw in my mind's eye were those enormous hooters she carried around, not her face.

"Apparently, it looks like a tornado hit the place."

"Why would vandals break in and destroy the set?"

"Funny, I asked Rita that. She said she was not Dr. Joyce Brothers and didn't know why people do things. Anyhow, I thought you'd like to know. I'm on my way to the theatre."

"Stop by and pick me up," I said. It might be a little tight, but I figured I could get back from downtown in time to meet my lunch date. Gee, my life was getting so exciting.

On the cab ride down I told Marty I was having lunch with Becky. "Good, good," he said, distracted. Then he said he'd had another disturbing call right after Rita's. It was from the director Wayne Galafant. Sounding anxious, Wayne wondered if Marty planned to come to the theatre that night. Marty told him he was on his way out the door and would be there in twenty minutes.

Twenty minutes? Wayne didn't know what Marty was talking about? He hadn't heard. He'd had his ringer turned off and hadn't checked his messages. Marty filled him in, and Wayne said he'd meet Marty at the TASSQ shortly.

When Marty and I dashed into the theatre and down the aisle, people were standing on stage shaking their heads. Rita, Wayne, and others, including Julius Moss, the talented set designer. His was the most important shaking head.

Marty hopped up onto the stage and surveyed the damage. Somebody, or some gang, had gone on a rampage. Walls, or flats as they're called, were torn down, and set pieces broken. A chair had been thrown through the "window," and an expensive (borrowed) pinball machine had been smashed and overturned. The dozens of newspapers and magazines that were part of the set dressing were torn to shreds and flung all over the place, and various vulgarisms had been spray-painted all around. Even some hanging lighting instruments had been shattered with a broom stick.

"Have you called the police?" Marty said.

"Of course," Rita said. "They're upstairs talking to Dori." Dori, the box office girl who had never taken one minute of her life to watch a Prell commercial.

We didn't know, of course, that two of the cops upstairs were Flannigan and Rivo. At first, they had ignored the report of a 10-21 when it crackled over their radio, but then they heard the incident had occurred at the TASSQ Theatre in the Village, and it grabbed their attention.

"Who breaks into a theatre? What's the point?" Marty said.

"Turns out they didn't break in," Rita said. "No signs of forced entry. Somebody let them in or they were already in or they let themselves in. Who knows? They didn't break in, that's all."

An inside job? Hard to believe.

"Julius," Marty said, "there's a show tonight. You have to put this set back together."

"Yeah, right," Julius said, "let me snap my fingers." He wore a black T-shirt, jeans, and black boots. He folded his arms over his chest and stood there as defiant as Brando.

"We can't cancel this show, not even for one performance. It's too important to too many people who've worked too hard to let some mindless punks stop us. Besides, the theatre can't afford the loss of revenue, right Rita?"

She seemed to concur.

"How's the house tonight?"

"It's sold out. The whole run is sold out."

"There's a waiting list," I added. People looked at me.

“Excellent,” Marty said.

“Yes, that’s the way we like it.”

“See?” Marty said to Julius. “The play has to go on.”

“This set can’t be rebuilt in a day, Marty,” Julius said.

“I agree,” said Wayne.

“Of course it can,” Marty said to Julius. “I know what you designers can do with a handful of help in a very short time. You’re the best, most efficient carpenters, painters, and craftsmen in the city, Julius. I’ve seen you do too many amazing things in a matter of hours, so don’t tell me you can’t put this set back together. You’re a magician, Julius. You could build a house in a day if you had to.”

It took what seemed like another ten minutes of blandishments and flattery before Julius’s head stopped shaking. But it finally did and he leapt into action.

Rita gave Marty a sly grin as she left to go back upstairs. She never gave much, but she gave that.

“Are you sticking around today?” Wayne quietly asked Marty.

“No, I don’t want to be in the way. I’ll come back tonight, and let Julius surprise me.”

“Could you come a little early? Say ... six?”

“Is something else wrong?”

“It can wait. I’ll meet you upstairs at six.”

Wayne hurried down off the stage and out of the theatre before Marty could ask any more questions. It wasn’t even noon yet. Marty had more than six hours to wonder what was on Wayne’s mind and Julius had about seven hours to fix the set.

That night, Tuesday, would be the first performance of the second week. There was no show on Monday; the theatre had been “dark,” in theatre parlance. Although watching the set being demolished would have been quite a show in itself. Marty said it wouldn’t be unusual for the director to call in the whole cast at six, just to have them run their lines fast and furiously for an hour or so. Of course. That was probably it. He asked me if I agreed. I didn't know if I did or not. But why did Wayne want Marty there for a speed-through? He probably wanted some line changes, some cuts, right?

"Stop it already, Wayne," Marty said to me. "The play's open, and it's been reviewed. Let's let it 'breathe and find itself,' as the sage Stassie Simmons said." Besides, they were lucky to be having a performance that night at all.

Chapter 36

Shortly after one o'clock I buzzed Becky's apartment. She let me in and I walked up to the third floor and down the hall. She opened the door and said, "Don't look at me."

"Too late, I see you already." I thought she looked magnificent. I leaned in and pecked her with a kiss. As I pulled away, she was wiping the blue paint off me that had been transferred from her cheek and shirt.

She'd tried to clean herself up some and look presentable for me, even though I'd told her not to bother. We met somewhere in the middle.

I had with me a couple of bags from Zabar's. It was like I'd walked into the deli section and said, "Give me one of everything." I lifted the bags a little toward Becky like two buckets from the well. "Hungry?" I said.

"That's for us? I thought it was your groceries for the week."

"We don't have to eat it all. Most of it'll keep." She took the bags, as I surveyed the apartment. It was a large studio with southern exposure and a wood-burning fireplace. Well, once it burned wood. Now it was just a tiled indentation in the wall occupied by a vase containing a variety of long-stemmed ferns with specks of powder blue paint on their fronds. The windows weren't huge, but there were several of them, and early November's transitional light was coming through at the moment. Most of her furniture was covered by drop-cloths, but if a piece of the arm of a chair happened to be exposed, it had not escaped splatter.

"So this is Valhalla, huh?"

"It's what?" She was on her way to the kitchen to unpack.

"Valhalla, you know ... in Norse mythology, the hall of the slain? I mean, your name is Norse, right? So I thought ..."

She came back into the room, over to me, looked at me, completely deadpan. "What are you talking about?" she said, and it really threw me.

"Valhalla. I thought because your name is Norse."

Cold silence. Then, suddenly, she slapped my chest with both her hands and then took them to my cheeks and patted both of them three or four times. She laughed and said, "Yes, silly, I know what Valhalla is. And yes, this is the great, splendid hall where Odin fed and entertained the slain warriors. And that's what we're going to do, feed. Now come on."

She took me by the hand and led me. She uncovered a couple of chairs and a round, antique oak table. "Now sit down, Jackson Browne."

I sat and she walked away saying, "Valhalla ...," all in fun, just teasing me. And I'd thought I was so clever.

We ate everything from pastrami to potato salad, all of it delicious. I had even brought dessert, creampuffs, but Becky passed. I had one bite of mine, and she took a lick of it, but that was all.

We sat at the table with its drop-cloth pulled back until nearly three-thirty. We got to know each other. I even told her, without detail, about the lucrative horse farm deal that had soured me on my professional life, and I didn't go around telling that tale to very many people.

I didn't mention I'd been down to the theatre and the set of her play looked like a box of Tinker Toys. I thought it might alarm her.

Becky was from south Jersey, and her parents still ran a bed and breakfast in Cape May. She had worked there all through high school, then went off to Rutgers. And, although she was enrolled there on and off for five years and was moving toward a theatre arts degree, she never finished. Just before the start of her junior year, she had come into New York to see an agent who had stayed at the bed and breakfast that past summer. It was the agent herself who, in talking with Becky, had learned of the young Ms. Norse's ambitions and had detected something special in her (so had I). The agent set up the appointment. It went well, and before Becky knew it, she was not only going out on auditions but actually booking commercials.

As she was telling me all this I realized I had seen Becky Norse a long time ago. I interrupted her. "You were in that Pepsi ad!" I said, remembering a TV commercial from a dozen years back.

"You don't remember that."

"I most certainly do. You were the girl in the wheelbarrow."

"You remember me? You remember that ad?"

It was strange, indeed. Not only was I not a TV watcher, but the last thing I cared about was any television commercial. But here I was seeing it in my head. Not the whole one-minute spot, maybe, but certainly enough of it to remember the girl in the wheelbarrow being rolled around by some hunk at a cookout and other kids laughing and, oh, by the way, drinking Pepsi.

"That was, I think, the second or third commercial I'd ever done. I can't believe you remember that."

I couldn't either. Were there fated meetings on this earth, fated relationships and destinies? Did certain people, events, did some particular moments, stick in a person's mind instead of or above thousands of others for some reason? Did they remain in the mind to be recalled in the future when it was time to place that piece of life's puzzle into the others on the board? Or was everything chance? A chance meeting, sighting, a chance experience, coincidental and arbitrary?

Did my remembering that commercial, that girl in the wheelbarrow, mean destiny had put this young woman in my path all these years later? I didn't, for example, remember the girl in the Dr. Pepper ad, if there was one.

We very lightly touched on Harry. As long as he was gone, that's really all I needed to know. But I couldn't help learning he was an actor, too, struggling, and they had been together about four years.

Actors with actors. If it doesn't work in the big leagues, Hollywood and Broadway (it usually doesn't), how is it going to work down here in the minors? Down here where the frustrations are more abundant, the money drastically less, and the time to achieve stardom, or even reasonable success, flies by like a cruise missile. So you give each other comfort for a few years until it inevitably blows apart because one of three things has happened — you've both done very well, neither of you has done well, or one of you has done well and the other hasn't. In their case, Becky was working steadily in the theatre and still making good money doing commercials. The only job Harry had had in two years was selling jungle pants and shirts at Banana Republic.

Why had Jaysovich never married? I was "such a special guy, a professional, obviously interested in women, and physically not repulsive" — an expression she used because we had become so comfortable with each other and because Becky found humor in everything. I told her I'd had my chances. I mentioned a few (didn't mention Daisy), first because she asked and secondly, to counter Harry.

The simple truth? The right one hadn't come along. It's easy to marry. You have to escape the ones that aren't right. That's the hard part. It takes careful thinking, patience, sometimes strength, and always luck. I had, so far, escaped.

"You know what I have to do?" she said, finally, looking around the room.

"Yeah, I know, you have to get back to work."

"No, no," she said, "I have to take a nap." She had worked all morning, the proof was splashed and spilled and piled all around us. It had to have taken a lot of work to destroy the apartment like this. "I have to take a nap so I'm fresh for the show."

"Okay, sure," I said and stood up and looked at her.

She just sat there but looked at me, too. "I'm awfully glad you called, Jay Silverheels."

Jay Silverheels. Sounded familiar but I couldn't remember.

"He was Tonto on the Lone Ranger television series, way, way back. I had older brothers."

"Oh, yeah. Me Tonto. Except I didn't call, you did."

"No, you did."

"No, you did," I said.

"Oh, maybe I did. But you called me first and got my paint store message and tracked me down, and I'm glad you called."

Right. "Maybe I did," I said.

She stood up, still looking at me. She took both my hands and held them, kissed me on the cheek. "I want you to take these leftovers with you."

"No, you keep it all."

"There's enough food left to feed Eric the Red and all the little Viking men."

"You keep it, please."

"You'll have to come back."

"Nope, sorry, not interested." We were winding our way to the door.

"Next time maybe you'll call me. I'm tired of having to call you every single time," she said.

"What time do you leave for the theatre?"

"I like to get there early. So I leave around five. Why?"

"What time do you get home?"

"Oh, my gosh. You're not going to start stalking me, are you?"

"If I were going to stalk you, I wouldn't have to ask these questions. I'd just stalk you and find out."

"Oh. Okay. I usually get home around midnight, earlier if I don't go out for a drink or eats with some of the cast. Why?" she asked again.

"Just curious."

I left. But when Becky came out of her building shortly after five that afternoon, I was waiting for her on the sidewalk in front. She was surprised to see me.

"Jay Boy?"

"I decided I want the food back."

She looked at me a second, put her fists on her hips, her arms bowed out, and cocked her head.

"Let me into your apartment. I want to straighten up and organize things for you so it'll be easier for you to see what you're doing."

"Are you quite mad?" she said, like a young Bette Davis. She puffed on an imaginary cigarette.

"Not at all. I can help you. I want to help you. When you come home, you'll see what I mean. Let me help you."

It took some doing, but I talked her into letting me in. She left again, off to the subway. I stood in the chaos and looked around. Then I got busy and painted her apartment.

Chapter 37

At six o'clock Marty entered the theatre. He resisted the temptation to peek into the house where hammering and sawing were still going on and climbed the stairs to the upper lobby. He could smell sawdust and fresh paint.

I'd get a full report from him the next day on why Wayne wanted to see him before the show. A full report.

Wayne was waiting.

"Where is everybody?" Marty said.

"Everybody who? Becky's here, meditating or whatever she does. Let's not get her in on this."

"On what? Where's the rest of the cast? I thought you'd have the whole cast here."

"No, no. Come on." He motioned for Marty to follow him back toward the dressing rooms.

"Have you looked at the set?" Marty said.

"Yes, ycs, it's fine."

Ellen Rivo's door was mostly open. Wayne let his knuckles tap a couple of times, and he and Marty went in. Ellen shared her dressing room, but the other young woman wasn't there. In a show with a fairly large cast, such as this one, some of the performers might have to double up. Ellen was sitting at the long mirror, which was lined with a couple of dozen white-burning bulbs. She was staring at herself.

And for good reason. Her right cheek was swollen at the corner of her eye. It was about the size of a racket ball. Her right eye was half shut by the swelling. The whole mess was blue and black, with just a dash of orange and yellow. She wasn't in pain, but she sure looked like she should be.

"Good lord, what happened?" Marty grabbed a chair, turned it around, sat close to and facing Ellen.

"She ran into a wall."

"What?"

"She ran into a wall, Marty."

"No, I heard you. I'm asking how you run into a wall and do this?"

Ellen hadn't spoken yet. She still didn't. She shrugged.

"How do you feel, Ellen?"

"Okay. Doesn't hurt."

"I gave her a pain pill," said Wayne.

"How did this happen?"

"I ran into a wall."

"I want everybody to stop saying that. Were you drunk? Was it dark?"

"Yeah, I guess." She was subdued and more or less mumbling. She tried to look away from the mirror, but like a magnet it kept drawing her head and eyes toward it.

"Have you been to a doctor?"

"No."

"Wayne, she has to go to a doctor. Her cheek bone could be broken."

"It's not broken," Ellen said. "It's just sore."

"I'll bet it is." Marty placed a couple of his fingers under her chin, tilted her head back gently, and gazed at her face from a different angle. "Why didn't you tell me about this this morning, Wayne?"

"We wanted to see how she got along today. She got along fine, didn't you, Ellen?"

"Uh-huh."

"I was thinking," Wayne said, "when she makes her first entrance and gives the speech about 'running all the way over here,' well, we add a line for her. She says 'I was running and I fell.'"

Marty eased his fingers away from her face and stared at Wayne. "Are you out of your mind?"

"What? She fell, the character."

"She didn't fall and do this!"

"Why not?"

"In the first place it wouldn't swell to this size that quickly, and in the second place, it's every color in the rainbow, Wayne. That doesn't happen instantly!"

"We can cover it with makeup. They'll buy the swelling."

"What a crock. She fell on the way over and why, what does it mean, what does it have to do with anything in the play?"

"Okay, it doesn't, but it's an explanation."

"It's laughable. The audience is a little smarter than that, Wayne. They'll crack up. If, if Ellen even feels like going on tonight."

Wayne put a hand on her shoulder and said, "You feel all right, don't you?"

"Uh-huh."

"She'll be fine," Wayne said.

Marty looked her in the eye, in her good one, and said flatly, "You ran into a wall."

"Uh-huh."

"Have you put ice on it?"

"Yes," she said, and she rummaged through make-up, sponges, brushes and combs, hairspray, hair dryers, newspapers from the weekend, and a wig stand or two until she found the ice pack she'd been using, a clear plastic bag packed full and zipped shut. She put it to her cheek, closed her eyes, held it there.

"Keep the ice on it," Marty said.

"There's just one thing I'm worried about," Ellen said. "My dad. I know he'll come to the play again. He'll pop in, maybe even tonight, and I don't want him to see this."

"Why not?" Marty said.

"Because there's so much on his mind and everything. Seeing me hurt will just upset him."

"Well, he can't just pop in. The show is sold out. He'll have to get a ticket through you or me."

That seemed to cheer her a bit. "Oh. He probably won't know any of that. So if he comes to the box office at the last minute, he won't get in?"

"It's possible he could get on the waiting list and get a seat from a no-show, but it's not likely."

"Oh." She thought that over.

"I think you're being silly, though, Ellen. Accidents happen to everybody."

She looked at herself in the mirror again. She tried to make that dumb-looking expression from the first photo Marty saw of her. It didn't come off too well.

"Why don't you lie down for a few minutes?" Marty suggested.

"Right, Ellen," Wayne said. "Lie down for awhile."

There was a narrow bed built into a wall with a mattress on it, a reasonably clean sheet, pillow, and blanket. Ellen turned her neck slowly and looked back over her shoulder at the bed. Yes, she would lie down.

Marty looked at Wayne, Wayne returned the look, and they stared each other down for a few seconds. Then Marty left the dressing room. He went into an office up the hall, the one he had used when he called Ellen a month or so ago and asked her to come down and audition. He made another call, to someone else this time. The carpentry sounds from down below had tapered off.

At a quarter of seven, Marty was standing outside the theatre when a taxi pulled up and a strapping fellow with curly hair and pallid skin named Tommy Kloover bounced out. He was about Marty's height but heavier. Under a black coat he wore a dark blue sweatshirt with MICHIGAN printed across the front in maize letters. He carried a black bag. He stuck out his other hand and shook Marty's.

"Thanks, I appreciate this," Marty said.

"Sure! Let's have a look." He had a strong, Steve Canyon-type face. When he smiled, his teeth were prominent, white and straight. He and Marty had the same kind of energy, positive and kinetic.

I know because I had played football with Thomas Kloover, M.D., internal medicine. He had played in the Sunday game with Marty for five or six years and was a marvelous athlete. When sides were chosen on those Sunday mornings, Marty and Tommy could never be on the same team. Otherwise, the other team wouldn't have a chance, no matter who comprised the rest of the rosters. I had figured that out all by myself and quickly.

They went into the theatre. A minute later they were upstairs in Ellen's dressing room.

"Ellen, this is a friend of mine, Tommy. He's a doctor. Can he have a look at your face?"

She was sitting at the mirror again and had started to dab at her cheek with a flesh-tone make-up sponge. She took a moment before answering. Finally she said, "Well, okay."

Tommy sat in the same chair Marty had used. Marty stepped back into the door frame and watched. Wayne wasn't around.

"Got bonked, huh?" Tommy said, looking closer at Ellen's cheek and eye, comparing them with the normal ones on the other side of her pretty face.

"I ran into a wall."

"Uh-huh." He touched her cheekbone gently, here, there,

here, and asked her if it hurt. It didn't seem to hurt much. "Has your nose bled?

"No."

He took a miniature flashlight out of his bag, clicked it on and peered into her injured eye. "Can you see normally? Any blurriness or double vision?"

"No. I see fine."

"Open your mouth for me." She did, and he lit it up and looked in. He picked up her upper lip with his thumb and forefinger and examined her teeth and gums. "Any numbness or tingling in your mouth?"

"Huh? No."

"You weren't knocked unconscious, were you?"

"Heavens, no," she said.

"Are you slurring any words?"

She shook her banged up head.

Tommy turned off the flashlight and replaced it in his bag. He took out a thermometer and took her temperature. Normal. He noticed the Glad bag and picked it up. There was a little ice left, but mostly it was a pouch of cold water now. "Wouldn't hurt to refill this and keep it on there for awhile."

"Her cheek's not broken, is it, Tommy?" Marty said.

"I don't think so, but we'd need an x-ray or CT scan to know for sure."

"It's not broken," Ellen said.

"Why don't you come by my office tomorrow, we'll work you in. We'll x-ray it and depending on how it looks by then, we might want to put you on some antibiotics."

"I can take you tomorrow," Marty said. She didn't say no, but she didn't commit to it, either.

"Ellen, let me ask you something else," Tommy said.

"Okay."

"Who hit you?"

Chapter 38

Marty once said, "An audience is a strange creature, capable of almost anything. It paid to see you. It wants to love you. It needs you; it depends on you; it wants to believe you. And it will, given the chance. It wants to follow; it wants to be fooled; it wants to applaud. If you tell it there's a door there, when actually there is no door, it will accept what you tell it as long as you are consistent and don't break the illusion.

"Or if you should, the creature is merciful and will forgive you. If you perform in front of it and make a mistake or two, it knows that we all make mistakes, and it will cut you slack. But you must be honest with it. If you lie to it, it has an uncanny sense of knowing. And it will turn on you.

"If that happens, it can become an angry, ugly, even dangerous creature, and there's no soothing it. It wants to kill you and will."

That's why, on that Tuesday night, the first night of the second week of the TASSQ play, Marty insisted someone (it turned out to be Rita Wauller) stand up in front of the house before the show and explain that because of a minor accident the night before, Ellen Rivo, in the part of Annabel, would be performing with a swollen cheek and partially closed eye. The "creature" was assured the actress felt fine, had seen a doctor, and was going on, despite the noticeable injury to her face.

There were no understudies in a situation like this, and so it was either let Ellen do the role or have the ASM walk through the part reading Annabel's lines from a script.

"Please bear with her," Rita said, "and with the rest of the cast. Thank you."

The creature loved it. It applauded, even before the play started. It watched the show knowing it, the creature, was special. It was privy to something the previous creatures had not been privy to. This was live theatre, and the performance was under stress. But the performers had a huge heart, and the creature showed it did, too. It paid special attention; it laughed harder; it felt more deeply. The creature, God bless it, gave itself to the performance. If the beast had also known the set had been rebuilt and painted that very afternoon, it might have gone into convulsions of glee. But that information was kept from them.

The actors had all been told, of course, but they took it pretty much in stride. What could they do? Besides, everything was back the way it was supposed to be, and they had a job to do.

Marty didn't stick around for the show that night. He listened to the announcement (he had told Rita what to say), and then he took a cab up to 21st Street and Ninth Avenue. He rang the bell of a particular apartment on 21st and, after an exchange or two, he was buzzed in. He walked toward a door on the ground floor. The door opened about halfway as he approached, and Wayne peered out.

"What's up?" Wayne said.

Instead of answering, Marty shouldered the door and went into the apartment. He turned and slammed the door shut with the flat of his hand. He grabbed the front of the white T-shirt Wayne was wearing and nearly ripped it off him. He held him that way for a moment, not saying a word. Then he released him with a shove, and the director stumbled backward, hit the sofa's end-table, knocking the lamp to the floor and breaking the bulb.

"You don't understand, Marty."

Marty was furious, a millimeter from out of control. "I don't understand?" Marty kicked the lamp and sent it sailing. "Make me understand how it was acceptable under any circumstances to hit that girl!"

Marty came at him again. Wayne put both his hands up in front of his face and backed away. "She came in here. She started coming in here, and before I knew it, she thought she owned me. Thought she owned me."

"What are you talking about?"

"She came over last week and threw herself at me. She threw herself at me. What am I going to do?"

"I know what you did, Wayne." Marty walked back and forth on the wood-plank floor.

"No, no, before it happened, before it happened, Marty. So I slept with her. What was I supposed to do? Don't tell me you wouldn't have done the same thing."

He hadn't done "the same thing," as a matter of fact, but he wasn't going to go into that. His heart was in his throat, and his chest was heaving. He started to become aware of his condition and got a hold of himself. He let Wayne continue.

"By the second time she came over, she practically thought we were married. I'm lucky she didn't order wallpaper. Did we get into a fight? Yeah, we got into a fight. But don't stand there and accuse me of hitting her for no reason. I had to hit her to get her off me!"

It was Wayne's voice rising now as the recall seemed to fuel him. "Look at this," he said, raising his T-shirt. His chest was scratched from the base of his neck to his navel. "She clawed me, man, like an animal. Okay, I hit her. I didn't mean to but I did. I sure didn't mean to hit her that hard."

The lightning had passed, the electricity had dissipated some, but the air remained charged and heavy.

"Her old man's a cop," Marty said.

"Yes, I know that."

"She's afraid of what he might do if he sees her like she is now."

"Afraid of what he might do to me."

"Yes."

"See?" Wayne said. "I hit her, busted her face, and she still wants to protect me. I tell you, Marty, the girl has problems. Well, anybody could see that the first day she came down to the theatre looking like she'd just stepped out of an old *Life* magazine."

Marty stopped pacing and watched Wayne pick up the lamp and table and replace them. The relationship between these two had never been perfect, but it had been a good one as playwright/director relationships go. Wayne had worked hard and, though Marty hadn't always agreed with him, a fine production had come out of it all, even the reviews said so. There had been the one casualty, Louise MacArthur, but there was nothing unusual about that.

But next play, Marty knew he'd need a new director.

Chapter 39

Okay, I didn't finish the whole apartment that evening and night. I might have if I hadn't had to go back to the paint store before they closed to get more paint for the walls, ceiling paint, enamel for the shelves, and some other goodies. That set me back.

But the place was looking pretty darn good when Becky came home, just before eleven. There was an order to it all, and much of the furniture was back where it belonged with the cloths removed.

She was so pleased and excited, she danced en pointe for about ten minutes. It put an odd feeling in the pit of my stomach when she did that because it reminded me of Daisy's waltzing around the sitting room at the McNoel, and I couldn't tell you why, but I felt a little guilty.

But Becky, too, had reason to dance. When I showed up with lunch earlier in the day, the room looked like Henry Alden Sherwin's laboratory where he and Edward Williams were trying to come up with the world's first ready-mixed paint. Not anymore. There was considerable touching up to do and some detail work, but as Becky twirled around on her toes, she was thrilled with how it all looked.

When she calmed down, I asked her how the show had gone, and she said, "Great! Best one yet. The audience was fantastic, even though Ellen, who plays Annabel, hurt herself before the show and had a swollen cheek and eye. Plus, somebody had trashed the set, and it had been put back together that very day and some of the paint wasn't even dry. Didn't matter," Becky said, "they loved us." She excitedly spilled all the details.

I hadn't talked to Marty yet and so hadn't heard anything about Ellen Rivo's injury or his visit to Wayne's apartment.

"Was Marty there tonight?"

"No, yes," she said. "He was there, but I don't think he saw the show. Not all of it, anyhow. I heard him say he came late. He was talking to Ellen when I left. Are you hungry? I seem to have a ton of food from Zabar's in the fridge," she said.

"Maybe we could just have a drink."

"A drink." She thought about it.

"Do you have anything to drink?"

"Don't you know?"

"What do you mean?"

"I assume you rifled through all my drawers, cabinets and cupboards. You probably know what liquor I have and my underwear size and style."

I looked around the room. "What do you have, video cameras?"

"Come on," she said, taking my hand. She dragged me into the kitchen and brought down a couple of glasses. "What do you want? Just name it."

"Bourbon."

"Bourbon." She opened a lower cabinet door, reached way in the back and pulled out a dusty bottle of brandy made from plums. She uncapped it and poured two shots. She held up her glass, "Here's to you, Dr. J!" and we drank. Robitussin-CF goes down easier and tastes better.

"Would you like to stay here tonight?" She asked it a few minutes later, just as I was leaving.

I looked at her and smiled. "Not on your life," I said.

Walking away, down the hall outside her apartment, I looked back. She was standing at her door, watching me go. "I'll come back at your convenience and finish the job."

"No hurry," she said. "Anytime tomorrow morning, early."

I stopped and thought a second. Why not stay over? No. No way was I going to sleep with her that night. Sweet of her to offer, thinking, of course, it was the sole reason I had broken my back on the apartment. But I had to make sure she knew I didn't do it for payment of any kind. I just did it because I liked her.

Home, I was dog tired and went quietly into the apartment. The bowl of popcorn I'd left out untouched was still there, but Kate had helped herself to it. It also appeared she had watched one or two of Marty's movies. She'd left the TV on, sound off. The blanket from the sofa was on the floor along with several unpopped kernels. I stepped lightly to the bedroom door and peeked in. She was sleeping. I stood there and admired her for a moment. Maybe I was adopted. I was glad she was home. She'd been out too much lately. Back off, Jay, she's not twelve years old.

I eased out of the doorway, went into the bathroom, and threw some water on my face pretending to wash it. I took a slug of pale yellow mouthwash, rolling it around in my mouth until it set my tongue and cheeks on fire. Too beat to brush my teeth.

I went back into the living room. I threw most of my clothes over my screen and fell into bed. I wanted to go to sleep thinking about Becky, but I closed my eyes and saw Preston Hondonada's big, wide face. I shook my head quickly a few times to get rid of the image.

Chapter 40

Here's a piece of good advice if you happen to be playing the game of Monopoly — buy everything you land on. Sure, it's scary to be sitting there with most of your cash gone, but your deeds are much more important.

I don't know how true this story is, but supposedly, in the late 1960's, a thirty-year-old Italian carpenter and craftsman named Franco Ossi came to America from the province of Parma with his wife and two young sons. He brought with him the tidy sum of nearly twenty-two thousand dollars. It was every penny he had managed to save since he first started working at the age of fourteen, plus a bonus his grandmother had slipped into his tattered pocket the day he left.

Five weeks after landing in New York, he signed a piece of paper at the Manufacturer's Hanover Trust bank and became the owner of a dilapidated and vacant four-story brownstone building on West 78th Street, west of Columbus Avenue. It was a bad area, seedy, dangerous after dark.

With the help of two young men he met, also recent immigrants from Italy, he gutted the building and began its renovation. He divided the building into apartment units. When the first two were finished, he moved his family out of the Times Square hotel where they had lived for three months and into one of the new apartments. He rented out the other one.

Twenty-five years later, Franco Ossi's first-born son was arrested for a murder he did not commit. The victim was a bookmaker and Franco's son owed him thousands. The son seemed to be the last one to see the victim alive. They had argued, the son had fled, and the evidence against him kept mounting until the cops finally picked him up and charged him.

But before he went to trial, a homicide detective named Paul Rivo, who had never been convinced of the Ossi kid's guilt, found a hidden ledger belonging to the murder victim. It was a duplicate, almost, of the book they had found at the scene of the murder, except this one had notes written in it about everyone who had ever placed a bet with the bookie. It contained some names that did not appear in the other ledger. They were the names of bettors whose credit was no longer good.

Rivo's superiors did not want him to muddle the case by coming forward with the second ledger. So on his own time and dime, Rivo began tracking down and talking to the customers in the book, the ones viewed unfavorably by the dead man. When he began interviewing a nineteen-year-old Hunter College student, the young man flabbergasted Rivo by breaking down, crying, and confessing to the murder within fifteen minutes, his guilt and conscience having just about eaten him alive.

Franco Ossi, multi-millionaire, owner of eight apartment buildings on the now-oh-so-fashionable Upper West Side, came to Detective Rivo privately and insisted he, Ossi, owed Rivo a debt he could never repay. If there were ever anything, anything the landlord could do for Rivo, he hoped the detective would not hesitate to ask.

That tale was told to Marty and me at a table in an Amsterdam Avenue bar in 1990. We had stopped in for a quick one, and who came in but Detective Paul Rivo himself. We asked him to join us. He did, and as the shots and beers kept coming, Marty asked Paul about Ellen's apartment. Marty had for several years been curious about it.

Marty didn't know anything about Frank Ossi when he had taken Ellen and her banged up face home that night after the show back in the 80's. But he escorted her into her building and up to her apartment. It was a coveted one-bedroom with a river view on the corner of West 77th. It was modestly furnished and decorated, but it didn't matter because the apartment itself was so special. Marty stepped in and was shocked and impressed, and Ellen could tell.

"I know," she said, "Isn't it great? My dad found it for me. And it's so cheap, you wouldn't believe it if I told you what I pay. Let's have something to drink."

"No, no," Marty said, "I have to go."

"I told you I wouldn't do anything stupid."

"I know, but ... Ellen, I'm so sorry about what happened. I apologize for Wayne."

"It's okay. I guess I brought it on myself."

"I don't believe that. He didn't have to hit you."

She shrugged. Maybe he did, and maybe he didn't.

"I'm going to talk to your dad tomorrow."

"Oh, please don't."

"No, not about you. Something else."

"The murder?"

"Yeah, maybe. As they say in the movies, 'It's probably nothing.' I won't mention this ...," and he gestured toward her face, "if you don't want me to."

"I don't. It's over and it won't happen again."

"The thing is, if he sees you before you heal, he'll know I was holding out on him."

"It's improving fast, Marty. By the time he sees me, it won't be anything. If you tell him, it'll just cause trouble. I don't want trouble for Wayne or you or the theatre or anybody."

"He knew you were at my place, huh, in the bedroom?"

She lowered her head.

"Makes it a little harder for me to talk to him again. Why didn't he say something? Why didn't he tell you to come out?"

"You have it in your head I'm sixteen. I'm twenty-two. So that's the first thing. The other thing is, he loves me and watches over me and wants the best for me, but ... he's very insecure about how to handle the women in his life because of my mother. So ... so if I wasn't going to come out that day, he wasn't going to push it. And I wasn't going to come out because I knew it would upset you."

Marty shook his head very quickly a few times. Weird. At the door, he said, "Can I take you to see Tommy tomorrow?"

"The doctor guy? No, thanks. It's not necessary. I'd go see him if I thought it were."

"How's your mother?"

"I talked to her. She likes her new room."

"Good. Good night."

She probably wanted to hug him and kiss and keep him there, not that he ever said so. Just a guess. But he ducked out and put the door between them.

Chapter 41

Next morning, Marty hoped Detective Massgrave or Mossgrove, whatever it was, wouldn't answer the phone. He didn't.

"Flannigan, homicide," the voice said.

Perfect. With everything that was going on with Ellen, Marty had almost forgotten about Flannigan. Now he could get the bothersome piece of information about the ring off his chest and not even have to deal with Rivo.

I was home watching *Learning the Body*, but I'd hear about all this shortly.

"Detective Flannigan, this is Marty Sequatchee."

"Hey, how you doing, Marty?" the big Irishman answered.

"Yeah, good, uh ..."

"You want Paul, right?"

"Well, actually ..."

"Paul!" Flannigan yelled, his mouth away from the phone. Then he came back to Marty. "He was just leaving. I caught him. Hold a sec."

Marty sighed, rolled his eyes, threw his hands up, doing all the things you do when there's nothing you can do.

"Paul Rivo," another voice said.

"Detective Rivo, it's Marty Sequatchee."

"Marty, what can I do for you?"

“I’ve got a little something.”

“A little something, huh?” Marty had the feeling Rivo had repeated the line for Flannigan’s benefit.

“One night Patsy, my friend Jay, his sister, and I went out for something to eat.”

“Uh-huh.”

“We went to a place in the Village called Sandolino’s.”

“Sandolino’s,” Rivo repeated, as though he were writing it down.

“That’s not important, you don’t have to write that down,” Marty said. “The point is ...,” and Marty related the incident to Rivo.

“So you’re saying ...?”

“The amethyst ring was given to her by some guy, some guy who left town. Since he left town, it might be someone you’re not aware of. Who knows? It might be the person who killed her.”

“Came back to town and killed her, huh?”

“Well, yeah.”

On the other end of the line, the general hubbub of the precinct.

“Are you there?”

“Yeah, I’m here, Marty. Who do you think this person might be?”

“I don’t know.”

“She didn’t say anything else about him? No other little detail you may have forgotten?”

“No. I’ve been over it a hundred times in my head. That’s all she said.”

“And you didn’t pursue it?”

“No, why would I do that? It was an old boyfriend or someone she had been seeing. He was gone, so it didn’t matter.”

“Uh-huh,” Rivo said and Marty didn’t like the way it sounded. Rivo said “uh-huh” with the same inflection and connotation as Tommy's "uh-huh" when Ellen told him she'd run into a wall.

"I'm not holding out on you. That's all she said."

"Why would you be holding out on me?"

"I'm not." Neither of them said anything for an uneasy two seconds. "I guess it's nothing, huh?"

"You still getting those calls? Nobody's there?"

"Yes."

"Say, Marty, long as you're on the phone, let me describe someone to you. You tell me if he sounds familiar."

"Okay."

"He would be a big guy in his thirties, tall, with muscles. He wouldn't be very handsome, but he'd have a dark tan and blond hair. Know anybody like that? Seen anybody like that around?"

Blonde with muscles. That's the guy Ellen saw outside before she rang Marty's bell, the guy that gave her the willies.

"Uh ..." Marty said.

"Say what, Marty?"

"Somebody saw a guy like that outside my apartment building recently. But I don't know him, haven't seen him. What's going on?"

"The investigation, Marty. The investigation's going on."

"I suppose you know somebody ripped our set apart at the TASSQ."

"I heard about that."

"The blond fellow, did he have something to do with that? Or did he have something to do with Patsy's murder?" It seemed like a fair question.

"Both," Rivo said.

The phone call ended, and Marty stood there with the cordless Uniden in his hand.

Down at my place, I sipped at some coffee and thought about the movie I'd just seen. I had really enjoyed it. No, I didn't. Why say so? The story was fine, though a little soft, I thought. The characters were well-drawn and diverse, but the players weren't up to it, I didn't think. There on the screen was some kid I had once seen for five minutes in a situation comedy on TV. Now he wore an old-timey white smock, mask, and cap and hurled in the middle of an appendectomy, while the seasoned surgeon yelled, "Get him out of here!" The seasoned surgeon, by the way, was a mid-level actor named Hernandez. If he hadn't been sizzling in Hollywood years earlier when the movie was made, he had at least been warm. The problem was, he was Hispanic and spoke with a trace of a Spanish accent. Look, I understood political correctness, but I also understood reality, and Hernandez in that role just wasn't kosher.

And the production itself, the director's responsibility, Marty would say, did not capture the mid-depression era, not even a little bit. You could feel the lack of authenticity in everything from the hospital to the automobiles. The suits were too classy (YSL?), the fedoras phony as theatre sets. All added up, it made enjoyment of the picture, belief in it, an uphill battle. But I watched the whole thing and did admit to being touched (lightly) at the end.

Then, while the tape was rewinding, I realized something. Dr. Hernandez in the movie reminded me of Hondonada, Preston Hondonada, who himself was one-quarter Hispanic, I had read. Did that color my perception of the film? I wasn't crazy about the actor Hernandez. Why? Maybe because I wasn't crazy about the TV personality Hondonada because ... ah, it was all too jumbled up in my head. Kate could go out with anyone she chose.

Maybe I just didn't like the movie.

The phone rang, and I said hello to Marty. "I just finished watching *Learning the Body*," I said.

"Oh, yeah?"

"I really enjoyed it."

Ignoring the comment, he said, "Want to know why Galafant wanted me to come to the theatre early yesterday?"

Sure, I wanted to know. So Marty walked me through it. Poor Ellen Rivo, that lovely face.

Then he told me about his conversation with Flannigan, then Rivo, the ring, and so forth.

"What did he say?"

"Little. But Jay, there's a connection between the set being torn apart and Patsy's murder. I know that much."

We hung up in another thirty seconds, and I threw on my painting garb. I hadn't told Marty I'd turned into Michelangelo.

As New York days go, this one had barely started — it was just after ten in the morning. By mid-afternoon Becky's apartment was finished. Her shelves were dry and put back, and I was sitting with a cold bottle of beer.

Decades later I can close my eyes and see her carefully replacing all her books. The day before, I'd left a flannel shirt behind and when I showed up that morning, she was wearing it, unbuttoned, over her own outfit. I'd seen Kate in one of my shirts a hundred times and, of course, never gave it a thought. But seeing Becky draped in one was more meaningful than a hug and a great big kiss. It was as though she had accepted me, taken me in, wanted me close to her. I was proud of myself, so proud I might even get around to doing the bathroom and kitchen one of these days, I thought.

As she arranged her books, I sat back with my legs stretched out, crossed at the ankles, feeling like I owned the whole town. It was a great feeling, but I didn't want the whole town. I just wanted Becky Norse.

Chapter 42

Tuesday of the next week, still in early November of that long-gone year, Kate and Preston Hondonada were in his suite, sipping a cocktail. It was just after five in the afternoon. The sun had punched the clock and was heading west in a hurry.

Kate was wrapped in a luxurious McNoel bathrobe, he was mostly dressed, and they were having some delightful conversation about dinner. "There's Deep Ocean, if you feel like seafood. I haven't been there in weeks," he said.

"I don't know restaurants on the East Side, so whatever you say, Preston."

"Fish?"

"Fine."

"I've been thinking about Dover sole. Or there's Monroe's, of course. Hard to beat his prime rib. Last time I was there, Woody Allen was at the next table. He was with a large group, so we didn't havc a chance to chat."

"Was Mia with him?"

"I believe she was, yes."

"She is so beautiful."

"You, you are so beautiful," and he would lean in to kiss her, checking his watch at the same time. "There's always Escargot, but I'm not feeling French, are you?"

"Not really."

"You decide." He finished his vodka gimlet and headed for the bedroom. "I have a brief meeting downstairs in the bar, and when I come back, we'll go."

"Okay."

As Kate told me all this a week or two later, I cringed with every word. Maybe she just gave me the broad strokes and my imagination kicked in as it sometimes did. Nevertheless, I wouldn't doubt a word of it.

Can't you just see him in the bedroom, buttoning up and checking himself out? He liked what he saw, as usual, and came back to Kate. "Are you going to take a bath?"

"I might."

"Relax in a hot bath. I won't be too long. I just have to set this guy straight about a couple of things."

"Who is it?"

"No, I won't talk about it just yet. Soon. Soon I'll tell you all about it. For the moment, I don't want to jinx it. Are you going to have another drink?"

"No, I don't think so."

"Have another drink. I won't be long."

Hondonada's appointment was either waiting for him in the bar at one of the two square, glossy-black tables opposite the mahogany bar itself, or would arrive very shortly. There was one other customer, slumped on a barstool. He was a man in proper but jostled attire. He was working on his third, maybe fourth martini. He was Don Toswell, my old college pal.

I'd say the bartender, a young man who had probably won an Olympic gold medal for high diving, came out from behind the bar at the first sight of the TV personality. "Good evening, Mr. Hondonada. The usual, sir?" Or words to that effect.

"Yeah, thanks, Crey."

Meanwhile, I was in my apartment but on the way out the door. Becky and I had been spending a lot of time together. A lot of time. Just about the only thing that had kept us apart lately was the play, but I'd even done a good job of working that out by being in the audience two of the last three performances. Yes, the play was sold out, and there was a waiting list, but I knew people.

Seeing a play three or four times was a new experience for me and an eye-opening one. About halfway through the show the other night, something had hit me. I said to myself, "Wait a minute, this play is about the futility of war. This is an anti-war play, and more specifically, it's about the Viet Nam war — Marty's war. The girls in the show? They represent Lyndon Johnson's daughters! The older man, that's ole Lyndon himself." Was I blind, for God's sake? Was I an idiot?

No. Because nobody in the show was in the military, there was no mention of guns, bombs or Napalm. The setting was Tennessee, not the Mekong Delta. This was an old-fashioned domestic play, the well-built play, one critic had called it. But it was about the tragedy of Viet Nam, and I finally got it.

The names began to leap out at me. Lionel, the patriarch, that was Lyndon. Annabel. Was that Linda Bird? Sure. The two friends he talks about in the play, men never seen, are named McManus and Russell. They would be McNamara and Rusk, secretaries of Defense and State under Johnson, no question about it. I began to realize the play was written in code. Lionel was a stepfather. What did that mean? Surely someday scholars would pick it apart. What a discovery! I felt like Copernicus, formulating the heliocentric theory.

And not one reviewer understood it. Whose fault was that? Was it a fault? Had Marty meant for everybody to know the play was an allegory? Or had he meant to bury that intention so deeply no one could uncover it without a steam shovel?

It's the first thing I said to Becky after the show, after my awakening. She came out from her dressing room, skipping into my arms, and I said, "This play is about Viet Nam."

"Yeah?" she said with mock surprise.

"I have to know. How much did you talk about that? How much emphasis was put on it when you rehearsed the play? Were we supposed to know at some point during the evening? Was it supposed to dawn on us? Because it just dawned on me tonight."

"The first day of rehearsal, after we all had read the play through one time together, Marty talked about it for all of about two minutes. Then he told us to forget about it."

"Forget it?"

"Yeah, forget it. Both he and Wayne said, 'It's there, but if we play to it, it'll get in the way. It'll kill us. Some people will get it. Most won't. But subliminally, it'll pack a wallop.'"

"Holy moly," I said.

In the 1950's, when I was a little boy, Hollywood poured out a slew of pictures about invasions from outer space, monsters from another planet, creatures from Mars. I was in college when I read an article in *Time* magazine about those movies. They were all really about the fear Americans had of being invaded by Russia. Huh? It was news to me.

"There's a lot I don't know about fiction, subtext, and interpreting literature," I said to Becky.

"Let's eat," she said.

But that had been Sunday. We ate a late dinner, then went back to her place where I spent the night. Kate was away from home, too, so the Bluffing apartment was spending some time by itself.

At the moment, I was on my way out the door. I was going to grab a cab, pick up Becky, and take her down to the theatre. I wasn't going to see the show again, enough already, but I thought I might look around the Village and buy her a present. No occasion, just a present. The phone rang. I hesitated, then decided to answer it.

"My turn," the voice said. "I'm here. Get over here right now."

My stomach tied itself into a knot you couldn't pick apart with a crochet hook. The voice spoke again and said, "Jay? Are you there?"

"I'm here, Daisy," I said. "Where are you?"

"I'm in our suite at the McNoel and I'm waiting for you. This one's on me, old boy."

"Well, the thing is, Daisy ..."

"What? What is the thing? The thing is what? I don't want any excuses. I want you over here."

I bumbled around with her on the phone for another fifteen or twenty seconds until I finally told her I'd be there in half an hour. I hung up and called Becky.

"There's someone I've seen off and on for a couple of years. She just called and wants me to meet her in a fabulous hotel suite on the East Side. I told her I would."

No, I didn't say that to Becky on the phone, just to myself. Instead I told her, "Change of plans. I can't take you down to the theatre. I have to go across town."

"Is everything all right?"

"Fine, yeah, sure, everything's fine."

"Will I see you after the show?"

"Probably, yeah. I just don't know how long this is going to take."

"You mean it might take five hours?"

"Probably not."

This was the first time Daisy had ever called me to say, "Let's get together." I called her. She didn't call me. Good timing, huh?

While I sat in the taxi as it shot through the park, over to Second and down, I wondered what Daisy would have done if I'd said, "Sorry, can't make it." Did she have others to call? Was I at the top of a list she could have gone down until she found a partner? Was I even at the top? I remembered her sour doorman. Was he rude because I wasn't his favorite of the six or seven or eight?

I shouldn't have been thinking about any of that. I should have been thinking about what I was going to say to her, how I was going to tell her it was over. But it wasn't going to be a problem, was it? I mean, we didn't have a contract. We had a lady's and a gentleman's vague agreement, which was by no means binding.

Around that same time, Marty Sequatchee was finishing up some work on an outline for the rewrite of the movie script and thinking about his date. Earlier in the day he had had a call from Louise MacArthur, the short-haired knockout who had been fired by Wayne. She had called to congratulate Marty on the play, the reviews, and to say there were no hard feelings. She had sneaked in and seen the play and thought it was wonderful. Three minutes into the conversation, Marty asked her to dinner. He'd be paying the bill with red ink, but a person had to eat.

He showered, shaved, all that, and left his place with plenty of time to walk down to Louise's. She lived on 68th, West of Columbus, with a couple of roommates. He could take his time, stroll along, and make it easily in thirty minutes. They were going to have an early dinner, mainly because the only reservation he could get at the restaurant he chose, Carolina's, was for six forty-five.

Would he end up sleeping with her? He was conflicted. If it worked out that way, fine, but she was as young as Ellen Rivo, and isn't age the reason he had turned Ellen down? Age? What was he thinking about? He wasn't sixty, he was thirty-eight. Bogart had been forty-something when he first met the nineteen-year-old Bacall. You can picture me shaking my head in disgust when he got around to telling me all this. Gosh, Marty, I'm sorry you have so many decisions to make.

It was chilly but not cold, and the walk south was refreshing. On the sidewalk behind the Natural History Museum he recognized another young woman from his neighborhood coming his way. She was an actress named Kristy Adams with whom he had worked on two different occasions. They had had a wild night or two along the way, but it hadn't amounted to anything, and now they were casual friends.

She saw him coming, wrapped her Levi's jacket a little closer to herself, and scurried over to him. Marty kissed her soft cheek and gave her a hug. She was from Oklahoma originally and still had an open-range look. But her voice was trained and carried no trace of an accent.

"I read about your new play. Congratulations."

"Thanks, Kristy. How are you?"

"Better than Patsy Holton, the girl who was murdered a few weeks ago," and she looked south, back over her shoulder. "I don't even like to be out by myself after dark."

"It was someone she knew, Kristy, so it's probably one killer you don't have to worry about."

"I guess. One killer among many, though. I knew her."

"You did?"

"A little. We worked the car show together at the Coliseum once, and I'd run into her on the street. We didn't hang out or anything, but I knew her. She was hard to get close to."

"I knew her, too."

"Oh, my, you did?"

Marty took his eyes off Kristy and gazed down the street.

"Were you close?"

"I hadn't known her long."

"I saw her that very day," Kristy said.

"You did? The day she was killed?"

"Yes!" she said with special articulation. "On Broadway. She was standing outside that store, Pauline's Dream, over there," and she pointed west. "I stopped, and we talked for a minute. A couple of hours later, I guess, she was dead."

"Did you talk to the police?"

"The police? No, I didn't, of course not. Why would I?"

"She was standing outside the store?"

"Yeah." Kristy closed her eyes to conjure the scene. "She had her arms folded on top of a parking meter, and she was just sort of leaning there."

"Doing what?"

Kristy opened her eyes. "Just ... standing there."

"Why?"

"I don't know. We said this and that, laughed about an old acting teacher we both knew. It was nothing, really. I have to go, Marty. Call me sometime," she said.

And they parted. After a few steps, he looked back to see Kristy moving quickly away, hurrying home. He checked his watch and realized he'd have to hurry, too, to get to Louise's and then Carolina's on time. He felt like cutting over to Broadway and walking past Pauline's Dream, but there wasn't time, and besides, there was no sense in it. And he wouldn't even phone the cops about it. He felt stupid he had called them about the ring. He wasn't going to call now with more meaningless blather. But he would tell me what Kristy had said, later that night, and it's a very good thing he did.

Around this time, across town, Kate was out of her bath, dressed, and waiting for Hondonada to return.

Chapter 43

Not long before I moved out of New York in 1994, I was strolling through the old Coliseum Bookstore at Broadway and 57th Street. On a remainder table a non-fiction book called *Solving Murder* caught my eye, not so much because of the title, but because of the author. The book was written by Michael Flannigan, a retired New York City homicide detective. In the head shot on the back of the jacket, he looked vital and relaxed, and his cheeks showed not a trace of red.

I read most of it that very afternoon, concentrating, of course, on the section devoted to the Patsy Holton murder. I gave the book to Marty, and we had quite a time integrating Flannigan's recollection of the case with our own. He didn't contradict anything Marty and I had learned or figured out long before, but some information and details he provided we never would have known. Marty and I were in the book as M.S. and J.B.

Good ole Flannigan. His personal life was going very well, and he had woven scenes of it into his tales of mystery and violent death. He wrote about sitting in a room's tattered easy chair, drinking a can of Hamm's, the beer he had grown up on. The nineteen-inch TV was on with the volume very low. The local news, all of it bad, colored the slightly fuzzy screen. A hit-and-run in Murray Hill, a robbery in lower Manhattan, an argument that led to a fatal brawl in the Bronx. Flannigan was looking at the screen but not really seeing it. He was thinking about Patsy Holton's murder and drinking his Hamm's.

The old and cluttered apartment on Ninth Avenue was directly above the meatloaf-and-mashed potatoes diner owned and run by blue-eyed Phyllis Bolsky. Six or seven years earlier, Phyllis and her husband had packed their meager belongings, abandoned their state-owned farm, and ventured to New York City after Gierek was toppled in Poland and martial law was imposed.

After working for a couple of years, Phyllis as a waitress and Rafal, her husband, as a short-order cook, they leased the long, narrow restaurant space with its living quarters above. They quickly turned the White and Red Diner into a thriving concern, serving a practical and inexpensive breakfast and lunch to, for the most part, hungry laborers.

But one day Rafal, who was fifty-two, stretched out for a nap upstairs after the diner closed at three p.m., and he never woke up.

Phyllis didn't know what to do except keep going. She had help from a sporadic customer named Mike Flannigan. He stepped in, arranged for the funeral of Rafal, found her a sober, dependable, trustworthy cook, and saw to it that there was a more noticeable police presence in and around the White and Red since the neighborhood was dubious.

Flannigan, fifty-five and recently divorced, easily made the transition from occasional customer to twice-a-day regular and within a few months, he and the thirty-nine-year-old Phyllis were providing each other solace and more.

Phyllis was slightly plump, appealingly so, with creamy and youthful skin, a round face, and those enormous blue eyes. She was bright, honest, tireless, and had a work ethic to be admired. She gave Flannigan more attention and tender care than all of his ex-wives put together. He had fallen for her in a very big way.

About six-thirty that evening she came into the apartment via the stairs from the kitchen below. She had closed up as usual at three, cleaned up, and prepped for the next day, which for her began at five a.m. She came in with one hand resting backwards on one of her kidneys, her elbow sticking out. She smiled at Mike, went over to him, leaned down and kissed him on the cheek. She took his beer from him and drank the last of it.

"May I get another beer for you?" she said, her eastern European accent not thick but noticeable.

She walked into a tiny, lime green kitchen, dropped the empty into the garbage, and brought a fresh, cold can out to Flannigan, who was still staring at a barrage of flashing images. She popped it for him and he took it. Then she stood behind him and massaged his stiff and chronically pained neck. After a moment he reached up and pulled her around and down into his lap. He put an arm around her.

"The murder, the murder, always thinking about the murder. Who dunnit, who dunnit?" she said.

He smiled at her, ever amused by her sincerity and her innocence. "Sweetheart, we know who did it. We just can't prove it yet."

"You know who killed the girl?"

"Sure we do."

"Arrest him! Go out now and arrest the man!" She took the beer away from him and held it at a distance. "Let me up." He wouldn't. "Let me up from here, you bear! Let me up from your lap and go arrest the murderer."

His grip around her tightened. He tickled her until, giggling from the torture, she returned the beer.

"I'll tell you what I'll do," he said. "I tell you who murdered Patsy Holton, and you go out and make the arrest."

"Okay, I will. Tell me who. I'll take your badge and your gun and arrest him or shoot him up."

Flannigan leaned into her ear and whispered. She listened, her eyes getting even bigger than they usually were.

"No!" she said, aghast.

"Yep. We know it. We just have to prove it."

Chapter 44

I arrived at the hotel, saying a little silent prayer I wouldn't run into Kate and Hondonada. How could I ever make her believe I wasn't there to spy on her?

A different doorman, but one just as groomed and gracious as the other one, opened the taxi door for me. Richard Gere's twin was standing outside again. He glanced at me, then discreetly slid a flat hand inside his topcoat and down one side of his torso as though he were checking to make sure his Uzi was still there.

I walked into the lobby and looked around. I didn't see anyone I remembered from the last time. A new flock of Ford Agency models with Master's degrees stood in the appropriate spots. I wondered if I could just get on an elevator and go up. Did I have to identify myself, give a name or suite number? I wondered how Daisy had done it when she came to me. I'd never asked. I stood there doing my wondering when I heard my name and a voice that almost sounded familiar.

"Jshay! Jshay!"

I looked to my right to see Don Toswell wambling out of the bar. He was swaying like Trump Tower in a cat 5 hurricane. At eight bucks a drink, Don had about forty-two dollars' worth of gin and vermouth in him. The wrestler from Teaneck tried to put a smile on his face. I said the only thing I could think of. "Don," I said.

"What are you doing here?" he wanted to know. "What are you doing here?"

We were shaking hands by this time, and I felt I was the only thing keeping Donny boy on his feet. An alcohol vapor seemed to emanate from the guy like swamp gas. It engulfed his head and face, and he was talking a little too loudly.

"What are you doing here?" I said quietly.

"I ass you fursss."

"A friend of mine is staying here. I came to visit her."

"A friend of yours is staying here?"

"Yes," I said, trying not to look around at whoever might be in the audience.

"A friend of yours is staying here?" Don was finding it hard to believe. "Thass a coincidence. Isn't that a coincidence?"

"That's New York," I said with a grin.

"Thass New York," Don repeated. Then, giving it a little guarded laugh, "Thass New York."

"Why are you here?" I said, changing the wording of the question.

"Oh!" he said. He put his arm around my shoulder, pulled himself closer, got conspiratorial. I didn't mind since it brought his voice down. "I think she's here. I think she's here. I'm waiting for her to come down."

"Your wife?"

"Susan. I think she's here."

"Don. What are you planning to do?"

"Huh? Confound her. Confront her, I mean. Confront her. Both of them, if they come out together." He balled up a fist. "I might even take him out. I might take em both out."

"Come with me," I said, guiding him back toward the bar.

"Okay. I'll buy you a drink."

We entered the den, and I saw Preston Hondonada. He and the other man were getting up, just leaving. Hondonada let several bills float out of his hand and land on the table. I thought of the night Marty had pulled out the wad at Sandolino's. I sat Don down at the other table. Then I sat with my back to Hondonada and company.

Hondonada said, "Crey, thank you," and I could picture the pseudo-Eric Severeid making his finger and thumb a pistol and pointing it at the bartender.

"Thank you, Mr. Hondonada."

Hondonada and the other guy walked out. I had my head down. I could have said, "Excuse me, Preston? I'm Kate's brother." Not on your life.

"Stay here," I said to Don, and I turned to the bar.

"He knows what I'm having," Don said. Then he said it to Crey, "You know what I'm having."

Before Crey could start mixing, I said, "Could I have a cup of black coffee for him, please?" and the hot, fresh coffee was on the bar in a wink. "Thanks."

I walked it over to Don, who seemed to be nodding to music only he could hear.

"What do you call this?"

"Drink it."

"I know what it is."

"Coffee. Drink it."

"You drink it," he said, scooting the cup away and sloshing an ounce out of the cup.

"I'm your lawyer, and I'm advising you to drink the coffee." The cup moved back toward Don.

"You're not my lawyer."

"Let's pretend I'm your lawyer, and I'm here to get you out of jail."

"I'm not going to jail."

"No, you're not, because your lawyer's here."

Don slapped a hand onto his forehead and pulled it all the way down his face to his chin. He stopped it there and rubbed awhile.

It gave me a moment to think about Kate. She had said earlier she was going over to "Preston's place," and they were going out to dinner later, so what did this mean? She was probably upstairs. Hondonada was going up to get her. Don took a sip of the coffee, realized he liked it, and sipped some more.

He decided to talk again. "I followed them. They came out of his office and got in a cab. I got in a cab. I followed them. They were coming this way. Then my driver, some moron with a fez on his head, lost them. Who drives around with a fez on his head? So I just had him bring me here."

"So you don't even know she's here?"

"Pretty good idea."

"You're unbelievable, Don. Excuse me." I went back to the bar. "Do you have a house phone?"

"Yes, sir," Crey said, pointing to the end of the bar.

Daisy picked up, and I told her I'd run into a friend downstairs. I'd be up shortly.

"I'll join you," she said. "Order me a white wine."

I knew what was going to happen and it did because it could. Except I thought Kate and Daisy would probably run into each other in the hall. They didn't. The elevator carrying Kate and Hondonada stopped on the way down and picked up Daisy.

So three minutes after I hung up the phone, Daisy, Kate, and Hondonada strolled into the lounge. Don, sobering but not yet there, looked up at Hondonada and said, "Hey, you're on TV!" He hadn't even noticed Hondonada earlier.

"Thank you," said Hondonada, his face expressionless.

The necessary introductions were made all around. Then we pulled the two tables together, and everybody sat down. Don sat so he could see out into the lobby in case Susan passed through, with or without her boss.

There were a couple of other drinkers at the bar by that time, and they casually looked over, disapproving. You didn't push tables together at the McNoel. It wasn't the Pig N' Whistle. Then the strangers seemed to recognize Hondonada, and that made it okay. Pull some bar stools over, too, if you need them.

Kate looked at me suspiciously for a moment, wondering if I had come there to keep an eye on her, but Daisy mentioned something about inviting me over, and that seemed to satisfy my sister.

Crey appeared and took drink orders, except for Daisy's and mine since her chardonnay was waiting for her when she came down, and mine was in front of me as well. I had told Crey to make it two. Don decided he needed a glass of beer, and Kate and Hondonada each requested a vodka gimlet. Crey darted away like a goldfish.

The chitchat didn't come easily. It was like trying to drive uptown on Columbus Avenue, a southbound street.

I didn't like Hondonada and didn't go out of my way to hide it. Why didn't I like him? It wasn't even something I could put into words. And Kate and Daisy still couldn't warm to each other. They seemed to miss connecting by a mile. Chemistry. Don didn't pay much attention to anybody. He just glared through the opening into the lobby.

I found myself watching Don more than listening to anything being said, until I heard Kate say, "Preston has some big secret he's keeping from me, and I can't wring it out of him." She did something to precious Preston under the table, and it made him jump a little and squeak.

"All I can say is it's a new plateau for me, maybe a whole new world. It's very exciting." Maybe it wasn't gravel in Hondonada's mouth but a pint more saliva than a person needs.

"And you can't share the excitement?" I said, flat as a tone-deaf tenor.

"Soon, brother. Soon."

Hearing him refer to me as "brother" was hard to swallow. I tried to wash it down with wine.

Chapter 45

Marty was a semi-regular at Carolina's. If their waitress didn't know exactly who he was, she knew he looked familiar. Dinner with Louise was comfortable and pleasant once they were past reviewing one more time her departure from the show. Wayne was a jerk, they both agreed. The murder came up because Patsy had seen the first act of the play while Louise was still in it. But neither of them wanted to talk too much about that.

The food was delicious, the service excellent, and sexual innuendo dangled over the conversation like the carrot on the end of the stick that the donkey keeps heading toward. Marty was the donkey.

Or they were both the donkey. Because there was no charade here. They were going back to his place, and they both knew it by the time they'd finished their piquant shrimp-in-sesame-sauce appetizer. And so what? That's the way things were in those days. Maybe they're still that way.

They climbed out of the cab in front of Marty's building and started up the outside steps. From up the block a double-parked no-frills Plymouth slowly rolled down in their direction. The passenger window came down, the car stopped, and Detective Rivo called up to Marty.

"Marty? You got a minute?"

Marty stared down at Rivo, then over at Louise who just stood there waiting.

"I suppose I do."

Rivo turned to his driver, Flannigan, and they mumbled a line or two between them. The Plymouth stopped idling. The two detectives got out and clomped up the steps.

"Marty, how you doing?" Rivo said, extending his hand.

Marty shook it, then shook Flannigan's. "This is Louise MacArthur."

Both Rivo and Flannigan said, "How do you do, Miss," at the same time.

The four of them went up and into Marty's apartment. Flannigan and Rivo didn't do much looking around this time. They'd seen it. But Louise hadn't. She gave the place the once over. Her eyes landed on cool cat Bob, who had been asleep on the couch but was now awake and blinking. She went over and sat down, put Bob in her lap, and scratched the top of his head.

"What's your name?" she asked him.

"Bob," Marty said, "that's my friend, Bob."

"Bobby," Louise said, kissing his neck.

Marty told the detectives to sit down, but they didn't. Then he said, "Do you guys ever work during the day or just stalk the city at night?"

Flannigan offered no response, and Rivo said only, "Yeah," meaning something, probably, but Marty didn't know what.

"Paul says you were getting some phone calls."

"Phone calls, yes, I was," Marty said.

"Yeah, Marty, you still getting those annoying calls?" said Rivo.

"Yes, but not as often. I've had three, I think, since I told you about them."

"Did you happen to write down the day and time like I asked you?"

"Yes, I did." He was already at the living room desk,

looking for the piece of paper with the entries. Flannigan's notebook came out of a pocket of his tweed jacket, a jacket that wasn't brown for once but was a regular and should have been a long. So said Marty. Not to Flannigan, of course, but to me, later on.

He found his sheet of paper, handed it to Rivo and, with Flannigan, began to make some kind of comparison, silently, except for an occasional "uh-huh" or a "mmmnnn."

"Is the person who's been calling me the person who killed Patsy and the one who wrecked the set?"

Flannigan and Rivo looked up at Marty, as did Louise who had to stop kissing on Bobby to do so. So they didn't like the question, so what? What were they going to do to him?

"A murder case," Rivo said, "you find yourself putting this together with that, that together with this, maybe you trade this for that. Eventually you've strung four or five pieces together, right Mike?"

"That's right."

"Like a puzzle," Marty said.

"That's exactly right."

It was okay. Marty could handle a little sarcasm. He didn't have an answer to his question, but it was all he was going to get. He walked over to the fireplace. Five or six logs from the local International food market, about five bucks a bundle in those days, were on the irons, ready to burn. Marty wadded up some newspapers, stuffed them in under the logs, struck a match, and had a decent fire going quickly.

Louise dug around in her handbag for something, found it, and went over to Flannigan. "You see this?" she asked, holding up a plastic tube about half the size of a tube of toothpaste. "Sometimes I get a little hairline crack behind each ear, right here, where my ear curves around my head. It can be very painful, especially with winter coming on. I'm not going to say the word. Let's just say it's a common skin condition.

Well, a tiny bit of this cream behind each ear, the cracks heal up overnight. My dermatologist gives it to me. It comes from Europe. Miracle stuff. Works on lots of skin disorders. They use it over there, but we can't use it here. Don't ask me. Except he sneaks it to me. Anyway, I bet it would work for you." She uncapped the tube, squeezed out just a smidgen onto her index finger, applied a little to each of Flannigan's cheeks. "No fragrance, non-greasy, it completely disappears. There. How does that feel?"

"Good."

"Don't be surprised if your cheeks are smooth in the morning, and the redness is gone."

"Okay. Thanks." Marty thought Flannigan was probably flabbergasted. Rivo, too. Marty certainly was.

Marty wondered if that had anything to do with why she wore her hair so short. Did it hurt if hair touched the thin cracks behind her ears? "Is that why you cut your hair so short?"

"Why?"

"To keep it out of the cracks behind your ears?"

She paused, staring at him. "No." Then she laughed, and both detectives joined in.

Marty told me, more than once over the years, it was one of life's surreal moments, so surreal that sometimes you think you dreamed it.

The detectives apologized for interrupting their evening and headed for the door. Marty followed them over. Flannigan stepped out into the hall first. Rivo turned to Marty and said, very quietly, "She eighteen?"

"Yes. She's twenty-two."

"Good. Just looking out for you."

"Thanks." Marty and Rivo stared at each other, and Marty knew they were both thinking the same thing — Ellen. Then again, Rivo could have been thinking about tomorrow's lunch.

Flannigan leaned back into the room. "This cream works, I may need some more of it."

"Oh, you will. It's not a cure. It just controls the condition."

Flannigan stepped out into the hall again. Rivo joined him, and Marty stood in the door frame to watch them go down the hall.

On impulse he said, "You might want to talk to an actress named Kristy Adams." The men stopped and looked back. "It's probably nothing, but she talked to Patsy on the street, briefly, shortly before she was killed. Outside a store called Pauline's Dream."

"Kristy Adams?" Flannigan said, writing it down.

"She lives on West 82nd."

Rivo said, "Maybe we'll look her up."

"Patsy knew her killer. Do I know him, too?"

Marty seemed to think Rivo nodded, but it was almost imperceptible. Then the two men went down the stairs.

Marty joined his date and his cat, and all three of them cuddled there in front of the flames. They had had a perfect dinner, and now everything was warm, sexy, clean, and safe.

Several hours later, Becky and I would be there with Marty, Louise, and Bob. The fire would have burned itself out except for a rogue ember or two. Marty had mentioned Kristy to the detectives, but he would tell me about running into her in more detail. I would put the information to very good use.

For the moment, it was Marty, Louise, and Bob. Then the phone rang. It was me calling about Ellen Rivo, and what I had to say wasn't good.

Chapter 46

If Susan Toswell was at the McNoel on the evening I went there to meet Daisy, I never knew it. Kate, Daisy, Hondonada, Don, and I sat in the bar long enough to finish our drinks, making talk so small we could have all been Lilliputians.

Hondonada suggested everybody join Kate and him for dinner, but somehow he didn't sound as though he meant it. Anyhow, I was dying to get Daisy upstairs and explain things to her.

"We have the suite only for tonight," Daisy told Hondonada. "I think we'll eat in." She looked at me, and I knew she was thinking about our last visit to the hotel. So was I, but not exactly in the same light. It was just about time for the half-hour call at the TASSQ, and Becky would be getting prepared for the show.

Don didn't comment on the dinner invitation, no need to. Daisy had declined for all of us. He just sat there like a bottle of white vinegar, looking out into the lobby.

Kate and Hondonada, Daisy and I, all scooted back and rose at the same time. I pulled out some cash, but Hondonada wouldn't hear of it. "Crey? On my bill."

Crey was over there wiping glasses that already shown like diamonds.

I shook Don's hand and said, "Will you please go home? I have to go upstairs now."

"Do I have a home? What is a home?"

Oh, God.

"Don't worry about me, Jay. I'm a big boy. You don't by any chance have a license to practice in New York, do you?"

"No, I don't."

"Too bad."

I didn't mention I could get permission from any reasonable judge to handle one divorce case in New York, pro hac vice. I didn't mention it because I'd had enough of Don Toswell for six months ... or a year ... or two.

So Kate and Hondonada left for dinner. Daisy and I went up to the suite. There was a bottle of some other fancy wine, uncorked and on ice. She poured each of us a glass, and we sipped it.

She sat me down and sat opposite me. She set down her glass and shook her head quickly a time or two. I didn't know why. Her thick, red hair barely moved. She leaned into me, looked me dead in the eye. What in the world was she going to say?

"Jay," she began, "there's something I have to tell you. Something I finally have to tell you."

I took another sip of wine without taking my eyes off her. Years before, in Kentucky, I had had a client who had made a fortune in the mail order business in the 1960's and 70's. He sold magic tricks, illusions, and escapes. Everything from Houdini's famous Metamorphosis to simple card tricks. Sound silly? He made millions. He came to me one day and said, "Jay, there's something I have to tell you."

Yes, the very words Daisy had just uttered. In the mail-order millionaire's case, I made sure my lawyer's face was on tight, and I braced myself because I knew whatever I was about to hear wasn't going to be good. It wasn't. The gentleman proceeded to say he had for years performed a dangerous stunt— he had hidden hundreds of thousand dollars from the IRS. They had somehow become suspicious and had now come calling. I managed to keep him out of jail, but, including my hefty fee, it cost the magician everything he had. The last I heard, two or three years later, the guy had made himself disappear.

I didn't know what Daisy was about to say, of course, but I put on the same face I used when a client had something tricky to relate. And I braced myself the same way.

"I have a boyfriend, Jay. I have and have had a boyfriend."

I said, "Huh," flat and dry, not as a question but as though she had just said, "Tomorrow's Thursday."

"I've had a boyfriend since, well, since before I met you. And now ... we're getting married. So, my old friend, this will be our last night together."

What do you say to that? I didn't say anything. Not because I chose to keep quiet, but because I really didn't know how to respond. So we just kept looking at each other.

"I'm sorry to shock you, but I don't think I've hurt you, have I?"

"Huh?"

"I've deceived you. I've deceived you for a long time. I'm sorry. But I don't think I've hurt you, have I?" she said again.

It registered the second time. "Hurt? I don't know, Daisy. I probably won't know for a while."

"You're not hurt. You're just disappointed in me."

I tried some more of the wine and looked at my glass. "This is very good," I said.

"Sauvignon from the Colchagua Valley in Chile," she said.

"It's good." She orders wine from Chile but avoids the West Side of Manhattan. Okay.

"We, you and I, we ... were never going to go beyond what we've had. Isn't that right?"

I couldn't disagree with her, and she knew it full well.

"It was inevitable it would end. We both have known it for, well, I guess we've always known it."

"Is he a good guy?"

"He is. He's an architect. He designs giants. Paul Goldberger has written about him."

Even I knew Goldberger was the architectural critic for *The Times*. "He's older than you," I said, figuring he must be.

"Yes. He's older."

I didn't ask for more, didn't want more.

"So ... our last night together, okay?" She came over and sat in my lap.

"Daisy, I'm going to leave. I want you to get on the phone, call the architect, get him over here, and you two have the time of your lives in this joint."

"It wouldn't be his kind of gig, Jay."

"Oh. Well, anyhow, I can't stay."

I made a move to get up. She stood and let me. We had a hug and a kiss.

"I'm inviting you to the wedding."

"No, no, don't do that."

Then I had a thought and felt like a heel. "Does he know about me?" She hesitated. Then she broke out a smile and said, "No, silly person, he doesn't know about you."

"Good."

She walked me to the door. We looked at each other with the sudden knowing this was the last time, probably, we would ever see each other. In the elevator on the way down, I flashed ahead twenty, thirty years, and felt myself wondering about Daisy Leiber, what she looked like, how she was, where she lived, if she still chewed Aspergum ...

When I arrived in the lobby, there were no police and the hotel wasn't taped off. Don was gone, and I hadn't heard any gunshots, so I assumed, for better or for worse, Don's situation had dissolved like a miner's paycheck.

A white-gloved hand opened the door and a helpful voice asked if I needed a cab. I didn't. I was going to walk for a while.

I turned left onto Second Avenue and a wind from the south hit me like tiny steel shavings. It was cold for a minute, but I got used to it and walked all the way to Greenwich Village. The night was just beginning. It would be a harrowing one, climaxing with Ellen Rivo near death in Roosevelt Hospital.

Chapter 47

I was in the upstairs lobby at the TASSQ. The show ended, the applause was enthusiastic, and there were even some whistles. The sound came drifting up, muffled, from the house below and lasted at least fifteen seconds after the curtain call, always a good sign. Nobody knew it, but it was to be Ellen Rivo's last performance.

After walking all the way down from the McNoel, I had hit a couple of different bars and listened to some more or less improvisational jazz on 8th Street. Jazz. I liked the big band swing of the 30's and 40's, but beyond that, I didn't get it.

So I killed some more time window shopping, going into the occasional establishment to warm up when I needed to. I passed the store on MacDougal where Kate had bought my privacy screen. They had an antique dresser in the window, taller than the one I had, and I wondered if I needed it. I decided I didn't.

What had Daisy done? Did she check out and go home? Did she call some other boyfriend? Did she order room service and curl up alone?

I was considering the possibilities when the actors started coming out from their dressing rooms. They all recognized me by now, and most usually said hello, sometimes with a chuckle, a teasing chuckle I thought. So what?

Becky came out, slowly, almost peeking around the corner first, afraid I wasn't going to be there. But I was and she smiled and did a dumb little Frankenstein walk over to me and gave me a hug.

"I'm glad you made it," she said, and I knew she had thought I wasn't going to show. The thought had actually frightened her. Good, I thought.

Ellen Rivo was with her but didn't do the monster walk. Her eye injury was still noticeable.

"I invited Ellen to eat with us, okay?" Becky said.

"Great."

"Are you sure?" Ellen said.

"Absolutely. I'm so sorry about your injury."

"It's nothing. I ran into a wall."

I knew the truth but, of course, didn't let on.

"Oh, she's such a trooper!" Becky said.

It would be the first time someone else would be with us since that afternoon in the bar when I had become smitten with Becky. Here I was going out for an after-theatre supper with two lovely young women, one of whom I adored. I owed it all to Marty Sequatchee, really. I wondered where Marty had been all my life.

We flagged a cab, wheeled up Amsterdam, and got out near 81st. That neighborhood was in its early stages of urban renewal in those days, and hip new restaurants had started to open. I had found one called West Texas, and that's where the cabbie dropped the three of us.

We went in and were seated at a table by the window. The girls each ordered a glass of white wine and me, a bourbon on ice. We talked over our drinks and over the hum of the crowded restaurant. From what I had learned about theatre people in the last several weeks, Ellen didn't quite fit the mold. Not that she should have, since this play was her first experience. If she stuck with it, she'd probably become as idiosyncratic and flaky as the rest of them. For the time being, she seemed a little too straight.

I complimented her on her performance in the play. Yes, I had on opening night, too, but you can't say it enough. I knew what I was talking about since I had seen the show repeatedly. It really was impressive how she had stepped up there and into the role with no previous experience, especially considering the thousands who train, study, work, and struggle, and still just don't have it.

She thanked me for my comments and said, "I didn't know enough about the process to fear it. I didn't know it was supposed to be terrifying."

We talked about Becky and some of her previous roles. We laughed about the fact that, when Becky started doing TV commercials, Ellen wasn't even a teenager yet. It made Becky say at one point, "God, I'm so old!" Yes, well, dear, no one is young forever. She was thirty-two.

My illustrious life came up and got the once over. But I managed to muscle the wheel and steer us into something else fairly quickly when the image of an elderly gentleman's charred remains flashed in front of me, a gentleman to whom I had given my word and broken it.

We each had the house specialty, fried chicken with mashed potatoes and a second vegetable. I can think about that crisp, golden-brown chicken even today and salivate. I had grown up in a land where southern fried chicken was as common as Pepsi, but I'd never tasted anything that could compare to a serving of it at West Texas on Amsterdam Avenue. Ditto the mashed potatoes.

Halfway through the meal, Ellen scooted her chair back on the hardwood floor and stood up. She put the tips of all ten of her fingers on the top of the table and said, "Excuse me, please."

I made an effort to stand. Then Ellen went limp and collapsed like a marionette, taking a few utensils and her dish of black-eyed peas down with her.

Chapter 48

The paramedics wouldn't let both Becky and me ride in the ambulance to the hospital, so Becky said, "You go. I'll come down in a cab."

Before I hopped into the back, one of the medical guys asked, "Are you her father?"

My instinct was to say, "I'm only thirty-eight," but I suppressed it. "I'm her lawyer," I said.

"Right," he said, instilling the word with less respect than he would have if I had said, "I'm her rapist."

I rode with Ellen and held her hand. She had not regained consciousness in the restaurant, and she still hadn't. The ambulance screamed down Columbus until it turned into Ninth. Then we swung into the emergency entrance of Roosevelt Hospital.

We got her into a treatment cubicle. A Dr. Fleming came in right away with a large, black, female nurse. Fleming looked like a young version of Larry Fine, but he worked quickly and seemed to know his stuff, and I saw right away the doctor was considerably more competent than any of the Three Stooges would have been in this situation. Before he threw me out, I told him Ellen had had a trauma recently to her cheek and jaw, not that he couldn't see that for himself, but I knew the injury had looked much worse a few days before. On his way to the other side of the curtain, I heard Fleming say to the nurse, "Dr. Brenniman was here. See if he's still around." She bumped into me on her way to find Brenniman and said, in a deep-south accent, "Scuze me, sweetheart." I figured her for Alabama.

Out in the reception area there were several rows of people waiting to be patients. I surveyed the group, avoiding eye contact. The last thing they wanted was some fool gawking at them and wondering what affliction had brought them there.

No one seemed at death's door, and I didn't notice any gunshot wounds or stabbings. I turned to a woman behind the admissions window, who was doing paperwork. "Excuse me?"

It took her a few seconds, but then she looked up.

"Dr. Brenniman? What's his specialty, do you know?"

"He's a neurologist," she said, quietly. "Are you with the young woman who just came in unconscious?"

"Yes."

She slid a clipboard through the opening. It had a pen and some papers clamped to it. "Fill this out, please."

Becky hurried in, came up and grabbed me. "How is she?"

"A doctor's with her and has asked for a neurologist." I held up the clipboard and said, "I'm going to call Marty, let him get in touch with her dad."

Marty, Louise, and Bob were cozy by the fire when the phone rang. I explained things to Marty, who calmly said thanks, said he'd find Rivo, said he'd be down to the hospital himself shortly.

Marty hung up the phone and called the Flannigan number. It rang and rang. It was after eleven. He couldn't expect Flannigan or Rivo to be there, but somebody should answer.

"Homicide, Masgrove," a voice finally said.

"Detective Masgrove, this is Marty Sequatchee ..."

Rivo was at the hospital and had already talked to Dr. Brenniman by the time Marty arrived, and Marty was there before you knew it. Louise had come with him, and the first person she saw was Becky. They embraced, held each other's hands, and stepped out of the way somewhere to talk.

Becky, being who she was, had called Louise right after the younger actress had left the show to say everyone would miss her, but the two hadn't spoken since. Louise had not gone backstage after she saw the play. She didn't want pity. Now there they were in the hospital, discussing the girl who had taken Louise's place.

Rivo, whose badge gave him total access, led Marty and me into a corridor. It was empty except for a gurney with a broken wheel and six or eight cylinders of oxygen that stood against the wall like soldiers. "How is she?" Marty said.

"What do you know about this? Either of you," Rivo said.

I explained that Becky had invited Ellen to have supper with us. I told him where we were and what had happened.

Rivo looked at Marty. "Her eye and face?"

She had begged Marty not to tell, and he hadn't. But now, he had no choice. He told it all, and Rivo and I listened. Marty tried to avoid saying who it was that had struck her, but there was no chance he could get away with that.

"She didn't have a follow-up with your doctor friend?"

"She wouldn't let me take her."

"Okay," Rivo said. He nodded a couple of times and said it again. "Okay." He started to walk out.

"Paul? What do we know about her condition?" Marty said.

"Nothing yet."

And Rivo left, leaving Marty and me standing there.

The blow to the head could have caused internal bleeding, bruising, swelling, even tearing of brain tissue. You didn't have to be a neurologist to know that. Everybody knew it. On the other hand, maybe the smacking around had nothing to do with her fainting. People pass out all the time.

Marty, Louise, Becky, and I hung around for another

hour or so without any word, before deciding to go home. All we were doing at the hospital was taking up space. Rivo had disappeared, and we assumed he was with his daughter. That's who she needed, along with her doctors.

We all piled into a taxi and went back to Marty's. He pulled out the Jim Beam, and even the girls had a taste (and hated it).

We sat around, glum and worried. I could tell Marty was feeling personally responsible for Ellen's condition, but I didn't feel like bringing it up and trying to convince him not to blame himself.

"Something happened," Becky said, "when she ran into that wall. It took this long to manifest."

Marty and I locked eyes. Marty didn't want to tell it again, but he wanted the girls to know. "It wasn't a wall," I said. "It was your director."

Then I told Becky and Louise all about it, even about Ellen's provoking him. It was relevant, though no cause for physical abuse.

"I never trusted that guy," Becky said.

"I never trusted him or liked him," said Louise.

"I don't think many people do," Marty said. "I guess it's a testament to how talented he is that he gets such good performances out of everybody, even Ellen."

Everybody was quiet for a moment. Then my shrewd, plotting brain intervened. I looked at Louise and said, "You're back in the show."

Marty was way ahead of me. "Will you step in?" he said to her. "Keep the show open the next two weeks? You know the words, the blocking. You've seen the show. You'll fall right back into it, Louise. What do you say?"

"Well ... I guess if I had a few days' rehearsal ..."

"The show's at eight tomorrow night, honey," he said. "We could get together at noon, work till, say, five."

"You can do it, Louise," Becky said.

"I saw you do the first run-through," I reminded her.

"Oh ... yeah ...," she didn't remember me from the bar that day, I could tell. Oh, well.

"You were terrific."

Louise raced through the three scenes in her head, and we all watched her do it. Then she said, "Okay, sure."

I said, "Would you guys mind if I came down and watched you work? I'd like to see how it's done."

"Sure, fine," Louise said. Then she jabbed her index finger into Marty's chest. "You have to work me into the show, Marty, not Wayne. You have to rehearse me."

"Unless, God forbid, Ellen dies," he said. "Then it's over."

Chapter 49

Marty said he woke up about nine the next morning, and young Louise was gone. That wasn't unusual. Girls, young women, who stayed over were up, dressed and gone quickly. Marty had long noticed the pattern. Who knew why they hurried away? Maybe when the whole night's depravity was exposed by sun and sobriety, the female just had to get out.

On the other hand, if they were still there, chances were they'd be there all day. Marty rose to his feet and called her name, to be sure. No answer. He wandered into the living room and gave the room a quick look. He saw a slip of paper by the phone. The note said, "See you downtown at noon."

He stood there a second or two, reflecting. Then he picked up the phone and called Roosevelt Hospital. He couldn't get through. He went into the kitchen, started a pot of coffee, and hoped Ellen Rivo was all right.

The phone rang. It was early, too early for people to call people in New York City. He stepped back into the living room and picked up the receiver, expecting it to be the mystery person who remained on the line but never spoke. Was it the big, blond stranger? And was he the person who had killed Patsy and attacked the stage?

"Good morning," Marty said, surprising himself with the

deep, raspy voice that came out of him. He covered the phone and cleared his throat. "Hello," he said.

"Mr. Sequatchee?" It was a male voice but high-pitched.

"Yes."

"You probably don't know me, but you might have heard my name. I'm Tad? Tad Arnett?"

"I'm sorry," Marty said, "your name doesn't sound familiar."

"I was a good friend of Cherry's."

"Who?"

"Patsy's. We came to New York together, years ago. I drove her here."

"I see."

"She probably mentioned my name to you."

"Yeah, okay, sure, maybe." Never, Marty thought.

"Did she tell you I'm a playwright, too, but not in your league?"

"Uh ... I don't think so."

"After she met you, I asked her to give you a couple of my plays to read. Did she not ever do that?"

"No, she didn't."

"She was going to. I guess she was going to get to know you a little better first."

"Uh-huh."

"I'll never get over Patsy being killed. I'll never get over it."

Beautiful, sensual Patsy. "I know what you mean," Marty said.

"I wonder who killed her, don't you?"

"Yes." Marty tried to match the voice up with a mean-looking bruiser, some male and muscle-bound Goldilocks, but it didn't fit.

"Anyway, why I called. Do you think you could read one or two of my plays and tell me what you think of them? I've been in New York more than six years, same as Patsy, and I haven't been able to get anywhere. No doors have opened for me. I thought if I had a helping hand from somebody like you, it might make all the difference."

This had happened to Marty before, of course. Aspiring writers or actors or actresses had either asked for help or hoped to ride his wave with him. How about Ellen? Or Patsy? Or even Kate? Who could blame them? You had to have the talent, the training, the skill, all that. But you had to have a break, too, and you had to look for that break anywhere and everywhere you could.

"I'll read a couple of your plays, Tad, sure," Marty said. "Why don't you drop them in the mail to me?"

"I could come up there and give them to you right now," Tad said. "I don't mind at all."

"Well ...," Marty said. How do you say no? "Do you have my address?"

"Yeah. You're on 85th Street, right?"

"Tell you what," Marty said, "there's a coffee shop on the corner. Why don't you come on up, and I'll treat you to breakfast?"

"You will?"

"I'd be happy to."

As soon as Marty got off the phone, he tried the hospital again. He managed to get through to someone who said Ellen's condition was stable. No diagnosis, no prognosis. I had called, too, and been told the same thing.

Marty phoned me and asked if I had anything on Ellen other than "stable." I did not. Then he told me about the call from the guy that had actually brought Patsy to New York in the first place. He asked me to join them for breakfast. Are you kidding? I had to.

Chapter 50

Half an hour later, we were sitting in a booth with coffees, waiting for him. He came through the door. The clod might as well have been wearing a sign that said, “I’m down but young and a believer.” Marty motioned him over. Tad’s skin was what you might call ecru, his eyes sad, and his mouse-brown hair proved the existence of static electricity. He wore a ratty blue sweater much too big for his slight frame. He wore another sweater, green and stretched like taffy, as a coat. His unwashed jeans were torn in the days before it was fashionable. His shoes were black, low-cut Keds’ tennis shoes somebody had likely thrown out. His socks almost matched but didn’t. A little chimney dust on his face and he’d be the perfect Dickens’ character. It would have cost him ninety cents to get uptown on the train, and I wondered if the poor guy had ninety more to get home.

Here was irony for you. Marty was more broke than this guy. How many tens of thousands of dollars did Tad Arnett owe?

They greeted each other, shaking hands. Marty introduced me, and Tad slid onto the vinyl beside me and opposite Marty. He had two play scripts with him, and he handed them to Marty right away. The copies had been passed around and were as tattered as Tad’s jeans. Everybody had moved to word processing but these scripts had come page by page out of a typewriter. Marty did a quick page-through of one of the plays and saw misspellings, smudges, coffee cup rings, white out, and inconsistent margins. He tried not to wince.

"I'll look forward to reading them," Marty said, setting the scripts beside him on the red seat.

"Patsy was going to give you a couple herself, but ...," and there was no reason to finish the sentence.

"You called her Cherry?" Marty said.

"I've always called her that since high school. Do you know the William Inge play *Bus Stop*?"

"Oh. Yes."

I nodded, too, because I had heard of William Inge and had once seen part of the movie on TV.

"I played the character of Bo, and Patsy was Cherie. So I always called her Cherry."

I had to ask: "What?"

"In the play, Bo can't say Cherie, so he calls her Cherry," Marty said.

I'd hear all this again and more, years later from Patsy's mom and high school friend.

Marty ordered scrambled eggs, bacon, toast, and hash brown potatoes. Two over easy sounded good to me. Tad studied his menu like a six-year-old seeing his first Marvel comic. He ordered what Marty was having, then heaped on a side of pancakes and sausage. Oh, and a large orange juice. The waiter, in a red vest, poured Tad's coffee and warmed mine and Marty's as he memorized the orders.

"I don't get many offers from people to buy me breakfast, Marty, so I'm going to take advantage of you, if you don't mind."

"Whatever you want."

"To tell you the truth, I've missed a meal or two lately."

"You're not working?"

"I was busing tables downtown until a week or so ago. I dropped some dishes, and they let me go."

We sensed there was more to it than that. Maybe it wasn't the first time he'd dropped dishes, showed up late, or maybe even copped an attitude — sometimes the Tads of New York could be overcome with the belief they should be on Broadway instead of by the dishwasher. Tad seemed like a sweet young man, but you never knew what thoughts people might have, how much anger brewed inside, or what five or six years of frustration and resentment could do to them.

"I haven't looked for another job yet. I've been finishing up another play. Did Cherry tell you how many plays I've written?"

"I don't believe she did."

"Nine now. Nine whole plays. Three before I came to New York and six since I've been here."

"That's impressive."

"Thanks. I really appreciate it. Thanks a lot. I've never seen any of your plays, but I've read several of them. A lot of them are published. They're good, I think."

Marty was glad to know a number of his plays were published and that Tad had read some of them and, in Tad's opinion, they were good. Yes, Marty would read two of the young man's plays and think of something to say about them. But what he and I were really interested in was Tad as Tad related to Patsy.

"How did you find out about her death?" Marty asked him.

Tad's eyes shifted to me then back to Marty. He looked down at his flatware, then up again.

"Just wondered how you learned about it."

"I talked to the cops. They tracked me down through Eileen, Patsy's mother. I talked to them."

"So they told you she had been murdered?"

"No, I knew it. I told them I had heard it on the radio ... and I did, except ... I first heard about it from a phone call."

"I don't get you," Marty said.

"This guy called me and told me she was dead, and I couldn't believe it. Told me I better go up to her place. I turned on the radio to 1010 WINS news, but there was no mention of it, so I thought some boyfriend of hers was playing a joke on me. I called her number and didn't get an answer. I figured if anything had happened to her, there'd be a lot of people around and somebody would, you know, answer her phone. I hung up before her machine picked up."

"You didn't come uptown?"

"No."

"You don't know who called you?"

"No. And since there was nothing to it, I didn't mention it to the police when they came to me."

"You should have, Tad."

"See, the police scared me one time. I met this girl at this dive where I was working, and she thought I followed her home or something. I didn't, really I didn't, 'cause I didn't care anything about her. But she called the cops, and they talked to me and scared me. This time, boy, when they asked me questions, I didn't know anything, nothing. I was afraid they wouldn't believe me, and I'd just get in over my head."

"Did two detectives talk to you? A large one with short hair and a smaller one, dark?"

"That sounds like them. They just talked to me for a minute or two."

Our food came and was thrown in front of us by the waiter who had carried all three orders in his hands and on his forearms. He got most of it right.

"Oh, boy," Tad said, and in half a second he had a mouthful.

"You don't know who called you?" I repeated Marty's question, fighting the food now for Tad's attention.

"Some guy, I don't know. Looking back on it, I guess he was just being nice to call and tell me, but we were disconnected."

"How did he know?" Marty said.

"Huh?"

"How did he know to call you?"

"I don't know." Tad poured syrup over the pancakes, thick and messy. "I guess he knew we were friends, and she used to live with me and everything."

"Patsy lived with you?" I couldn't keep my mouth shut. Maybe I could please be quiet and let Marty handle the kid?

"No, not really. But ... yes and no. It's hard to explain." He was eating and loving it. "Aren't you guys going to eat?"

"What did you think when you got that phone call?"

"I ... I just figured it was a bad joke, a cruel one. But then when the cops came a few days later ..."

Marty and I realized for the first time we had no idea how the body was found. It was found quickly, that much we knew. Had the police also received an anonymous call?

Marty said, "Tad, can you remember exactly what the caller said?" I tried to eat, so did Marty, but listening seemed more important.

"The guy who called me? He said ...," Tad chewed again, very slowly, as he thought back. He swallowed, carved out a pie-shaped piece of pancake, impaled it, and sent it home. "He said, 'Is this Tad?' I said it was and he said, 'She's dead, Tad. Patsy's dead. You better get up to her place.' I asked him who he was, but like I said, we were disconnected."

"Maybe he hung up." Marty said it looking at me.

"Why would he hang up? He had just called me," Tad ripped a slice of bacon apart with discolored teeth and said, "I think that was about the last call I got."

"What do you mean?"

"They disconnected my phone. For non-payment, I guess."

"They hadn't found her yet?"

"Huh?

"When you turned on the news, you said there was nothing."

"Right."

"But the man who called you knew."

That made Tad stop eating again. "Yeah ... you're right. How'd he know?"

"Do you think you'd recognize his voice if you heard it again?"

"I might," Tad said. "I don't know. I might."

"If those detectives came to see you again, would you tell them everything this time?"

"Ah, see, I don't know."

"Tad, you didn't kill Patsy, did you?"

"Of course not."

"But that phone call might be important. It might help them nail the person who did. Just tell them what you've told us. They're not going to hurt you."

Tad piled it in, chewed, swallowed, shrugged. "Okay."

Marty picked up one of the scripts again and referred to the cover page. "You're still at this address, right?"

"Yeah. I have another place, a penthouse on Park Avenue, but I'm usually down in the East Village."

A rapidly filling stomach had unveiled the kid's wit, and it made us smile. Tad pointed his fork at the script Marty was still holding. "I think you'll like that one," he said, "and the other one, too." To me he said, "You can read them, too, if you want to." I nodded, sort of, but didn't really commit.

Marty leaned back in the booth, and his napkin slid from his lap. "Oops," he said. He ducked under to retrieve it, and when he came up there was a crumpled fifty-dollar bill in his hand. He held it up to Tad. "Did you drop this?"

"What?"

"This was by your foot."

"I didn't drop it."

"You must have."

"Believe me, I did not drop it."

"Well, there it was. It's yours."

Tad looked at me, and I don't think he was even breathing. "Is it yours?"

"I don't carry fifties."

"You found it," Tad said to Marty. It was Christmas morning and here Tad was telling the other kid to take the new bicycle.

"Yeah, but it was on your side," Marty insisted. "I think it's yours."

Tad stared at the money as though Woodrow Wilson's picture was on it and it was a 100,000 dollar bill. But it was a fifty, the last large bill my friend had on him.

I paid the check. I insisted.

When Marty got home, there was a phone message from Stassie, his agent. Good news. The producer of the romantic comedy script was back in town. Could he and Marty try again to get together later that day?

Before he returned Stassie's call, Marty called Flannigan and told him he should talk to Tad Arnett again. And did Flannigan have any new info on Ellen? She'd had surgery, that's all the detective said about it.

Then Marty called Stassie, who told him he was to meet the film producer in the Oak Bar at the Plaza that afternoon at five. The Oak Bar at the Plaza. These producers, if they were spending a studio's money, had to spend it in the most pretentious way possible. It was absolutely necessary to impress the poor little writer, lord over him that the producer was the king and had the power. Marty would rather have had a beer with the guy at the Blarney Stone, with a plate of meatballs, the ones with a toothpick through the center and soaked in that special Blarney Stone sauce. But then that would have been too loose, too comfortable. The producer wouldn't want Marty to feel either of those things.

Because of what had happened to Ellen the night before, Marty had to be at the TASSQ at noon, which he told Stassie.

The plan was for him to be at the theatre till five, but he could cut it short.

"Cut it short," Stassie said. "I'll tell the guy you're leaving the theatre early to meet with him. He'll like that."

Chapter 51

According to author Michael Flannigan in his Chapter Sixteen, the second visit to Tad Arnett found him wrapped in an Army surplus blanket which was heavy, wool, and moth-eaten. His brown hunter's cap with fake-fur ear flaps was pulled on tight, but the cap was meant for a kid of about twelve. His red-tipped earlobes stuck out.

It wasn't that cold, but the electricity and heat were off. It wasn't January. It wasn't New York's blood-freezing, Siberian arctic-death, which would be along in a couple of months. This was just an early rehearsal.

The Bowery Mission was over on Avenue D, several blocks from Tad's Avenue A sublet, but Tad was one step away from it. If they took one look at him, they'd have to offer him a hot shower and a cot. It would be better than the apartment's stained mattress with its ticking worn through, here and there, to the stuffing.

Food wasn't a problem for the moment, thanks to the breakfast M.S. had bought him earlier in the day and the money found on the floor. All Tad had in the house to eat was half a can of Campbell's chicken noodle soup, but he could remedy that with the fifty he clutched in his fist. Thirty dollars for food, ten dollars for typing paper and a ribbon, ten dollars for cigarettes and beer.

That's the way Flannigan broke it down. I had to assume there was some speculation on his part sometimes (as there was on mine), along with his notes and research, but it was easy to go along with everything he wrote.

The knock on Tad's door startled him. If it was the landlord about the rent, he didn't know what he'd say. He hadn't paid the old guy in Latrobe in two months, and before the phone was disconnected, they had had an unfriendly conversation about it.

Tad wondered how that would work. Would the rightful tenant tell the landlord Tad hadn't paid, so the landlord couldn't get paid until he, Tad, settled up? No, that couldn't happen. The sublet was probably illegal in the first place, so the failed novelist in Latrobe would have to pay every month whether or not Tad paid him.

Whoever was at the door knocked again. It couldn't be the old guy from Latrobe. He wouldn't bother to knock. He had a key; he'd just come in and demand his money.

Tad got up, not relinquishing his blankets. He was a cold, tired, lonesome, worried Indian, stripped of just about everything he once had or hoped for. He shuffled to the door, the floor chilly on the bottoms of his feet, even through his socks. He might have stuffed the fifty-dollar bill deep into a pocket of his pants in case somebody was looking for it. "Who is it?"

"Tad? It's the police. You remember us."

He unlocked the door and opened it. Flannigan and Rivo entered Versailles. They weren't smiling, but they weren't frowning either. Their faces were blank but open. They looked right at Tad. Rivo looked exhausted, as though he hadn't slept lately. He hadn't. He'd been up all night at the hospital with his daughter.

Flannigan didn't even need Rivo along for this interview. Neither of the detectives thought there was reason to talk to Tad again, since he couldn't give them the hard evidence that was needed. But Rivo, worried and exhausted, wanted to come along.

Things hadn't changed much in the apartment since the cops' last visit. They hadn't changed much since Tad and Patsy had arrived that afternoon more than six years before. Everything was older, that's about all. There was a horizontal board across stacked, blue-plastic milk crates. On top of this makeshift desk was a beige IBM Selectric typewriter, not new. That might not have been Tad's sole contribution to the furnishings, but if not, it was close.

Rivo dragged himself around, sightseeing, while Flannigan just stood and kept looking at Tad.

"It's cold in here," Tad said.

Flannigan didn't respond, but from the kitchen area, where Rivo was looking at the bathtub, he turned and said, "Yeah, it is."

"The heat's off," Tad explained.

"How often does that happen?" Rivo said, wandering back over to Tad and Flannigan.

"Not often, thank goodness," Tad said, "or I couldn't stay here. You guys want to sit down?" If they did want to, their options were limited.

"We're fine," Flannigan said. "So you have more to tell us, is that right?" He pulled out his little notebook and pen.

"Not much."

"Why don't we start at the beginning," Flannigan said.

Flannigan regretted saying it because to Tad the beginning was the day he had asked Patsy to try out for *Bus Stop*. Then he backed up from the beginning and talked about how he had admired Patsy from afar for a very long time in high school. But so had just about every guy in town.

The detectives indulged him, let him talk, let him ramble. An anecdote or two from the *Bus Stop* rehearsals tried their patience, but they didn't push him. Finally, he and Patsy arrived in front of the building on Avenue A, and the tale became a little more interesting.

Tad told it all; how Patsy wasn't happy here in this apartment, how she was hardly ever there, and so on. She kept in touch with him, barely. He always knew where she was working but didn't know much at all about her personal life or where she slept most nights. At least not until she got her own apartment uptown.

"I'll tell you guys something," he said, almost in a confessional tone. Then he paused.

"Tell us what?"

"I guess the only reason she didn't abandon me and this place completely was just-in-case."

"Just in case?" said Flannigan.

"You know, just in case there was an emergency and she had absolutely nowhere else to go." A moist glaze washed over Tad's eyes. He stared off past the detectives into nothing. It was probably the first time he had ever admitted it to himself.

"When's the last time you saw her?" Rivo said.

"The last time I saw Cherry ...," Tad thought a second, "was one day shortly after she had started seeing Marty Sequatchee. She came by one afternoon with two cups of coffee, and we sat right over there and drank it." Tad looked over at the spot and stared at it. "I can still see her sitting there."

"What'd she have to say that day?" Rivo said.

"Not much."

"Why'd she come by?" Flannigan said.

Tad looked again at the detectives. He didn't have an immediate answer.

"Just touching base?" Flannigan gave him an out.

"No," Tad said, surprisingly. "No," and he paused, thinking. "She came by to tell me she was seeing Marty Sequatchee," he said slowly. "That's why she came by."

"But you just said she never told you anything about her personal life."

"That's right, she didn't. But she wanted to tell me she was seeing Marty Sequatchee because he's a playwright and screenwriter, a successful one." Tad was putting this together as he talked. "She wanted me to know she was with a real playwright, 'cause I'm a playwright, too, see, but I've kind of struggled." He paused again. "That's exactly why she came by that day. She made a special trip down here ... just to hurt my feelings."

Flannigan and Rivo sneaked a peek at each other. They both felt sorry for the kid.

Tad laughed at himself, short and not very sweet. "I asked her if she'd give him one or two of my plays to read, and she said she would real soon. I'll bet she never mentioned me to him."

"She ever mention Preston Hondonada?" Flannigan said.

"Who's that?"

"Preston Hondonada?" Flannigan said again. "He's on TV. He does reports, special assignment shows. She ever talk about anybody she might have met through Hondonada?"

"I was going to get a television set, but ...," then he just shook his head.

"Of all the guys she might ever have known, Marty Sequatchee's the only one she ever mentioned?" Rivo asked.

"He's the only one she ever mentioned," Tad said. "And I never asked 'cause I didn't care to know. Don't tell me she was going out with a TV star, too."

"She may have had a fling with Hondonada, but she was also involved with someone else after Hondonada and before Sequatchee."

"Oh, yeah?" said Tad, unsurprised and cynical.

"Were you ever in her apartment on West 74th?" Flannigan said.

"No. She told me when she moved into it, but she never invited me over. I went up there one time and rang her bell, back toward the end of the summer. She didn't even let me in. She came down and we sat on the stoop for a few minutes."

"You found out she was dead when some guy called you, right?" Rivo said.

"Yeah. That was spooky, looking back on it."

Flannigan and Rivo looked at each other, communicating silently. Okay, that was it. They made their way toward the door.

"Are you working, Tad?" Flannigan said, just before he opened the door. Maybe the kid was a deadbeat, or maybe he had just hit the wall like so many young people who flooded into the City with great expectations. He wasn't going to sit down with you and explain that nuclear fission was the splitting of the nucleus of a heavy atom while nuclear fusion was the combining of the nuclei of light atoms. But he had survived in the toughest town around, at least until now. Why not give him a hand?

"You mean at the moment?"

"Yeah."

"I was working. But, uh ... not at the moment."

Flannigan stared at Tad long enough to make the young man nervous. "Ever work in a restaurant?"

Tad lit up and his sad eyes widened. "Yeah! That's where I was working. Just busing tables, but restaurants? Sure."

"There's a place on Ninth Avenue between 38th and 39th called the White and Red Diner."

"The White and Red Diner," Tad said, excited, committing it to memory.

"Think you could come by there this evening?"

"This evening? I could come by there right now."

"Wait till this evening. I'll be there, and we'll get you squared away."

"This evening," Tad said.

"Why don't we make it six?"

"All right. And look, I'm sorry I wasn't completely forthright with you guys the first time."

"No harm done. Don't worry about it. We should have pressed you, but we were already focused elsewhere by then."

Flannigan and Rivo left. Downstairs and outside, they could breathe nature's air again, not the dry, brittle, depressing air of a tenement with no heat.

Back in the car, Flannigan fired it up. Rivo looked at him and said, "Old softie."

"What are you talking about?"

"I think I'll make a call or two, get the heat turned back on in that building."

"I'm the old softie, huh?" Flannigan said.

"Drive me back to the hospital, will you?"

Flannigan put the car into gear and pulled out.

Chapter 52

As for me that Wednesday morning, after the wretched night and the eggs with Marty and Tad, I stood on Broadway in front of Pauline's Dream. So Patsy was standing right here, huh, shortly before she was killed? That's what Kristy Adams had told Marty, and I couldn't seem to let it go.

I watched a customer or two go in or out. Then I went in myself. That song by the Police was playing over the sound system, "Every Breath You Take." Incense burned like they were expecting the Dalai Lama, but the place still smelled like fish.

I glanced around for Kate but didn't expect to find her there. She was working less and less.

I browsed like any regular customer, but that's not what I was. I was there to ask a few questions. A little detective work. The cops might show up here eventually and do it right, or they might not. Kristy's encounter probably wasn't at all important.

After pretending to be interested in the clothes, none of it my style, I wandered over to a gum-chewing woman standing at some shelves with a yellow pad and pencil. Another pencil was jabbed into her dark hair. Could have fallen from the ceiling and landed there. She wore glasses and seemed serious and dedicated enough to be more than just sales help. I didn't know her, and she didn't know me.

"Excuse me," I said.

The woman, she was about forty or so, looked at me over the top of her glasses. It made her look older. She was fairly attractive but could improve herself in that department ten-fold in three months if she'd join a gym.

"Yes?" she said.

"Are you Pauline?" I said, just for kicks.

The woman took a deep breath and exhaled slowly. "No," she said, "I'm not Pauline. I'm Diane von Furstenberg, okay?"

"Okay, lady," I said. I had just asked a simple question and didn't think there was any need for attitude.

She backed off quickly. "I'm sorry," she said. "I'm in the middle of something."

"I'm sorry for interrupting."

"It's all right." She lowered her pad and pencil. She was writing down pants sizes. How important could it be? "Herb is the owner; would you like to see him?"

"Well ...," I didn't know if I did or not. I'd met Herb before, of course.

"Herb Leech is the owner. He's in the back. I'll get him if you want to see him."

"Okay," I said, "thanks."

"Hold on." Departing, she puckered, then popped her gum at me, smiled, reached out, found my hand and squeezed it. Her fingertips were calloused, coarse as denim. Guitar player, I thought. She headed for the rear of the store through stacks of apparel. See, I knew Herb was the owner, but maybe she was Pauline, his lifelong love, and he had named his store ... okay, forget it.

I wandered in the general direction of the rear, glancing at some shirts, some slacks, a rack of jackets.

Herb Leech came scooting out on skinny legs, looked around nervously with a little suspicion. I was standing right there.

"Herb, Jay Bluffing," and I offered my hand.

"Oh!" Herb said, shaking the hand, "how do you do?"

He didn't remember me and had, obviously, paid no attention to the name.

"I'm Kate Bluffing's brother."

"Oh! How do you do?" he repeated. "What is your name?"

"Jay."

Herb was a little confused. He had probably been in the back cooking the books and was distracted.

"I was also a friend of Patsy Holton's, the young woman who was murdered on 74th a few weeks ago."

"Oh, heavens ...," Herb said.

"The afternoon of her murder, on her way home from downtown, she was seen standing outside your store."

"What?"

"That's right. It's possible she was waiting for someone, someone who was inside here."

"Who says?"

"Well, me. I just said." It was a thought I had about three o'clock in the morning. I had awakened from a nightmare about a man burning inside a truck in Kentucky. I got up, had a glass of water, paced around, and heard myself mumble, "... waiting for someone ..."

"What are you getting at?"

"The person who killed her might have been in your store not long before it happened."

"Oh, heavens," said Herb, "don't get me involved in this." He nibbled at the cuticle on an index finger, then took his hand away to examine it and the other nails.

"It's all right, Herb. But were you here that afternoon?"

Herb's head went loosely back and forth a few times on his Ichabod Crane neck. He wasn't shaking his head "no." He was just relieving tension as Detective Flannigan was given to do. Who doesn't have a neck problem? "Yes, I was here, I usually am."

"Do you remember any particular customer that day? Anyone who was acting strangely or maybe looking out to the street at someone?"

"Look," Herb said, getting more annoyed. He was a busy man and, anyhow, he didn't like these questions. "Do you have any idea how much merchandise you have to move to stay in business in Manhattan?"

"Must be a lot."

"Tons. You have to constantly be selling, constantly selling." He glanced at the cash register where a sale was being rung up at the moment. Two other people were in line. "That means you have to have a constant, healthy flow of customers. What's your name? Jay? Jay, I couldn't begin to tell you who was in the store that day, okay?"

"How about one of the clerks? Would any of them remember?"

"Why of course not."

"What about Diane? Was she working that day?"

"Who?" Herb said, looking around.

"Her." I pointed.

"Flora?" He said it loud enough for her to hear, and she came over.

The gum, glasses, and pencil from her head were all gone. She seemed to have sneaked on fresh lipstick. Had she done that ... for me? Impossible. She must have accidentally glanced at herself in one of the mirrors and realized she needed maintenance.

"Yes?" said Flora.

"The day of the murder up on 74th Street, were you working?" I said.

"Yes." She didn't have to think about it. "We were busy that day."

I asked the couple of follow-up questions I'd asked Herb. Nothing. Three other clerks were working that day, but only one of them was there at the moment, a twenty-something fellow with caramel hair and slumping shoulders. I had seen him in the store before. He couldn't place me, exactly. I put the same questions to him, but it accomplished nothing.

I thanked everybody, but I had one more question before leaving. "Who is Pauline, anyhow, Herb?"

Turns out Pauline was his mother. She had been a seamstress her whole life, always wanted her own shop, never happened. She died at her sewing machine. Her arthritic fingers, bent and knobby, looked like a witch's kindling. Herb, who never got over her passing, opened this store with the money she left him.

Everywhere you turn there's a story, a history, success and failure, hopes and dreams, all sizes.

Back out on the street, I looked downtown in the direction of Roosevelt Hospital. Stable. That was better than critical. Was it better or worse than fair? I should know that. I'd chased a few ambulances in my time.

I crossed over to Amsterdam and down a few blocks to Vinnie's Pizza. Anybody could eat a slice from Vinnie's anytime. I didn't know it right then, of course, but my visit to Pauline's Dream was the key to nailing Patsy's murderer.

I didn't know it because I wasn't a psychic. If I had been, maybe I could have seen a series of events that transpired on the afternoon of the first run-through of Marty's play. After the case was closed, this is how Marty and I figured it:

Patsy had left at the half, intending to return for the second act. She just needed to make a quick, unpleasant, phone call. She went out onto the street, and the sun hit her. A few non-threatening cumulus clouds floated around the sky that day like balloons for Macy's Thanksgiving parade, except they were too high and too white. She looked around for a phone. Spotting one, she scurried to it, picked up the receiver, but heard no dial tone. Two or three phones later, she found one free and in working order. She made her call and connected with someone, but it wasn't the person she was trying to reach.

She ended the call, cleared the line, dug for a quarter, and dialed again. This time she reached her party and talked, unenthusiastically, for two or three minutes. When this call ended, she hailed a cab.

Fifteen minutes later she was standing outside Pauline's Dream on Broadway, unhappily waiting for someone. She saw an attractive young woman with the ruddy complexion of a cowgirl. It was Kristy Adams, someone she had once worked with at a car show and still knew well enough to say hello. Kristy stopped and the two of them talked.

"Did you ever work with David Roscoe?" Kristy asked.

"Yes," Patsy said, "for a while."

"So did I, for a while. Did you hear he was busted for shoplifting little girls' underpants? The guy turns out to be a pervert. I guess there was more going on under that cape than any of us knew."

"I had no idea."

"Who did? Oh, my, this business of show."

And that was about the extent of it. Kristy continued on her way, and Patsy continued to wait. Shortly, a taxi stopped. The door opened and a man emerged. He bubbled with joy, but Patsy did not melt in his arms.

"Aren't you happy to see me?" he asked, not thinking for a moment she could possibly be anything but overjoyed.

"I wasn't expecting you till later in the week."

"Surprise. When we're apart, I can't eat or sleep. The only thinking I do is about you. I'm in physical pain when I'm not with you. The possibility of you being with someone else enrages me so. My head gets thick with anger; I can barely breathe."

Patsy, ever cool, probably referred to Pauline's Dream and said, "You said you wanted something?"

"Yes. The last time I was here I fell in love with an item in there. Why I didn't buy it, I don't know. No, I do know. I was in such a hurry to meet you, I didn't want to take the time to buy it. Come in with me. I'll get it and something for you, anything. Then we'll go to your place."

Patsy knew Kate wasn't in there working, she was downtown at the play. But she still didn't want to go inside. She'd met the owner, Herb, before, and he might recognize her. Frankly, she didn't care to be seen by anyone she knew, not with this guy, not anymore. There's no question in my mind she had fallen for Marty Sequatchee in a big way. I'd say that for the first time in her life she was feeling deep and true emotions for a guy. The man she was with at the moment actually embarrassed her, and just looking at him made her feel like an opportunistic little whore. Which wasn't light years from the truth. She was going to disengage from him in a very few minutes.

"Come in with me," he said again, taking her hand and pulling her. "We'll spend some money, then go to your place."

"I'll wait for you," she said, resisting, pulling back.

"But how will I know if you'll like it?"

"Trust yourself." A snide remark he took as good advice.

The man left her and went inside Pauline's Dream, and Patsy waited some more. She probably stood there, forming the words in her head she would use shortly on the man. It didn't matter how she put it or how she said it; he was going to be crushed just like so many before him. Too bad.

She might have wondered about that crack he had made about her being with somebody else. Did he know about Marty? Maybe he did. Maybe he was following her. Was he that possessive, that obsessive? It didn't matter. Maybe she hoped he did know. That way, what she was about to tell him wouldn't come as such a shock.

But that had all taken place weeks before. Now, back at Vinnie's, I finished my pizza. Marty would be leaving shortly for the theatre. He had only a few hours to get Louise ready to go on stage that night. The plan was for me to pick up Becky and take her down to the TASSQ. I had time to walk up to her place.

Chapter 53

The three other actors who had scenes with Louise, including Becky, had showed up to rehearse with her. I brought Becky down to the theatre myself. After they talked about Ellen (nobody knew much about her condition), they went to work. I sat in the back and kept quiet.

Everybody pitched in, kind of like filling sandbags to pile against a crack in the dam. The first hour or so was shaky, mainly because some lines and blocking had changed since that rehearsal run-through weeks before. Plus, just as they were getting started, the ASM came up to Marty and said, "You have a phone call."

Marty looked at the poor kid. The ASM's eyes, puffy above the lashes, seemed so close together he looked like a Cyclops. "I'm busy, okay? Can we take a message?"

"It's your agent. She says it very important."

Marty looked up to the stage. He sighed and groaned. "All right, people, I'm sorry. I'll be right back." On stage, they were just getting revved up. Everybody shifted into park.

Marty walked up the aisle and out into the main lobby, the ASM behind him. I moseyed out also.

"I'll take it here," Marty said, stepping over to the box office window.

"Line two," the young man said.

Dori was on the phone, so Marty had to wait. And wait. Finally she hung up and looked at Marty.

"Could you hand me the phone? I have a call on line two."

She picked up the receiver, pressed the lit button, shoved the phone through the slot.

"Stassie?"

"Marty, I'm furious!" There came that voice again like a violin recital by a chimpanzee.

"What happened?"

"Leigh Teshler is in town and wants to see your play. Leigh Teshler, Marty. She called the theatre and was told it's sold out. She called me to get a ticket. I called the theatre, and they put me on hold. They put me on hold. Finally, someone came back to me." Dori could hear her, I know, but she didn't bother to react.

"Did you get her a ticket?" Marty said.

"No, I asked to speak to you."

"I'll get her a seat, Stassie. Is that all?"

"No, that's not all. I'm coming with her. We'll need two seats."

"Done."

"Leigh Teshler, Marty, you might be a little excited."

"I am excited, Stassie. I'm all giddy. But right now, I have some work to do. I'll put the tickets in your name. Again."

"Fine. Marty? Don't you dare be late for your meeting at the Plaza."

Marty gave the phone back to Dori and returned to the theatre. Tonight's performance had to be good. It had to be.

I'd never heard of Leigh Teshler at the time, but Marty had. She was one of the nicest people in Hollywood. She had once been an agent for CUA, the most powerful agency in the business, but forget everything you've ever heard about agents. Leigh was honest, kind, above board. She had worked tirelessly for her clients and had helped turn several of them into big stars. Then she married one of CUA's co-founders. Several years later she was working at home much of the time, so she could be with her baby and her two-year old.

Then her husband divorced her, because he was a poisonous snake, and forced her out of the agency. She got the beautiful house in Pacific Palisades, surrounded by more tropical foliage than there is in all of Bermuda. And she got loads of money and she still had lots of Hollywood friends. They were always sketching her in *People* or *Vanity Fai*r, but I'd missed those profiles.

So she was a nice person, so what? It was almost impossible to be a truly nice, caring, thoughtful, compassionate person in Hollywood because, if you were, people would kill you. If you were struggling and trying to get somewhere and you were nice, people would trample you, reading nice as weak.

If you'd made it in the land of dreams and were nice, look out. The minions would reach out for you, beg and claw at you. They were like the multitudes in various stages of Dante's hell, looking up and screaming for help, wanting you, needing you, but hating you because they were suffering. So most people in Hollywood weren't sweetie-pies because they couldn't be. People wouldn't let them.

But Leigh Teshler was, by all accounts, a wonder. She rose above it all with a warm smile, open arms, and an intelligence she didn't flaunt. She found a script she knew was good. She interested one of her ex-client/stars, attached him to it, set the picture up at Warner Brothers, and she was off and running in her new career, producer. She had produced six or eight films, all quality hits. When Leigh Teshler had a property she wanted made into a movie, it seemed to get made.

When she called the box office at the TASSQ that day, there was none of that "Do you know who I am?" business. She was disappointed but understanding. Even when she called Stassie to see if there was anything that could be done, Leigh was actually willing to stand in the back, if that was possible.

She wouldn't have to stand in the back. Marty put his two allotted house seats aside for them, then turned to me. "Of all the nights," he said. "Leigh Teshler's coming."

"Ah ..." I said, assuming she was someone important.

It was bad timing because a new play, still in its infancy, being done in a theatre-of-hope, was a terribly fragile piece of work. Yes, they had more than a dozen performances under their belt, the reviews were good, the seats filled, confidence was up. But putting Louise into the show could throw everything off for at least a night or two. The play could go flat and have the audience sitting there dumbfounded and silent, wondering what the buzz had been about.

If the timing was off, if the laughs didn't come and the drama didn't touch, the script itself would get the blame. If the evening died, no one in the audience would say, "Oh, it didn't work at all, but that's because they just put a new girl in the show this afternoon."

If the first act flopped, would Leigh Teshler be around for Act Two? Sure she would. Leigh Teshler wouldn't walk out. She didn't operate that way. But if she hated the show, it wouldn't help Marty's Hollywood career. Word gets around. And at least until Marty had a Broadway smash, he had to have movie money.

That November he needed it more than anyone knew.

Chapter 54

A movie came out in the late 1970's called *Camp Stinky*. It was directed by a nobody and starred nobody anybody had ever heard of before or since. Kids flocked to it and howled with laughter at the non-stop scatological jokes and slang for certain body parts. The number one movie in America for three weeks, it made eighty million dollars. That's two hundred million today, easy. The producer of that film and its sequel, *Camp Stinky ... Next Summer*, was the same mogul in possession of the movie script Marty might have the high honor of rewriting.

Marty wrapped up the rehearsal about four-thirty and threw on the conservative necktie he'd brought with him to the theatre. He brushed off the front of his jacket and came down the stairs. I was sitting on the bench in the lobby with Becky. She had one of her legs intertwined with one of mine like a vine around a fence post.

"Jay, come with me."

"Huh?"

"Come on, come with me to the Plaza and meet the man behind the movie script you love so much."

"No, I'd be in the way."

"You don't stay. You meet him and leave. I'd like to get your impression of the guy."

"Marty?" Dori interrupted. "It's for you ...," and she shoved the phone receiver through the bars of her cage again.

He stepped over to the phone. He'd gotten into the habit of waiting a second before saying anything, just to listen. That's what he did this time. Then he said, "Hello?"

Nothing.

"Hello?" he said, one more time. Open line, no response. Assuming part of the caller's purpose was to upset him, Marty covered the mouthpiece and said to Dori, "Hang this up very quietly, will you?"

She did. In fact she overdid it, moving her arm in slow motion, taking about ten seconds to do a one-second job.

"Thanks," Marty said, the word sprinkled with exasperation. "Got a pencil and paper?" He jotted down the date and time. Just before five, Marty and I stepped into the Oak Bar, which was exactly what it sounded like, oak and venerable. Marty wasn't at all nervous. He'd been through too many of these meetings in New York and L.A.

He'd been given a brief one-sentence description of the producer and the guy wasn't hard to spot. We walked straight over to the table where he was sitting. Stassie must have given him a heads-up on what Marty looked like, also, because His Honor half-stood and stuck out a hand, which Marty accepted.

"Byron Flank," he said.

"Marty Sequatchee. I just ran into a friend of mine. This is Jay Bluffing."

Flank wasn't thrilled I was along and who could blame him? Supposed to be a business meeting, not a frat party. But we shook hands, too. He looked about forty-nine or fifty but could have been older because he had had some work done around his little eyes, and it may have taken years off him. Flank's smile was as artificial as Cool Whip but revealed expensive teeth. So this was the guy who had nearly knocked me over on Sixth Avenue, I thought.

"Sit down, sit down."

"Not me," I said. "Got to run. Glad to meet you," I said to Flank. "Good to see you, Marty," I added, as though we'd just bumped into each other on the street. I hurried away into the hotel, pretending to have a purpose. Actually, I was thinking, I'd like to stay for this dance, but I would have to enjoy it later, secondhand.

Marty sat opposite the man who could offer a staggering amount of money for a routine rewrite, and baby, Marty was ready to grab it. Flank was about five-eight and pudgy. He was losing his hair and doing everything possible to try to make you not notice. His head and face were round as a ball; his cheeks were moons on either side of his too big, too flat nose. His eyes were green bb's but such a radiant green they kept attention away from the rest of a face he couldn't have been happy with.

The producer's outfit, which altogether had probably set him back a couple of grand, Marty figured, was curious — maybe not for Beverly Hills, but certainly for New York. His shirt was gold and his necktie black. His jacket was brown leather, boxy, stopped at the waist, and had extraordinarily wide lapels. It had to have come from some boutique on Rodeo Drive, or maybe Marty was giving it too much credit, and it was from a discount bin in some junk shop on Melrose. Flank's slacks were beige with more pleats in front than a school girl's skirt. Marty preferred not to look at the guy's shoes.

A waiter, an old-timer, came over for Marty's order. Flank already had a cocktail in front of him in a heavy, square glass. Marty ordered a bourbon and water.

"I drink rye and soda," Flank said. "I acquired a taste for it after ordering it when I was younger because I liked the sound of it, rye and soda."

How interesting.

"Okay," he said then, seeming to mean they should get down to business. "I'm a fan."

"Thanks."

It was a standard Hollywood line, Marty would tell me with contempt. Anytime you met someone you had vaguely heard of but couldn't quite place what they'd been in, written, directed, or otherwise tinkered with, you simply said, "I'm a fan." And although it had been uttered ten million times, it never failed to flatter and please. Except maybe if you said it in New York to a playwright who also happened to know a little something about the movie business and its people.

"I believe you can make this script crackle," Flank said.

"I'd like to try," said Marty.

"Where are you from, Marty?"

"East Tennessee," he said, "near Knoxville."

"Sequatchee sounds like an Indian name."

Marty went through the usual explanation about the Tennessee county spelled Sequatchie.

"How long have you been in New York?"

Marty told him and wondered why they were back to this-is-your-life talk again. But did he really wonder? Marty knew these guys like Flank, and he'd never met one with an attention span of more than ten seconds. So by the time Flank had finished saying he believed Marty could make the script crackle, he was tired of talking about it for the time being.

The waiter came back and set Marty's drink in front of him. "I grew up in the mountains outside of Albuquerque, little place called Cedar Crest," Flank said. "Its claim to fame was a non-union dinner theatre. I worked there as a teenager. Maybe that's where showbiz seeped into my blood. The theatre burned to the ground, and I took it as a sign to move on."

New Mexico might help explain Flank's attire. It could be interpreted as having a mildly Southwestern flavor to it, in a dude-ish sort of way. Marty leaned back in his seat and glanced at Flank's footwear. Sure enough, he was wearing pointed, yellow cowboy boots, so fancy they made the ones Ellen once wore look like a pair of Bob Dylan rough-outs.

"I've spent my whole adult life in California. Well, and New York, I come to New York, of course."

Marty wanted to say, "I know that, Flank. You're sitting here. We're in the Oak Bar, remember?"

They sipped their drinks, and Marty waited for permission, or at least an opportunity, to offer his take on the script.

It never came. They had one more drink each, and Flank talked. He would ask Marty a question to which Marty would give a short, polite reply. Then Flank would take off on answering the question as though Marty had asked it of him.

"Where did you go to school?" Flank asked.

"University of Tennessee," said Marty, and then he listened to five or six minutes about Flank's brief stint at New Mexico State where he majored in "girls." That's "girls" with a wink and a laugh, as though it were a quip worthy of Dorothy Parker.

"I can tell by looking at you," Flank went on, "your curriculum was probably along similar lines."

Marty hoped the "script meeting" would end with a deal and a handshake. It didn't. The only further, and elliptical, mention of the job came as Flank paid the tab, checked his watch, and stood. "I'll give Stassie a call," Flank said.

They stepped outside and down the front steps of the Plaza Hotel. "Which way are you going?" Flank said.

"Uptown," Marty said, gesturing toward the park.

Flank, thank God, pointed the other way. "I'm glad we got together. I've been wanting to meet you," he said.

Marty had to say what he said next because the money at stake was so considerable. "I hope we can work together."

Flank had turned to leave by that time, but he looked back, gave a quick nod of his bubble head, and smiled. And that was it. He walked away. No mention of the afternoon he was a no-show at the theatre, no mention of Marty's play, or any previous play or movie.

Marty shook his head and touched the knot in his chest as the Hollywood Legend vanished. So many trips to L.A. Countless meetings with agents, producers, directors, and studio executives. Original scripts, rewrites, and movies actually made. Oh, yes, he had played the game. After a dozen years or so, he knew he hadn't seen it all, but he really never expected to run across a sort like Flank. Live, until it kills you, and learn.

The first available working phone Marty could find was around the corner on Central Park South. He called Stassie, and she picked up right away.

"How'd it go?" the artificially cheerful voice asked.

"I don't know. Listen, is this a real project?"

"As far as I know." Which meant, "I have no idea."

"The script was barely mentioned. He asked me some personal questions, but mostly we just had a couple of drinks as we listened to him talk about himself."

"Huh. Maybe that's his style. Maybe that's how he learns whether you're right for the job."

"Right. That's not something you can glean by reading or watching my other movies or by reading or seeing my plays or by maybe listening to me talk about the script."

"I'll give him a call."

"He said he'd call you. Honestly, Stassie, I doubt it's a real assignment. I'm afraid he's running around, trying to stay active, trying to kid himself and the business into believing he's still viable."

"Yes, well, there are those."

"If the studio is serious about the property, why don't you find out which exec is handling it and give him a call?"

"The problem with that is, Marty, if Flank finds out, he'll think we don't have confidence in him and don't trust him."

"We don't. Do we? I don't."

"You sound like you're starting to panic. What's the matter with you? I'll give him a call," Stassie said again and then, "got to go." She hung up.

Marty wanted to go home before going back down to the theatre to see as much of the play as he could stand. It was Louise's first performance; he had to be there. He hopped a cab up to 85th. He served Bob a fresh dinner, took a quick shower, dressed, and headed back downtown.

Toward the end of the performance that night, I came into the theatre with a cup of coffee from across the street. I started up the stairs to the other lobby, but I hesitated because inside the house it was deathly quiet. This part of the show was crucial, and there was always minor activity in the audience at this point. There was a low murmur, the clearing of a throat or two, sometimes even a mild ripple of nervous laughter. Tonight, nothing. I was suddenly worried for Becky, for Marty, for the play itself. Had Louise ruined it?

I had watched most of the rehearsal in the afternoon. Louise was phenomenal. At least, I thought so. She knew all the words, picked up the blocking in no time flat, and by four-thirty was putting layers on her character and adding nuances I had never dreamed of. Maybe it all fell apart in front of an audience.

I stepped lightly up the stairs. Nearly to the top, I spotted Marty, pacing, and as I did I tripped on the last step and spilled coffee on the front of my jacket. Yes, that jacket. Any night now I'd need an overcoat on top of whatever else I was wearing but not yet. So the Saint Laurent from Barney's was soiled again.

I went up to Marty, brushing away coffee with my hand. "How's it going?" I said, keeping my voice down.

"It's a quiet house," he said. He was worried. You never knew when the creature would turn on you.

I took off the jacket. At the water cooler, I wet my hand and wiped at the stain. "How'd the meeting go?"

"It was absurd. What'd you think of that moron?"

"An odd-looking sort," I said.

Marty laughed but cut it short. We had to be quiet, and besides, it wasn't a pleasant laugh but one laced with anxiety. He paced some more, back and forth, ending up near me again.

"You're going to rub a hole in it."

I looked up. I knew I'd heard Marty say something, but I didn't know what. I just stared at him.

"You're going to rub a hole in it."

I was a zombie. My mind had suddenly left the premises.

"What's a matter with you?" Marty said.

Chapter 55

Preston Hondonada strutted into the studio where he would anchor his upcoming special about rats in New York City. He worked out of an office and studios in Rockefeller Center.

Kate was with him. He was showing her around. Standing behind the kidney-shaped desk, where he would sit interviewing city officials and cutting to video, was a blown-up photograph of the common brown rodent known formally as the Norway rat. Kate sat in the desk chair, and Preston pointed out where the cameras would be. He explained the teleprompter to her, told her how the stage manager would stand off-camera and count down the seconds till they were back on air, that kind of thing.

"We tell guests never to look directly into the camera," he said, offering the rudimentary instruction. Apparently, it was a guarded secret. "You'll learn all about that someday when you're acting in movies."

"Yeah, sure," Kate said.

Relating it all to me not long afterward, she opened her mouth and pretended to stick her index finger down her throat. She no longer had any feelings for Hondonada.

After the tour that afternoon, they had headed down the hall to Preston's office. Coming quickly toward them, a dozen things on her mind, was Lynne, Hondonada's secretary/assistant since Patsy's demise. Lynne was a temp who might soon get the job permanently. At least Hondonada teased her with that possibility.

Lynne brimmed with two qualifications, competence and comeliness, not necessarily in that order. She was a blue-eyed dumpling, whose weight would be a problem someday, but for the time being, it just meant she was properly filled out. She stopped twenty feet from Hondonada and Kate and said, "Preston, your friend is here."

"Good," said Hondonada, and he looked at Kate and smiled. "Speaking of the movies," he said.

He led the way as they strolled past the reception area where Lynne was already sitting behind her desk again fielding calls. They went into Hondonada's office. The man waiting for him was sitting in an electric chair, except there were no restraints, it didn't plug in, and it wasn't quite as comfortable as a real electric chair. He was the same man Hondonada had met in the bar at the McNoel the evening Daisy had called me to join her there. If I hadn't been trying so hard on that occasion not to look at Hondonada, I might have recognized him at the Plaza. The fellow stood as Hondonada and Kate came in. He stuck out his hand.

"I'm a little early."

"Good, good!" said Hondonada, shaking the man's hand. "Did you bring the contract?"

"And who is this?" the man said, referring to my lovely sister and ignoring the question from Hondonada.

"Kate Bluffing, Byron Flank."

The name meant nothing to her, of course. She tried not to laugh at his silly trousers. They ballooned at the thighs but were tapered at his ankles and were black with flecks of yellow. She also noticed something else about him (besides his soccer ball head and tiny green eyes). She wondered if she should mention that something or not. She decided not to.

"Hello," she said, extending her hand. Instead of giving it a comfortable, polite shake, Flank took it, clamped his other damp hand over hers and held it that way.

"What is it about New York women? They have a hardiness you don't find in Beverly Hills, a more substantial beauty. You need only to look into their eyes to see a strength, a complexity that's hard to come by on Wilshire Boulevard." And he bore his eyes into Kate's as he gushed.

"I'm from Kentucky," she said.

To which Flank inexplicably replied, "Exactly." Having been originally from New Mexico and having spent the bulk of his life in and around Los Angeles, maybe he thought Kentucky was a borough like Staten Island. Then he finally unlinked himself from her by releasing her hand.

"Byron produces movies, Kate," Hondonada said. "Remember *Camp Stinky*? And *Camp Stinky ... Next Summer*? Byron made those pictures."

"Really?" Kate said, trying not to sound too put-off. She had seen *Camp Stinky* as a teenager in Louisville and had found it to be utter trash. Pointless, lewd, disgusting, worthless. She told me I actually drove her and a girlfriend to the theatre and dropped them off way back when, but I don't remember that.

"I suppose I can tell you now, Kate, Byron's going to make my movie." Hondonada beamed.

"Your movie?"

"A script I wrote. And wrote and wrote," he said. "I think I've written four drafts, right, Byron?"

"I believe so."

"Writing is rewriting, Kate," he said, enlightening her with the platitude.

"I didn't know you were a screenwriter," Kate said.

"I've known for years I've had a screenplay in me, just never got around to putting it on paper."

"What's it about?"

"Two people coming from opposite ends of the country meet in middle America and fall in love. Two delightful characters. The story is silly at times, as silly as love itself, but it also has its serious and sad moments. This is the first time I've talked about it to anyone other than Byron." He pulled Kate close to him and hugged her. "I even wrote the script under a pseudonym."

"Why? I'd think you'd want to use your own name."

"See, that's just it," said Hondonada. "If Preston Hondonada writes a movie script, of course it's going to get bought and made. Where's the challenge in that for me? I wanted the screenplay to stand on its own first. Then after it gets set up, I can announce the truth and let everyone say, 'Preston Hondonada wrote that? I had no idea!'"

"So now it's all set up, huh?"

Hondonada looked to Flank again to let the producer answer. "Practically," Flank said.

"Can I read it?" said Kate.

"No one has read it," Hondonada said, as though it were a map leading to tons of gold. "I mean, except for Byron and the studio, of course. Right, Byron?"

Byron had turned his back and was pretending to examine trinkets on the chrome and glass shelves in the office. "Hmmm?"

"Kate was asking if she could read the script."

Byron looked at Kate. "Maybe you could say 'no' to her, Preston. I'm sure I never could."

Kate told me she tried to smile but couldn't. Hondonada went to a desk drawer and unlocked it with a key from his pocket. He pulled out a copy of the movie script, handling it with such care it could have been a fused glass mosaic from the fourteenth century. He presented it to her, holding it with both hands.

"Sweetheart," he said, "why don't you wander out into reception and start reading? We won't be long. And don't tell

Lynne what you're reading or who wrote it. It'll be all over town if you do."

"I won't." Kate went out.

Who knows exactly what Hondonada and Flank said to each other after she left the room? Only the two of them. But I can close my eyes, even today, and almost hear them.

"You didn't bring the contract, did you?"

"Preston, we're going to get the movie made. You need to let me handle Hollywood."

"My lawyer wants to see a real-deal, bona fide contract."

"We have an agreement, Preston."

"A one-line memo. We want to see particulars, Byron, from the size of my name on the screen to how much I make per episode when it becomes a series."

"Who has fifty thousand dollars in his pocket? You do."

"Yes, you gave me fifty thousand dollars, but — "

"But nothing. That should buy me some time, Preston. I really think it should buy me some time."

"What it bought you, Byron, was not time," Hondonada might have said, quietly and through his teeth. "What it bought was my silence."

Chapter 56

Finding out who killed Patsy Holton was relatively simple for the police. Proving who the killer was, or even coming up with enough evidence to prosecute the murderer, was another matter.

As soon as they learned she'd left the theatre that afternoon to make a call, Detective Paul Rivo had the idea to check out the public phones nearest the theatre. Not for local calls, because in those days, at least, local numbers dialed could not be obtained. Sure, it's different today, since everything is technology and forensics. But way back when, long distance calls from a public phone could be traced.

It was a long shot, but in a murder investigation you often play long shots and hunches. Besides, since the time she would have made the call was known within five or ten minutes, there wouldn't have been too many long distance calls made from all those phones put together, if any were made at all, so it wasn't exactly a mammoth task.

The phone she likely would have gone to first was out of order the day after her murder. Safe to conclude it had been out of order the day before. The next phone had one long distance call made from it that previous afternoon. It was to The Grand Hotel in Stockholm. They didn't even bother with that one. Two of the other phones showed no long distance calls anywhere near four p.m., the approximate time she had left the TASSQ. But the fifth phone they checked had been used to make a call to a privately owned movie production company in Beverly Hills, California, called Amethyst Motion Pictures.

Rivo asked a detective from the Beverly Hills Police Department if he would swing over to Amethyst Pictures and ask about a call that came in, probably collect, from Manhattan on that certain date in late October, around four in the afternoon. All those places had phone logs and, surely, the call would have been entered. Maybe he could find out who in particular the call was for. Rivo could phone out to Amethyst himself, but a personal visit might be more effective.

The Beverly Hills detective did Rivo the favor but called back to report Amethyst showed no record of a call coming in from New York on that day at that time. To Rivo, that was odd.

A few days later Rivo and Flannigan were interviewing Patsy's boss, Preston Hondonada, in his midtown office. Rivo happened to ask the famous personality if he by any chance knew a man by the name of Byron Flank. It hadn't been hard for the detectives to find out Flank was the man behind Amethyst Pictures. Since they knew Patsy aspired to be an actress and actresses want to be in movies, the question was worth a shot.

Hondonada had seemed mildly surprised by the question but covered well. He said, yes, he knew Mr. Flank. The two of them were involved in a project together.

"So Patsy Holton knew Flank, too, right?"

"I believe she did, yes."

Flannigan wrote everything down. Rivo occasionally glanced toward the other detective's scribbling hand. "Did they see each other socially?"

"I really wouldn't know." Tiny beads of perspiration popped out above Preston's upper lip. "The thing is ...," he said.

"Yeah?"

"I believe Mr. Flank is married."

"So you don't want to talk about any of his outside activities."

"I don't want to, and I won't. Or, let me say, I wouldn't, if I did know anything."

"Uh-huh." Rivo noticed a five-by-eight photo on Hondonada's desk and picked it up at a corner by thumb and index finger, as though it were nasty. It was a picture, mostly a head-shot, of a brown rat. The animal stared right into the camera, its eyes wide and hypnotic. "A pet?" Rivo said.

"I'm doing a special soon on rats in New York. A blow up of that picture will be part of the set."

Rivo replaced the photo. "Would you happen to know if Mr. Flank was in town the day Patsy was killed?"

"No."

"No, he wasn't in town, or no, you don't know?"

"He's allowed to come to New York without telling me. It's not in our contract that I know where he is every minute of every day." Then Hondonada realized he sounded too defensive and sarcastic, so he tagged a phony laugh onto the end of it.

"What kind of a contract do you have with him?"

"Oh, it's not really a contract, exactly. We have a casual sort of informal option memo. We're going to make a movie."

Flannigan looked up from his notebook and said, "*Camp Stinky*. I missed that one."

A check with a few of the major airlines revealed Byron Flank had indeed arrived, first class, at Kennedy Airport on the day of Patsy's murder, about two o'clock in the afternoon. He had checked into his hotel off Fifth Avenue at three-twenty. He made three phone calls from his hotel room, one to Preston Hondonada's office, the other two to Patsy Holton's apartment, where he would have certainly left a message both times informing her he was in town and begging her to call him. Rivo and Flannigan began, as Marty would say, to piece the puzzle together. It wasn't really very hard to do.

Chapter 57

The first call Patsy made from the public phone that afternoon was to Flank's office in L.A. She was told Mr. Flank was in New York and had just arrived. She knew he was coming in later in the week to see her, but here he was, days early. Why had she called? Probably to tell him not to come, their relationship was over.

She didn't have to be told where he was staying in New York. She knew where he always stayed. So her second call was to his hotel. He was so excited about his surprise visit that even Patsy, who could be cold and ruthless when she had to be, couldn't bring herself to crush him over the phone since he had already made the trip.

Flank asked her to meet him on the Upper West Side at a store called Pauline's Dream. There was something he wanted to buy. Reluctantly, she agreed.

She waited for him outside the store, and when he came out with his purchase, they walked over to her place. Once inside the apartment, he tore open the box from Pauline's and slipped his arms through perhaps the ugliest jacket Patsy Holton had ever seen. It was brown leather, boxy, stopped at the waist, and had extra wide lapels. "What do you think?" Flank said proudly. Without waiting for a reply (and it's a good thing, since Patsy was probably speechless), he immediately began to paw her.

She pried him off her and shortly told him it was over. She couldn't see him anymore.

He went numb with rage, fought to keep it under control. "It's that writer, isn't it? That hack."

"What do you know about him?"

"I know about him," Flank said, trembling, mercury rising from the base of his neck to his forehead. "I know all about him, that country bumpkin. I keep track of you. I know where you are all the time, what you're doing. I know about the skinny little punk downtown. And I know you've been with that redneck, theatre faggot."

Patsy, cool under fire, kept her voice controlled but firm. "I've been with him. I am with him. I'm staying with him. How's that? You and I are through, Byron. It's over. Now get out."

Flank obsessed over Marty, was tormented by him. The cowardly phone calls were from Flank, of course. It's why the detectives wanted to know the dates and times they came in, so they could compare them with Flank's whereabouts and phone records. Maybe delusional, Flank was trying to annoy Marty into leaving the country.

The producer hoped more serious action against Marty would be taken by a fellow he had turned to for help, a hulking actor (now going to seed) who had played in *Camp Stinky ... Next Summer*.

It was the only movie part Lars Gundy ever had. During the filming he had become a sycophant to producer Byron Flank, and for a dozen years he'd licked Flank's boots, hoping that someday it would lead to another movie role, some part that would make him a star. He believed Flank could do it.

One day when Lars was changing the steam in the Hollywood maven's sauna, or doing some other menial job for the few bucks Flank doled out to him, Flank came home from New York. He was furious with some playwright that was ruining his life. He didn't tell Lars why or how the writer was ruining his life, just that he was. This was right after Patsy had started seeing Marty. After he ranted long enough, and after he'd let Lars guzzle a gallon of rye whiskey, a frequent habit, he got the aging house boy to say he'd go to New York and take care of the pansy. Flank paid for the economy class ticket and a cheap room at a shabby hotel.

Lars had no idea what he was going to do to Marty. Beat him up? Rent a car and run him over? He hung out for weeks and stalked, trying to decide how best to please Flank.

But now Patsy had only moments to live. The argument over Marty continued in her apartment that fateful afternoon. It escalated until Flank snapped and struck her, causing her nose to bleed. He tore at her clothing, and she fought him. By the time she decided she'd better scream, he was strangling her. He was out of his head, insane with jealousy, and he killed her. He paused, settled, got his breath back. He stepped around the body on the floor, pulled out his handkerchief, and began wiping down anything he might have touched.

He stopped before leaving and took one final survey of the apartment. He hurried over, erased her phone machine messages, and wiped off the buttons. Then he left. Escaping unnoticed from a West Side brownstone in the afternoon would be easy to do, with a little luck. No one saw him.

On the street he called Tad Arnett. The idea behind that was to get Tad uptown to Patsy's apartment. Placing him at her building or apartment about the time of the murder, Tad would certainly be the prime suspect. He waited half an hour or so, giving Tad time to come up on the subway. Then Flank called the police and, thinking a little more clearly, he disguised his voice. He told them he had heard a commotion in Patsy's apartment and thought someone should investigate.

Of course, Tad didn't make the trip uptown because he thought the call was a hoax. And he might not have had the ninety-cent fare, so Flank's attempt to incriminate the young man was fruitless.

Flank spent the night in New York gathering himself together. He even made one of his calls to Marty that night, just hours after he had killed Patsy. He flew back to L.A. the next day and eliminated the record of Patsy's call to Amethyst from the Village the day before.

A couple of weeks later, he sneaked back to New York. He couldn't get Marty out of his head. Marty was the reason Patsy was dead. Marty, Marty, Marty. Marty had spoiled his life. Marty ... young, handsome, talented, successful Marty Sequatchee. He didn't even know Marty, but he hated him, so he continued to make silly telephone calls while waiting to see what Lars was going to do. He called the big guy a time or two to nudge him, but didn't mention he was in New York and staying at a somewhat nicer hotel. He was probably hoping Lars would kill Marty, but he never actually ordered that.

The fifty grand given to Hondonada was, ostensibly, option money for the screenplay. What it really was, of course, was hush money. It was insurance against Hondonada mouthing what he knew about Flank and Patsy: how Hondonada had introduced them, how Flank had tumbled for her like a high school kid, and so forth. But Hondonada wasn't about to say or do anything that might bring Flank down and jeopardize his movie, the fifty thousand dollar gift notwithstanding.

Of course, the great TV personality had given Flank something, too — Patsy herself. She was a token to please the producer and help lure him into town regularly where he and Hondonada could have one-on-ones about Preston's masterpiece.

That worthless script. Flank kept from Hondonada the fact that the producer couldn't get through the gates of any studio in California with that drivel under his arm. The money Flank dropped in the Oak Bar and everywhere else was his own, contrary to what Marty thought.

Flannigan and Rivo, with the help of the L.A.P.D., were tracking Flank. When he came back to New York after the murder, Rivo arranged to meet him at the TASSQ for a brief one on one. With Flank's busy schedule, it was really the only time he had, even on a Sunday, he said.

But Flank got cold feet and didn't show, phoning in his apologies the next day from Beverly Hills. The detectives could have pushed it, even gone out to L.A. themselves to talk to him. But they waited. They were patient.

Did Flank think he could get away with Patsy's murder? Of course he did. They always think that. A murderer can't believe he'll get caught any more than an actor can believe he's not talented or not right for a part. Maybe Flank decided if he avoided the investigation long enough and let time pass, the whole thing would just fade away. But then I, Jay the Magnificent, was able to give the detectives the break they needed.

Flank thought he had slipped into town unnoticed for that Tuesday evening drink with Hondonada at the McNoel, the Oak Bar meeting with Marty the next day, and the meeting with Hondonada on Thursday. But the detectives knew where he was.

They were on the corner waiting for him when he came out onto 51st Street after the meeting in Hondonada's office. Flannigan nudged Rivo and said, "Get a load of the pants."

"You need a pair of those."

"Yeah," said Flannigan. "Does this guy think he's in style?"

"His style's about to go out." Rivo looked a little better than he had the day before. Ellen's surgery had gone well, so he had managed to get some shut-eye.

They approached Flank and introduced themselves. The day was bleak. A light, wintry rain began to fall. They asked Flank if he'd step over to their car with them, and he did. The three of them ducked into the sedan, Flank in the back. There was a brown paper bag on the front seat between Flannigan and Rivo. Flannigan pulled out his pen and notebook.

"I may take a few notes."

"We've been wanting to talk to you," Rivo said, innocently. "You had to leave and all. Then we got busy, and we weren't sure when you'd be back in town ...," he said, sing-song fashion.

They were sure, all right, Flank thought. Otherwise, how did they know to intercept him here? "I don't have much time today, either. What was it you wanted to know?"

Flannigan said, "How well did you know Patsy Holton?"

"Patsy, yes ...," said Flank, like he'd nearly forgotten all about her.

"Did you see her socially?" Flannigan said.

"No, no. I knew her from Preston Hondonada's office."

"Really?" said Rivo. "We thought maybe you knew her well enough to give her a purple ring, an amethyst ring."

"To give her a ring ...," he tilted his head back and looked up, like the next thing he was going to say was written on the ceiling.

Rivo didn't wait to hear it. "Were you ever in her apartment on 75th Street?" he said, intentionally saying 75th instead of 74th.

"75th? Her apartment? No." He almost corrected the street number but didn't because he was so intelligent.

"Ever heard of a young man named Tad Arnett?"

"Tad? Arnett? I don't believe so."

"So if we called Tad Arnett right now and asked you to say a few specific words, he wouldn't recognize your voice?"

"I ... I mean, how could he?"

Rivo opened the brown paper bag on the seat and pulled out an item of clothing, held it up to Flank.

"Is this your jacket?" Rivo asked.

"Where did you get that?" a surprised Flank said.

"Is it yours?"

"It looks like my jacket, yes."

The night before at the TASSQ while watering my own jacket, I realized I'd seen another jacket exactly like the one Flank had worn to the Oak Bar. That's why this meeting was taking place.

Flank had bought the fancy brown leather jacket at Pauline's Dream, of course. Kate had recognized it, too, when she met Flank, but didn't say anything. It was Flank Patsy was waiting for outside the store the afternoon he bought it. It had to be. Anything else would have been a ridiculous coincidence. Flank might have been the last person to be with her. I didn't wait till morning, I called Flannigan that night. I didn't reach him, but he called me back ten minutes later at the theatre. The conversation between Flannigan and "J.B." would be essential to Flannigan's section on the Patsy Holton case.

On 50th Street just off Sixth Avenue, still holding up the tacky garment, Rivo said, "If this were Patsy's blood on this jacket, could you explain how it got there?" He adjusted a sleeve to show dried drops of a reddish brown substance.

"I ...," said Flank. "Unless ... she had a cut and brushed up against me, you know, in Preston's office."

"Uh-huh," said Rivo. "Except according to the sales record at Pauline's Dream, you bought the jacket on the same afternoon she was killed."

Then Flank said something smart. "Can you prove it's Patsy's blood?" DNA testing was practically unheard of in those days.

"Oh, if there were long, brunette hairs on the jacket, I don't suppose they'd be hers either? Maybe our lab guys are crazy. And maybe you never told Lars Gundy to go after Marty Sequatchee and report on his activities?"

Flannigan clicked his pen, put it away, closed his notepad. They had Flank and all three of them knew it.

"Byron, we've had some evidence for a while, but now ..."

Rivo held the jacket up just a little higher to indicate this was the clincher.

"What happened up there?" Flannigan said. "You didn't intend to kill her. We know that." Rivo was stuffing the jacket back into the bag. "It was Marty Sequatchee, huh?"

The producer looked at Flannigan and blinked half a dozen times, rapidly, then gave Rivo some of the same.

"We figure competing with Marty was tough," said Rivo. "For thirty seconds you lost your head. You were alone, right? Just the two of you in her apartment."

Byron Flank hesitated, nodded, then lowered his head and started to weep. And it ended, not with a shootout or mad chase through midtown, but as softly as Marty might have written it himself. The pathetic man's sobs and whimpers fit in well with the drizzle pattering the gray Plymouth from the low November sky. He would go on that day to tell everything, confirming much they already knew and filling in the holes with the sad details.

Chapter 58

When Flannigan and Rivo arrived at the TASSQ right after the vandalism was reported that particular Tuesday morning, a couple of uniformed cops were hanging around, and a young detective named Gossinger, green as crème de menthe, had just started to ask Dori a few questions.

Gossinger had established there had been no break-in, so maybe someone was inside the theatre when it closed on Monday, had torn the set apart and then let themselves out.

"Now Dori, did anything unusual happen on Monday?"

"No."

"Uh-huh. Nothing unusual?"

"No."

Gossinger's partner was ill, but no problem, he could handle this. The veteran homicide detectives hung back and listened.

"You were in the ticket booth all afternoon?"

"Yes. I answered the phone, put people on the waiting list, talked to anybody who came in and up to the booth." She tossed her head quickly a few times. Nothing fell out.

"Anybody special come in and up to the booth?"

"No. Except that one guy."

"Who was that?"

"I don't know his name. But when I was a kid, he was in

that movie *Camp Stinky ... Next Summer*. He played the big lug. I remembered him."

It never occurred to Lars that Patsy's murder had anything to do with Flank, since he didn't know Patsy was Flank's paramour. If he had, he might have turned and fled. But after being admonished by Flank for not taking any action whatsoever against Marty, Lars had the idea to put an end to the play by demolishing the set. So he went into the theatre on that Monday afternoon and tried to buy a ticket. Instead of leaving when Dori turned him away, he sneaked upstairs to the bathroom and hid there until the theatre closed. Then he came out, did his deed, and left through the rear emergency exit.

As soon as Rivo and Flannigan heard he had played in the *Stinky* movie, they knew the blond male brute Dori was talking about had surely been sent by Flank. It also explained the lurking stranger who had spooked Ellen outside Marty's apartment. They'd have him picked up eventually, and some judge would fuss at him and might even make him pay a fine.

* * *

Was it really blood on the monkey jacket they showed to Flank? Yes, according to Flannigan's *Solving Murder*, but it certainly wasn't Patsy Holton's. In fact, it wasn't even Flank's jacket. It was an identical one the detectives had procured from Pauline's Dream before they picked up Flank. Had they lied to him? Not really. Everything was worded carefully so as not to say anything untrue. They just dug a hole and let him fall in. It would have been worth a few bucks to have seen the expression on Flank's face when he saw the jacket he owned still in his closet. If he ever did. Maybe it was still hanging there when he slumped into Sing Sing.

* * *

Ellen Rivo survived and recovered. There was a weak wall in a blood vessel in her head, probably since birth. It's otherwise known as an aneurysm, and the blow to her face ruptured it, very slightly. A CT scan along with a lumbar puncture discovered it, and Dr. Joseph Brenniman repaired it.

Detective Rivo, P.R. in Flannigan's memoir, visited Wayne Galafant at his Chelsea apartment while Ellen was still in the hospital. Flannigan waited outside in the car, while Rivo went in. About five minutes later, Rivo came out and the men drove off. Wayne left New York soon after that. A couple of years later Marty would read in the *Hollywood Reporter* that Wayne was going to direct a low-budget, independent film. Who knows if he ever did?

* * *

Something startling happened the night Louise came back into the show. The play hit a whole new level and mesmerized the audience. Ellen Rivo, for all her competence, was really just being herself up there. When Louise stepped back into the part, she brought professionalism and, even at twenty-two, an expertise to the part, which added voltage to the production no one had realized was missing. The audience had been quiet that night because the play was much more involving, affecting, and satisfying. I was there when Stassie introduced Leigh Teshler to Marty, and I watched Ms. Teshler hug Marty as though they were old friends. She and Stassie struck a deal that night. Marty would write the screenplay, and Leigh Teshler would make the play a movie. Marty Sequatchee was solvent again.

* * *

Kate moved back to Kentucky. I knew I'd miss her and I did, but I was so happy to see her get away from the rat man,

I rejoiced. The screen came down, and I moved back into the bedroom. Becky and I talked about her moving into my place with me, but she never did. Smart in New York, if you can afford it, to keep two apartments. Kate went back to UK to see if she could get some kind of arts degree and became involved in the theatre department. She was cast as Grandma Lester in *Tobacco Road*, she said, because she was such a relic. It wasn't much of a part.

* * *

I stayed in New York another six or seven years, Marty a little longer. I studied for the New York bar exam but never got around to taking it. I loved New York but was no New Yorker, not really. I'd practice law again someday, below the Mason-Dixon Line, but my heart wouldn't be in it. I'd retire early, very early, thanks to a real estate deal I would forever regret and several other clients like the magic trick salesman who made tax money disappear into his own pocket.

* * *

In the late spring of the year following Patsy's murder, Marty insisted I start playing softball with him on Saturday mornings in Riverside Park up at 110th Street. Marty had a regular game with a whole other set of friends apart from his football buddies. Someday we'll be too old, Marty had said, but not yet, we weren't.

One sweltering afternoon in July after we'd finished two seven inning games (10 to 8, 12 to 4), we limped off the field and out of the park with a few other all-stars and headed over to Broadway. The others were going to hit a local bar, but Marty and I were going to drag ourselves back downtown. Marty had a date with, let's see, an actress, and it was Becky's birthday so

John Jay (that's what she had finally settled on calling me) was taking her to dinner. It was best we passed on pitchers of beer with the guys.

Walking to the bus stop, who did I see strolling along toward us but Daisy Leiber? And this was the West Side! Her red hair was pulled back and up to give the nape of her neck some air. She was eating a butter pecan ice cream cone, and it was dripping in the heat. She wore a T-shirt with no bra, shorts, and sandals. I guessed she and her husband, who was beside her, were slumming.

Or, being a prominent New York City architect, maybe he didn't have the same bias against the West Side as Daisy.

Daisy and I were delighted to see each other. We kissed, embraced. She introduced me to the esteemed Sidney Wycott who was in his late fifties, pale, thin, and skyscraper tall. I thought of the woman in Pauline's Dream who had asked for jeans with a thirty-six inseam. Wycott's nose pointed to the clouds like the spire of the Chrysler Building.

Marty jumped in and introduced himself. Daisy had read one of his plays published in an anthology and was very complimentary. Wycott didn't say much of anything, just stood there, haughty. Referring to the canvas athletic bags and the condition of our T-shirts and jeans, Daisy said, "Who won?"

"We did." I gave her the scores of the two games, and she tried to act like she cared.

We talked for another minute or two. Then she and her husband went their way, Marty and I went ours. Ten or twelve paces along, I turned back to look at her. The tower was stooped at her feet, adjusting a strap on her sandal. With her fingertips on his shoulder, she was looking back at me.

No, she wasn't. She was looking at Marty. I was sure of it. No way was I going to give Sequatchee the satisfaction of knowing that.

"Old girlfriend?" Marty said.

"Yep. I broke her heart. Long story."

A southbound bus passed us, slowing for the stop just ahead. Marty called "double time." We caught up to the bus and stepped aboard.

THE END

Publishing Division
P.O. Box 2884
Pawleys Island, SC

CPSIA information can be obtained at www.ICGtesting.com
Printed in the USA
LVOW12s0108250314

378616LV00001B/1/P